"Jaskunas creates a hauntingly intricate weave of events in his first novel, which has the quality of a fever dream. . . . As much as *Hidden* is a novel of suspense, it is also an elegant exploration of vulnerability when it's seeded by guilt and loss."
—*The New York Daily News*

"Tautly written . . . No simple story of good and evil, this novel keeps you guessing. . . . *Hidden* is a well-told story of what an experience like Maggie's would feel like from the inside—how it might feel to no longer trust your memory."
—*BookPage*

"*Hidden* is a far better book than Ian McEwan's *Atonement,* another novel that took on the subject of truth and memory."
—*LA Weekly*

"A beautifully written, haunting, and ultimately hopeful story of what's true and what's not."
—*Washingtonian*

"At the heart of this insightful, atmospheric novel are the complexities of truth."
—*Publishers Weekly*

"A literary novel of mystery and suspense . . . a prickly, unnerving tale that's perfect for a summer read."
—*Pages*

"Jaskunas, a man writing in first person as a woman, gets a grip on your sleeve from the first line."
—*The Honolulu Advertiser*

"The sophisticated and sinuous *Hidden,* one of the most hyped books of the summer, deserves the acclaim."
—*Metro New York*

"*Hidden* has created an early buzz in the book world, and for good reason. Jaskunas has written a page-turner with psychological depths that resonate long afterwards. *Hidden* reads like a thriller and lingers like literature."
—*The Buffalo News*

"*Hidden* is a joy to read: the prose, line by line, is breathtaking, the characters come alive in all their complexity, the plot drives to a conclusion both shocking and inevitable. *Hidden* is a truly wonderful debut."

—Dan McCall, author of *Jack the Bear* and *Triphammer*

"This remarkable debut novel from a fine young writer deals on a high level with issues of memory, love, and guilt."

—Alison Lurie, author of *Imaginary Friends* and *Foreign Affairs*

"Good news: Paul Jaskunas is here, and he's a wonderful new voice in fiction, lyrical, smart, and frightening. *Hidden* moves us past mere trauma to the very heart of a woman all but murdered. We watch, spellbound, as her intelligence and sensitivity and pure grace float her back again to the world of the living, where there's a mystery to solve, and even deeper wounds to heal."

—Bill Roorbach, author of *The Smallest Color* and *Big Bend*

"Jaskunas's masterful prose casts a spell on the reader. He transports you from reader to dreamer—then awakens you with a jolt. The truth."

—Nanci Kincaid, author of *Balls* and *Verbena*

"*Hidden* is a beautifully written and intriguing novel, one that takes us into the world of a woman traumatized, a woman fighting quietly for her life."

—Kim Wozencraft, author of *Rush*

"'All a lie needs is telling,' Paul Jaskunas writes, and his thoughtful narrator, Maggie Wilson, is living proof. She peels away the layers surrounding her own near-murder and resurrection so calmly it gives you chills. *Hidden* is a shifty, low-key thriller, half *Spellbound,* half Daphne du Maurier."

—Stewart O'Nan, author of *The Night Country*

"*Hidden* is a page-turner: poignant and powerful. I was transfixed by the tale Paul Jaskunas has written, and haunted by Maggie Wilson, the wondrous heroine he has given us."

—Chris Bohjalian, author of *Midwives* and *Idyll Banter*

Hidden

A Novel

PAUL JASKUNAS

Free Press
New York • London • Toronto • Sydney

FREE PRESS

A Division of Simon & Schuster, Inc.

1230 Avenue of the Americas

New York, NY 10020

First Free Press trade paperback edition 2005

FREE PRESS and colophon are trademarks of Simon & Schuster, Inc.

For information about special discounts for bulk purchases,
please contact Simon & Schuster Special Sales at
1-800-456-6798 or business@simonandschuster.com

Manufactured in the United States of America

1   3   5   7   9   10   8   6   4   2

The Library of Congress has cataloged the hardcover edition as follows:

Jaskunas, Paul Richard.

Hidden : a novel / Paul Jaskunas.

p. cm.

1. Married women—Fiction.   2. Victims of violent crimes—Fiction.
3. New Harmony (Ind.)—Fiction.   I. Title

PS3610.A84H53 2004

813'.6—dc22

2003064358

ISBN 0-7432-5748-0

0-7432-5780-4 (Pbk)

for Solveiga

Hidden

Part One

At three-twenty in the morning, I am unconscious on the floor, and Jacobs and Castle are coming in their car.

The almanac says there is a quarter moon. The newspapers say it is partly cloudy. The house the police car approaches is mostly dark, except for the entryway light glowing from the open door and guestroom window to the left. My neighbor, an old man in his pajamas, stands on my porch waving frantically at the car.

Entering, the officers walk around broken glass, spilled juice, an overturned wicker basket of flowers. They hustle down a hall and into the guestroom, where there is an oak bed with four brass posts. At the foot of this bed I lie on the floor, my body curled on its side. Hair covers my face, and my left foot twitches at the ankle, tapping the bedpost softly.

Castle will write in the report: "Victim wearing white nightgown, bloodied but intact."

I am proud of this room because of the bed, which I slept in as a child in my girlhood home, but most of all because of the painting by Nate's grandfather hanging on the wall. It's of our house, but more than our house. Standing before a lush forest, this gray Victorian home with its stained glass and red lattice has the gloss and glare of a vision that lacks nothing, that is complete and unified according to its own austerity and the generosity of its rooms. Out front, in the flowerbeds, marigolds bristle in the sun, and a boy and dog run through the grass. Nate says it's him, though it is hard to tell. The boy is just a few strokes of the brush.

When they find me, I am still breathing. My pulse is slow. I have three wounds.

The house around me is not so brilliant as the picture. The gray paint has blistered in the heat, and the lattice, dulled by dust, is encased in spider silk. The marigolds have since been replaced with red impa-

3

tiens that all summer have suffered neglect and wilted in the hot Indiana sun. The forest behind the house hides a ravine seething with crickets. Its tangled trees, crawling with vines, hold the night in their limbs.

The first cut is a laceration an inch below my left clavicle. The second, a long tear on my upper arm. The third, a deep gash, arcs from the top of my crown to the left side of my forehead, which is pressed against the carpet when the officers arrive.

"Intruder probably entered thru front door, seized/struggled w/ victim in entryway, forced her into 1st flr. b.r. on north side of house. Victim unconscious and bleeding."

When I think of myself on the floor, I imagine myself as a little girl. I can see her curled up on her side, her face and gown softened by the moon. Her fingers innocently grope, as if for an imagined Teddy, as her foot moves gently back and forth. I don't see her blood. I don't feel the pain. She is only sleeping in the moonlight, waiting for someone to touch her and say, "Stop dreaming, Maggie. It's time to wake up."

In New Harmony, I'm a local eccentric. You spy me in the grocer's and almost recall my story—something to do with a trial, the Dukes, a senseless crime. I might make you look twice, being a scandal of sorts, and you probably try to avoid my gaze.

Today I'm in Peterson's searching for dinner. In this catchall pantry of a market, cans of Dinty Moore Stew collect dust along with cartons of night crawlers and shotgun shells. By the beer coolers, two teenage boys gossip about me. One says to the other, Isn't she the one with a hole in her head? Something like that, says his friend.

In this town there are no secrets, not when you're the village freak. Moments like these steal my appetite. I give up on dinner and head for the door. Once safe in my car, I stare through the storefront window at the boys, strangers to me, yet familiar with their John Deere caps perched high on their heads, sunburned skin, and pimply faces. Young men in this part of Indiana all seem to look the same. I know nothing about them, yet they know too much about me. If I had a hole in my head, I'd crawl inside it and disappear.

I tear out of the lot. In the mood for a drive, I don't take the direct route home but turn at random down a gravel lane that winds for miles through the corn. Such roads are where I sometimes live. When you make your home in the country between one town and another, you have to drive a long ways almost every day. The car time is quiet, ruminative. The hours are full of haze and skunk. Sometimes, at dusk, when the muggy clouds mass low to the earth and no cars are in sight, I like to get lost. I rattle down weed-choked roads, into acres of land I didn't know were there, past rusty oracles, an abandoned church and its cemetery, a junkyard of pickups sinking into the mud.

Mine is a secretive country. It was settled by people who came here to hide. Utopians who thought the end was near, they traveled from Germany centuries ago to make a home in the wilderness, where the fire and brimstone wouldn't touch them. The end never came, but they left their mark. Not far from New Harmony is their labyrinth of hedges. The locals keep it pruned, and sometimes I go there when I'm upset. I now take a haphazard route around the county's dusty perimeter and park by the labyrinth's edge.

The good Christian was to commune with God as he made his way through the maze. I don't know about that, but if you go in the evening when no one's about, the labyrinth can be a peaceful place as it's surrounded by woods and corn. Children have forced holes in the hedges, so it's easy to walk from the outside straight to the brick hut in the center. To ignore the holes and pretend you have to find your own way can make you feel foolish. It helps to close your eyes and follow the path with a hand in the bush. I do this now. I concentrate on the sound of my feet on the soil, the breeze on my face, as I walk slowly through the maze. I let myself wind around corners, drifting away from the center, toward it, away again. In time, the labyrinth becomes more comfortable. I am only walking and breathing and learning the way. I feel the knot loosening, and my feet know before I do that I've arrived.

In all of Posey County, there's no place where you may feel so alone as you do in the center of the labyrinth at sunset. There is no noise but for the crickets in the trees, and as darkness gathers, June bugs float from the rings of hedges all around you and glow in the humid air. I go inside the brick hut and sit down on a bench. The blue paint on the walls peels off in shreds, and in the rafters is a hornet's nest. I've never seen a hornet emerge from it, but always it seems the gray, papery tumor may explode with black wings and buzzing above me. Still, I take my time here and try to remember how it was before. How I used to feel about myself on a lovely July night like this. I was not always a creature who sought solace in secret places. I had enthusiasms and friends. I recall swimming in a quarry pool, diving deep and touching rock, bursting through the water's surface to find stars above, a boy on the bank waiting to kiss me. That was college, less than a decade ago. Before Nate and marriage and so much more. For just a year and a half, I was a Duke. Now I'm a Wilson again and twenty-eight, but not the same girl I used to be.

For example, I never knew this trembling around my eyes. This summer, I've had the seizures almost weekly. One is coming now. It pulses softly at first, a kind of summoning, a storm gathering a long ways off. The right side of my vision fractures like a stained-glass window, and the colors roil into an elliptical, throbbing chaos. The weightless mass of light and shadow burrows inside my brain. It's as if my head is bound in bridle and bit, and someone is jerking at the reins. To brace myself, I dig my fingers into the bench, place a hand on the wall, but there's no stopping it. I am thrown to my knees. I let myself go down and convulse in the dust.

In a couple of minutes the seizure subsides. A hole in my head or not, I'm medicated. I get up from the ground and sit on the bench, brushing the dust from my legs. That's when I hear the child's voice.

"Are you all right?"

I look up and see in the doorway a boy with scabs on his knees. He's staring at me, frankly curious. I must have been a startling sight, a skinny young woman twitching on the ground. "I'm fine."

"Do you live here?"

"I'm only visiting, like you."

"I think you really do live here. I think you're a fairy," he says with a hop. "This is your hideout, and you're going to give me three wishes." A high giggle rises up from his tummy. He happily strides into the hut like he's going to move in himself.

Something about a seizure—you feel a bit remade after each one, energized, and it seems I've the power to grant a wish or two. "So," I say, "what will they be?"

"I wish you could live in a magic castle," says the boy, flashing me an elfin smile.

"I think I can handle that. And your second wish?"

"That I could be a prince inside the castle with you." He jumps onto the bench and beams at me.

"Granted," I say. "And one more. Be careful to choose what you really want."

"A great big bird to fly away to the castle on," he says, throwing up his little arms like wings.

I hear the mother coming. She ducks her head in, a squat woman with fearful eyes. "Don't bother the lady, Will," she snaps at her son.

Ignoring her, I pat the boy on his head and say, "It was very nice to meet you, Mr. Will. Will you take care of the maze for me? I have to go now."

I take my time walking back to the car. I could use a new castle, I think, and certainly a bird to carry me, but the prince I'd do without. I've had one already in this life, and it's to his castle, my home, I must return now.

Passing through fields fragrant with summer rot, I soon come to my sprawling gray farmhouse. Standing alone against a forested ravine, it can take on a haunted look at night, and so to cheer myself I sometimes leave the lights blazing when I'm gone. Now the windows are lit up, and you might expect to find inside a bustling family sitting down to a country dinner. The rooms are empty, though, and so I look elsewhere for company.

In the cottage next to my house lives an old bachelor named Manny. He's sitting on his porch, as he always does this time of day.

"Thought you'd never show up," he says when I walk over. "The mosquitoes are drinking up all your gin."

The cocktail he's made me sits next to the rocking chair, on an over-turned crate. He greets me with a kiss on the cheek, as if we haven't seen each other in months.

"Hello, lover boy."

"I like the ring of that."

We settle down, and the radio's talking about boys blown to bits in Afghan caves. It's been a summer of distant explosions and talk of more war. We lighten up our daily dose with stiff drinks. Every day he carefully parts his white, silken hair in anticipation of my coming. He dabs cologne behind his ears and prepares his porch with a bucket of ice and lime wedges and tonic water. He always has plenty of gin.

Grateful for it, I drink his offering. I look through the trees dividing his property from mine. He is not so far away that he wouldn't hear noises through an open window, I think.

I ask him, "Manny, can you try to remember something for me? Can you try to remember what woke you that night?"

"Not again," he groans. "It was my bladder, it was the wind, it was the Holy Ghost!"

He reaches over to turn up the radio.

"Was it a car? Was there a car door slamming?"

"This is a hell of a sunset we're having."

"I'm asking you a question."

"And I'm avoiding it. Drink your gin and watch the goddamn sun go down for once in your life."

He smiles at himself and smacks his lips. Were it not for the transistor, the creaking of his rocker, it would be quiet here the way it's quiet in wilderness. We are lost in low hills in the Wabash Valley. The corn fields are oceans, the crows our gulls, that radio tower a kind of lighthouse. We have been talking about war and recession and baseball. We've been talking about whatever comes along in the radio waves. But sometimes I make Manny talk about the past.

"Why can't you remember?" I say.

"Why can't you stop?"

I give up, sip my gin, and watch the goddamn sun as instructed. Manny turns off the radio.

"You stew too much. I can see how you stew. You know what I think?"

He thinks I should buy a plane ticket to the Caribbean. He thinks I should get laid on some beach and lose myself to a foreign city. Every Sunday he reads from the travel section of the newspaper descriptions of Bali, Morocco, Australia.

"When the time comes and you die, it'll all come out in the wash," he says. "What happened, why, how. But it'll be a thin story in the breeze. It won't matter one bit. Just a rumor in the breeze, whistling by, like the rest of your life."

I don't want to hear this. Manny doesn't have any idea.

"A breeze, Maggie. Maggie out on a breeze."

I wrap my arms around myself. "You think I don't know what happened."

Manny says nothing. He is afraid to answer.

"I do know."

"Fine, then, you know. You're still getting drunk on a porch with a seventy-six-year-old man."

I laugh.

"You're impossible," he says. "I see how you stew. Let it all go away like a robin in winter."

"Robins come back."

"Don't be smart."

He tells me I'm skinny and should eat more, a common complaint, and struggles to his feet to find me a hot dog. Watching him limp, I think that perhaps I love Manny because he is weaker than I. He needs me at least as much as I need him. In the mornings, I take him on the walks his doctor has prescribed. I find him at dawn spreading chicken feed on the dirt around his untidy coop, where a rooster and two hens reside. These birds are Manny's confidants, his family. He tells them about the adventures of his past, mumbling. I come to him and say, "Manny, why are you talking to the chickens?"

"Because they're my girls."

I take his hand and lead him slowly to the ravine behind our houses. We walk the heavily rooted path that slants into the high maples. Here it is shady and cool, and at the bottom is a parched creek. We make our way along the bed, hunting for the raspberries we know are here. As we eat them, he talks about his past—war days, Pacific memories like flashes of lightning illuminating his youth, and an Indiana girl who left him. I don't know much about Manny. He is a longtime divorcé, childless, who once taught high school and sold hardware before retiring to his abandoned farmhouse. He loved and loves women, brags about fantastical conquests in far-off cities I'm not convinced he's been to. At the end of our walks, he thanks me with fresh eggs and tells me I'm his beauty.

"One hot dog with everything," he says, coming out to the porch. "Do I take care of you, or what?" He hands me the unwelcome treat on a plate. I will nibble at it to humor him.

The sky darkens to a deep blue velvet, and soon the news will be over. I should say good night and go to bed, but I don't want to be alone. I think of how during the day, Manny is often not at home. He is playing blackjack on the riverboat casino or reading Jack London stories to children in the public school where he volunteers. And when he is home, he is fooling around with his guitar, or woodworking in the garage, and would he hear a noise if I was in trouble? Would I have time to call for help? Would I want help?

"He's free," I say.

"Who?"

"Nate. He's moving to Louisville."

"Louisville's a long way off."

"Two hours, if that. That's not far. It's a trip you could take on a whim," I say.

Manny turns his face to me, close enough that I can smell the gin and cologne. "I'm sure as hell not losing sleep," he says. "You losing sleep?"

It's no use lying to Manny, one reason I like him. "I am."

"Like a robin in winter," he tries again.

I walk home in the near dark, through high summer grass I'm too lazy to mow. All around me, in my backyard, dandelions sprout in clumps. Maple saplings loom here and there, and at the edge of the yard, where fireflies fade and burn, you can see the forest encroaching, floating its spores into the grass. By August, the bramble will be at my door.

The cool buzz of the gin is a blessing I've come to crave. One drink more, and I could face what's inside. Boxes and binders and stacks of history.

Today I picked up the copy of the case file, *The People* v. *Nathan Duke,* 1996. It was a big case. It's standing in white towers in cardboard boxes inside my dining room. Transcripts, affidavits, police reports, motions, countermotions, crime scene photos. And last week I went to the newspaper offices after hours and made copies of clips about the trial. That's not to mention what I found in the house. My journals, for instance, the wedding license, photos from the ceremony and reception. From the file cabinet: the house deed and car loan papers and bank account statements. You don't know what might count in the end, what detail might reveal some fact you need, so I gathered every record of our married lives. Electricity bills, photo albums, Christmas cards. I put it all in the dining room.

I go inside, and the sudden brightness of the kitchen makes my head throb. Sweating, I stand at the sink and splash water on my face and arms. I sometimes touch the scar beneath my shoulder-length blond curls and trace its trajectory from the top of my crown to the top of my forehead. I do this now. I don't know why. Maybe it's that when people tell you you've no control over your mind, you start thinking of yourself as flesh and bone, and there's comfort in resignation. The doctors say I've invented certain recollections out of half-fact. They say we do this all the time, even people who haven't been hit with a rock.

Standing in the kitchen, I can feel the pressure of my life sitting in the dining room, behind the door. It's waiting for me, the snapshots of the two of us in Maine, the good times on the beach. I can see for myself he was a handsome man with a winning smile, and I had a nice figure, and our bank account was full. I can understand what happened is a tragedy, and I am one of its victims.

But I'm suspended in the tragic action.

I walk through the door into the dining room and switch on the light. The documents are still here, standing in tall, imposing stacks, like a load left in the night by unwelcome visitors. Soon I'm going to go through everything.

Since the news in the spring I see Rita Corelli, my therapist, once a week in the afternoon. She works in Evansville, the city on the Ohio River about a half hour from my house. When I go there I never drive the most direct route, but take rarely traveled roads. I go easy around the curves and look at the fields. There is a rusty bridge along the way over a small creek, and once I stopped there. I got out and looked at the sunlight shining through the water, onto the smooth rocks and the coppery backs of crawdads moving stealthily beneath them. I take my time because to talk to Rita I need to feel close to myself, alone though not lonely, so I can speak about what happened and not be afraid.

I don't usually want to go, but once I'm there, I feel better. In the afternoon her office is full of light, so all Rita's jewelry shines back at me—long, silver earrings, turquoise bracelets. Slender and lithe in silk and suede, she moves with the pleasing assurance of a dancer. Seated on the edge of her chair, with unwavering intensity, Rita hears every word I say.

We are talking about the day this April when the media broke the news about Benjamin Hodge. While in prison, he confessed to prosecutors that he'd attacked a woman named Maggie Duke nearly six years ago. Once the press found out, Nate and I were the center of attention again.

"Do you remember the kind of day it was then?"

"It was a clear day, completely clear. The weather was cool and snappy."

"Did you go to work?"

"No. In the morning I went on a long drive to nowhere to avoid the phone calls from reporters. By the time I got back it was dark, and that night I watched the news."

She says nothing, as she always does when I fall silent too quickly. She looks at me dead on, her eyes bright with interest, not pity. I have often thought she is beautiful.

"Just to see. I was curious. I wanted to know who he was, what he looked like. I didn't care about the story itself. I knew what it was, and didn't believe it, so I turned the sound down all the way. I sat very still and thought about how it's only news, only television, and none of it matters. So I saw him. Ben Hodge came on the screen, and I watched."

"How did he look to you?"

"He was in an orange prison suit. He was real tall and skinny and wore tinted glasses. The news kept replaying the same footage—him walking from some government building with cuffs on, toward a van, then ducking into the van. He looked at the camera as he went. They kept replaying this, about four times. I remember his walk was very awkward—he sort of slouched, he seemed uncomfortable with himself. And I didn't recognize him. I'd never seen him in my life."

"Was there anything else about the newscast you remember?"

"There was footage from the trial—Nate and his lawyers, me in a green dress with the prosecutor, leaving the courthouse. I looked scared. I wouldn't face the cameras. Seeing that on television, I could feel very sorry for the girl and her troubles, as if I was watching someone else. When the segment was over, I didn't turn off the TV. I kept watching through the sports and the weather, and the national news and the entertainment news. I let the TV roll on without sound, and I didn't get up from the couch. While watching, I decided I was going to be strong. I'd get to the bottom of it. The thing was, Rita, the most important thing, like a stone sitting in my gut, was that I'd never seen that man."

My head's down. Sometimes when I ramble I can't look at her, so I look at my hands like I've got to convince my own flesh of something. I often get hot and tearful inside when I talk to her, though right now I'm being good and strong. I look up and meet her gaze, so she knows it.

Then I tell her how I've copied all the court documents. I tell her I'm thinking I'll go through them soon.

"And you feel that's necessary?" She shows no judgment.

"Yes."

"Tell me why."

I look at my hands. I'm searching for the right words, and this isn't easy. There are not many words for instincts.

"To get close to it all. To know it close, so I own every little fact, because I deserve to. And to justify what I did."

"What did you do?"

I keep looking at my hands.

"I don't know."

This is a lie. I know what I did. I told the only version of events I was aware of, and I did not do so weakly. I spoke from the gut, throwing my voice to the back of the courtroom so everyone would make no mistake. So no one would confuse me with the brain-damaged creature the defense described me as to impeach my testimony. I was, in the words of the papers that took care to report the story, "strong," "unflustered," "convincing."

And so I damned him. Mary Starr, the prosecutor, turned to Nate, pointed at him. She asked me, *Is that the man you saw in the doorway?* I did not look at Nate. I looked at the air around his body.

Yes.

What?

Yes, that is the man I saw in the door.

He looked at me then. I didn't look back. I was waiting for the next question, staring at Mary, who rocked back and forth on her heels as she does when excited.

And what did he do?

He hit me.

How did he hit you?

He hit me with something in his hand.

Which hand, Maggie?

His left.

Is your husband left-handed?

He is.

And where did he hit you, Maggie?

In the head.

I lied to Rita. I know what I did. I pointed at the man I'd married and asked the world to hide him. The world obeyed, and I've had to live with that.

Shortly after he was incarcerated, he began to send me letters—one, two, sometimes three a week. My mother—I was living with my parents then and would for four years after the injury—always got the mail. She handed Nate's letters over with reluctance, saying, "You don't have to open or read this, and I don't think you should, but you're a grown woman." She didn't need to say it. The first dozen letters I gave back to my mother, unopened, and she surely threw them away. After he'd been sentenced and the letters continued, I did not reject them, but wrapped them, unopened, in a silk scarf, as one would store love letters.

The day I finally opened a letter was the day I went running again for the first time.

I'd always loved to run, but for months after I was hurt I was reluctant to set foot outside my parents' house. That year, I became afraid of the dark, of being naked, of unlocked doors and windows. I turned that home into a box of phobias, staged tantrums when my needs weren't met. My parents coddled me. They let me sleep with one lamp on. They allowed me to stay locked up as long as I wanted, forcing doctors to visit me, rather than I them. But one day, staying still became more terrifying than movement. I couldn't hide any longer. When everyone was out, I put on my shoes and left. Coatless, hatless, I walked out the door, leaving it open and unlocked. I went down to the end of our street, crossed the highway, and moved stealthily into the next neighborhood. I walked through it and the next, then suddenly into some patch of woods, then along a busy avenue. By the time the sun began to set, I was like a stray dog, not lost, but choosing the way that would afford me the greatest freedom of movement. In the dark, I began to run. My stride was wild and lurching. I paid no mind to where I was going. Hours later, spent, I found myself on the other side of Indianapolis, unsure of how to return. I called home collect and reached my mother, who was frantic. Somehow she found me in her car.

Later that night, while my parents snored away in the next room, I sat down and ripped open one of Nate's letters.

Maggie, it read,

Are you reading this? Why don't you write, call, visit? Am I dead?
Your silence is incredible. It's this prison I'm in, the brick piled up to
the lights. I write every week, and still you're silent. You can free me.
I actually, fuck me, hope you will. You've got courage. I knew that
the first time I saw you. Now I'm waiting for you to act. Take one
step, write a letter and let me know you're there—N

I put that note in my pocket and carried it with me for days. Every
now and then I would take it out and reread it, as I considered the best
response. Writing back wasn't an option. I couldn't start a conversation.
The trick was to face the situation as it was, to endure him and refuse
him at the same time. I read the letter over and over until I'd memorized
the words, and by then, they had little effect on me. Familiarity deprived
them of force.

The letter felt heavy in my pocket. The words were stones. I felt their
weight and still do and can only hope I someday won't.

People wonder why I live here, but they're afraid to ask. No one can look
me in the eye and say, "Why would you return to the house where a
stranger did such things to your body?" Because if they did say those
words, I would be forced to reply, "It was no stranger." And they, if honest, would retort, "The evidence is clear on that point." At once, I would
turn away, thinking, "Mine were the only eyes that saw."

But who wants to talk about particulars? People dance around the
story, asking, "Have you thought of moving closer to town?" I dismiss
the question with a nervous laugh, saying, "The house I have is lovely. I
like my neighbor and would miss this rolling countryside." And all these
things are true. The house *is* lovely. I do enjoy the country. It's also true
that, seeing as I won the property in the divorce, I pay not a dime to
reside here, and that's been crucial for a woman of limited means strapped
with high medical bills.

But I returned to the land for other reasons.

After that first run in Indianapolis, I routinely left the house, often at
strange hours, early in the morning or late at night. I'd go running or on
long walks, and this habit drove my mother mad. Once, after I did not
return from one of my moonlit rambles until full dawn, she wept on my

bed, holding my head to her chest. I pulled away from her, took her hand into mine, and told her it would be best if I moved.

She shook her head in a fitful way, as if trying to scare away a bee on her nose. "You're not well."

"I'm well enough to walk all night long and still want more. I'm well enough to live alone."

For months, there followed much discussion between me and my parents about where I would move to. They tried to sell me on a housing complex a stone's throw from their backyard. They would pay the rent and visit every other day. I pretended to consider the suggestion, but I didn't want to be dependent on my parents or so close to home. One night at dinner I announced I would move back to New Harmony.

My mother went red in the face and told me I'd never, in all my years, said anything so ridiculous. I told her I was sick and tired of feeling weak. I didn't want to be a patient any longer. I wanted to live on my own, and where could I afford to do that? Only in New Harmony. And besides, I added, it would do me good to reclaim that house. "When I go back," I said, "I'll make the land mine, not his, not ours, just mine—the place where I live and work."

Of course, this, too, was not the full truth.

That I had begun to doubt, I kept secret. That I still, even now, must be sure of all that happened here, I've never revealed.

I did not tell my mother, for example, that I've much to learn from this house. I can't explain to her that I want to know how night falls, how the moon makes the halls glow. She couldn't understand why I roam the rooms when I can't sleep, trying to memorize how the floors creak beneath my feet.

It's not a healthy life. I know that. I'm not concerned. What I long for is clarity, and that doesn't come easily to one with a split-open skull. People of my condition must pursue uncommon strategies of survival. I live like someone enduring a siege. The high-ceilinged rooms of this house conceal me with their thick walls, wood beams, the cherry moldings around the doors. Every corner holds idiosyncrasies that are like treasures to me. The kitchen door moans like a cat in heat. The faucets cough when asked for hot water. And always in the morning and at dusk, the heating ducts amplify an attic dove's plaintive coo. Such curiosities I count as part of my own defense. The house, the land spreading around it galvanize me toward my central purpose.

Am I sick to live inside the heart of this memory? To reenact the moment at night? I sometimes do. I get up at two and go downstairs and imagine the sound of the car. I stand in the entryway and stare at the door, trying to remember how it opened, the expression on my husband's face.

Tonight is one of my sleepless nights. Well before dawn, I creep downstairs for milk and cookies. Sitting down with my snack in the dining room, I try to get used to the power of the documentation stacked around me. I pick up a transcript at random and thumb through it. Officer Jacobs, talking about the way he found me. Officer Jacobs describing the head as "split wide open." Talking about the blood in the carpet "squishing under our feet," and the nightgown "ripped, from the neck and halfway down." Saying, "there was this stream of drool coming out of her mouth and her foot was jerking, banging against the bed." I sit there and eat my cookies and read this. I say to myself these are only facts. I say to myself this is only evidence. It's only a transcript, words on paper, typed by Annie French, court reporter. I thumb through the transcript and say to myself it's only paper.

Officer Jacobs saying, "I arrived with Officer Castle at three-twenty a.m., approximately." Saying, "her pulse was extremely slow."

Months ago, while doing laundry in the basement, I came upon Nate's deer-hunting rifle. It was in its rack by the water heater, gleaming in the dark. At once, I knew I was going to keep it.

In the fall, he would go to the woods with his father and bring home deer. The rifle never left its rack but for those few times. After the trial, while I was still living with my parents in Indianapolis, his father came down here, boxed up his things, and took them away. Only he must not have seen the gun.

I forgot about it until they let Nate free. After I read in the paper how he's moved to Louisville, I bring the gun up from the basement. I put it on the kitchen table and get used to its being there.

Later that week, I watch the evening news with the gun in my lap. I eat Ritz crackers and watch Peter Jennings and put my hands on the metal to get comfortable with the feel. During one of the commercials, I turn it toward my face and look down the hole. I flip the safety off and on. The news is talking about the stock market sinking and how we might be "facing a long-lasting recession." The news is showing pictures of people on Wall Street, and I want to learn how to shoot this thing.

I ask Manny to teach me. One morning I'm outside looking across his backyard at five tin cans on a wood fence. Manny's different with his own gun in his arms. He is a relaxed man with more fluids flowing through him, eyes that see farther, a heart beating nice slow beats inside his caved-in chest. He's wearing an orange hunting cap even though it's eighty-five degrees and so humid you can't breathe.

"You look careless," he says to me. I'm standing with the gun pointing into the sky, the butt balanced on my toe like a pool cue. "You look like you're going to kill one or both of us inside a half hour," he says. "Listen."

And he tells me always to treat the rifle as if it's loaded, even when it's not, and never to point at anything I couldn't shoot. He tells me to direct it at the ground when idle, and to keep the action unloaded unless prepared to fire. He explains how to load so the cartridge slides into place. He shows me how to cradle the stock against the inside of my shoulder, how to stand with my feet apart and back straight. "Go ahead," he says. "There's no magic to it. You just aim the best you can and let go."

Shooting cracks me open. The crush of the butt knocks me back. I nearly lose my balance, and there is a pain in my shoulder.

"Did I hit something?"

"You hit something. I don't know what. But something."

"I didn't open my eyes," I say.

I fire again. This time, I'm almost ready for the bolt of the gun in my arms. The violence makes my insides shudder. Manny looks at me.

"Powerful, isn't it?" he says. I nod. "Maybe I'll take you hunting sometime. Whitetail in November. I haven't gone in years."

"Did you ever shoot a deer?"

"Sure. Not that often, though. I missed more than I hit. I always had the shakes." He holds out one of his hands, pale and bluish and somehow not belonging to the world around it. It trembles a little. "The shakes."

"What's it like to shoot a deer?"

"You're impressed with yourself for a while. You're a king. But then you've got a big mess on your hands."

I'm thinking about the woods in winter and seeing a buck caught against a snowy thicket.

Manny raises his rifle and shoots, and the fence splinters. I raise my gun, imagining the tension behind the trigger. I anticipate the force, and just knowing it's there in the gun is remarkable. When I twitch my finger there's a flash of light against my eyelids, and when I open them, pieces of can are falling into lazy onion grass.

Ready for bed, I walk through the house, switching off the lights. These rooms are too spacious at night. I can pace acres inside them. When Nate's father took away his belongings, he confiscated the furniture. All that was left was one table, a heavy walnut piece warped slightly out of shape and cracked. I kept that for the dining room, but had to raid secondhand shops and my parents' basement for the rest. And so I've half-furnished the house, designating some rooms for living, others for neglect. The living room, too large a space for me, is a dusty wasteland home to a tattered yellow couch I built forts with as a girl, and the master bedroom is for the ghosts alone. The cozy front parlor, though, is all mine, with a sensational red couch, walls lined with books, and a crumbling old fireplace. I've decorated the space with charms from my parents' home—a family of cornhusk dolls, tiny pewter mugs, a painting of the ocean by a dead uncle.

I double-check the lock on the front door and the windows, then go upstairs to the tiny bedroom I've made my own. Nothing in the room comes from our marriage. I dressed the new bed in my grandmother's quilt and hung two paintings of the Wabash River and New Harmony's hills. Paneled with lacquered oak, the room is fit for a B&B, and I feel safe here.

That night, I fall asleep and dream about the gun. I'm hunting. I'm following tracks in the snow. I'm in woods, which are full of noise— twigs exploding, trees creaking, snapping in the luminous gray. I don't have it in mind I'm out to kill. It's something else I'm doing. Searching for a deer, yes, but when I find it I'm going to take possession of it somehow, and this is what the gun is for. I'm young, with pigtails adorned with blue ribbons. I have ambition in me that is quiet and soft like the snow under my feet. The dark tracks are speaking to me like secrets. They are hidden and personal and unequivocally there. I move around trees, over logs, across a stream. I notice droppings and branches chewed raw by deer teeth. As I go on, I feel more and more acquainted. Until I see it. A sudden fact beneath a curved bough. It looks at me with dark eyes and blinks. I raise my gun.

I'm the deer. I'm outrunning the bullet. I'm leaping over logs and around trees, moving fast and deep into the thicket. I'm outrunning it. I have space to run forever, and leap. I awake winded and accomplished.

That morning I eat breakfast in the dining room and thumb through Officer Jacobs's testimony again.

Her foot wouldn't stop banging the bed.

Traces of blood on the doorknob.

Shards of glass and juice.

Reading the transcript, I realize I'm finally ready to do this.

The lawyers know how it works. They always start with the simple ones.

Like how old were we?

I was twenty-one, he was twenty-five.

What year was it?

Nineteen ninety-four.

And how did we meet?

I was majoring in history at Indiana University in Bloomington, and he was in the business school. One night I was a guest, he was a host, and there were a lot of people in the room between us. My roommate Julie, whose sister knew him, had told me a lot of older men would be there, and there would be plenty to drink.

He was the kind of man you notice at once. He wasn't a tall man or a stunningly attractive man, but he had presence. It was, I think, in the way he moved. As we came into the house, he was crossing the room to shake a man's hand. His steps were sudden, his face embattled and proud. He said his name, "Nate Duke," and flashed a smile that convinced you something very clever and delightful had just popped out of his mouth. "Pleased to meet you." That was the first time I saw him.

What was I wearing?

A black dress too nice for what the evening was—a beer-guzzling gathering of business school students in wrinkled denim and plaid. I shyly kept to the periphery, feeling conspicuous in my cocktail dress, which I'd worn only because my roommate wanted us to impress the older men. All I desired was to watch people and drink too much.

About that night there are only a few memories, touchstones that stand in sharp relief against the half-drunk recollection of a shadowy room, the mingling of young, anxious voices. Waiting alone for my roommate to bring me a drink, I have my eye out for the redheaded host, who's been circulating the apartment, chatting and laughing with friends. Then I see him through the door of the bedroom. A girl in a gray skirt is leaving the room, but he doesn't follow. He lingers in front of a mirror on the wall and looks at himself. I can see in the glass how he licks his lips, how his green eyes shine with vanity. His gaze suddenly locks onto my own, flickering with interest. This is how he first noticed me. Me admiring him admiring himself.

Not long after this I am thinking of leaving, but as I begin to look for Julie, he appears at my side.

"Nate Duke," he says.

He's confident in a way I haven't seen in a man before. I can't see him anywhere, and suddenly he pops up next to me, showing off his name like it's a gold coin.

"You're Maggie Wilson, aren't you?"

"How did you know?"

"I always know the names of my prettiest guests," he says. "You can't leave yet. I want to introduce you to people. You've been looking lonely all night."

"You've been watching?"

"How could I not?"

There's a quick, drunken familiarity between us. It's strange how I immediately want him to stay close, how I'm jealous of other women who might distract him away. I remember how he places a hand on the small of my back as he guides me through the kitchen onto a porch, where there are people he introduces me to.

"This is my friend Maggie Wilson. She's a very smart girl and she's trying to decide whether she likes me or not."

"Do you?" someone says.

"I don't think so," I lie.

Everyone laughs. "That'll have to change. I've got a feeling I'm going to like her," says Nate.

A short man with a mop of black hair and thick glasses lurches across the porch to Nate's side. "This is Tokes. We go to business school together. He's a real smart kid, aren't you, Tokes?"

Tokes's eyes are blurred with drink as he touches me on the wrist and says, "Be careful of this guy, Duke. He's an animal."

"Shut up, Tokes."

"Let me tell you about Nate. He knows *everybody*. And everybody knows him. Some people love 'im, some people hate 'im. Isn't that the size of it?" He throws his arm around Nate and pounds his back. Tokes staggers and spills his beer on my dress and shoes.

Cursing his friend, Nate grabs my hand and walks me into the kitchen. Soon he's kneeling on the floor with a wet rag, dabbing the hem of my dress.

"Tokes is an ass. Don't listen to him."

"Why do they love you? Why do they hate you?"

"Stick around and find out."

He wipes off my shoes, and I like the feel of his hand on my calf. I think he might kiss me when he stands, but Julie appears. She's holding my coat, ready to go home.

When we reach the door, he presses his mouth to my cheek and says, "Tell me where you live." I tell him, he lets me go, and soon I'm out on the street.

The next morning I answered my doorbell and found him standing there. His hair was slicked back, his face smooth and pink, shaved clean with a bit of foam by the ear. He put his hands on either side of the doorframe and said, How are you doing, Maggie Wilson? And I was doing fine. I was more than fine. Nate Duke was at my door looking jaunty and satisfied with the morning and me. He'd come to ask me out for dinner.

How did I get ready for him?

I chose a blue dress with white flowers and white hose, an outfit you might wear to church. It was all wrong. He wouldn't wear anything nice, but I didn't care. I had the idea I would take the risk of being extraordinary in an elegant way. I also wore a pin I've since lost—something blue and false with a little gold border. And I remember that I did not tell anyone about the date, not even my roommate or my best friend.

He took me to a Chinese place in a blue Camaro that smelled of leather and dark cologne. He drove fast enough to make the tires screech on the turns, and I wondered if he was showing off for me. At a stoplight, I looked the other way as his eyes wandered over my body.

Later, at the restaurant, he sat with his arms folded on the table, leaning toward me. He didn't care about the food. He cared about me. He wanted to see how I'd react to all he told me about himself.

When I asked him what he wanted to do after business school, he said, "I'm going to run for office. What do you think about that?"

"What should I think?"

"It doesn't matter."

"Don't you have better things to do than impress an undergraduate like me?"

He said no, not one like me, and did he have the face for politics?

"You have the face for any number of things," I said. And he did. It was a strong face, contained by a definite jaw. He had a tough little nose that gave you the impression it might have been broken a few times before. It was that kind of face. Aggressive and successful. A good mouth set straight and purposeful, and no fooling around in showing what he was after.

"I'm a Republican," he told me.

"I'm neither."

"My father's a Republican. He's big in the party down in Evansville, where we're from. That's why I think I could do it."

"Sounds like you could run for mayor," I said.

"I was thinking Congress. Washington."

"I've never been there."

"Where have you been?"

"Not many places," I said. "Ohio, Louisville, Michigan a lot. Not many places. Neither ocean. We never traveled."

"Someone should take you places, Maggie."

I learned a lot that night.

That his father owned a company called Duke Properties, which built office buildings and housing complexes and strip malls in Evansville. That Nathan was supposed to take over the business in a few years. I learned that he'd been a high school wrestler who'd beaten every kid in town, the small ones and the big ones, being "quick as lightning" on the mat. I learned that he had a mother in Atlanta he rarely spoke to, that he'd grown up with his father and younger brother. His friends called him Nut, because he had a hard head and was the most stubborn man they knew.

And that as we talked in our circle of candlelight he seemed to grin just from looking at me. That there was something very basic I liked about his arms, which were freckled and covered with soft red hair. He had a quiet, confidential way of talking that made me want him to touch me.

His arrogance seemed harmless. He smiled it away, neutralized his boasts with the light in his eyes. From the start, I wanted to hold my own with him, to match his dare to me with an equal will.

"What are you afraid of?" I asked, guessing he could not be as confident as he seemed.

"I don't know. What are you afraid of?"

"Dying, but I asked you first."

He shrugged. "I like to be in control of things," he said. "My father—he's also like that. When we're together, it's a disaster."

"Lots of fights?"

"Wars." He grinned. "He's a big shot, you know. A big fucking chief executive officer, and nobody tells him to shut up, but sometimes I do. And nobody tells him no, but sometimes I do." He looked down at his food.

"I'm sorry," I said.

"Don't say sorry. There's no problem. There's nothing to be afraid of. Here, to you—" His smile was suddenly convincing, it demanded trust. "To Maggie Wilson."

In the parking lot, I walked paces ahead so he would watch me. I wanted to be admired, to be found worthy. I wanted him to kiss me in the privacy of his car. He did so without hesitation, almost carelessly, and we kissed a long time in the dark.

Searching now, I can find no mention of that night in my journal. I recall shunning the blank page. I did not want to put into words the excitement of saying good night to Nathan Duke, of hearing him say he wanted to see me again. The only record is my fortune cookie message from that night's dinner, furtively placed between the pages of my journal: *Imagine you can get what you want.*

Of course, I didn't know what I wanted. I was a college senior spending her nights in bars, flirting with boys who meant nothing to her. I was playing drinking games with roommates in my pajamas. The future was a rumor we'd all heard about. We tossed around words like "job market" and "career" as if we knew what they meant. That's when Nate appeared, at the moment I was willing something big to happen.

The morning after our first date, he showed up at my part-time job. To help pay my tuition, I waitressed at a twenty-four-hour diner named Jake's. My shift was six to noon, and he was the only customer at six-thirty in the morning.

He sat down in a sunlit booth and opened up his newspaper, pretending he didn't know I was washing glasses behind the counter. He was unshaven and had kinks in his hair. His freckled shoulders showed through holes in his T-shirt.

I walked over and asked him, "What's in the news?"

He said, "You're in the news, babe."

"Don't call me that."

"You tell me what to call you, and I'll call you that all day long." He grinned.

"I can't really talk, you know. Jake'll get pissed off."

And Jake's voice came thundering across the empty diner: "What does he want?"

"The special," Nate said.

"He wants the special."

Jake took out two eggs and broke them over the grill, and while they sizzled he looked to the side at the greasy one-dollar bill taped to the wall. "How does he want them?"

"Over easy," Nate said, looking at me. He had a talent for making the innocent not so.

Customers started coming in, and I had to deal with them. Five minutes later I put the eggs and potatoes in front of Nate. He sat back and ate and watched me work. I stopped by after a while. "What do you want?"

"More coffee, thanks."

"You didn't come here to tell me anything?"

"No. But could I get some more coffee?"

I gave it to him, spilling some on purpose. He got up after a while and went to the register and paid. He put a dollar tip on the table and then waved to me as he left.

He made this a habit. He would come to the diner every morning I worked there, order the special, have two cups of coffee, read the paper, and watch me work. He said he liked how I did my job. He said, "You're kind of careless about the whole thing."

I wasn't careless. I just wasn't fussy. I'd say, "What can I get you?" like I'd been doing it for twenty years and had bacon grease in my ears. Playing the part was the fun of it. Nathan could see that. He could see because he was playing a part, too, coming into the diner and reading the paper and shouting hellos and good-byes to the staff like he'd just about helped open the place.

I think he thought it charming that I waitressed to pay tuition. He was a man who'd never had to work with his hands for a living. Later, I would keep this from my parents, for whom labor of one sort or another had been a fact of life. I'd taken jobs every summer during high school and for most of my college years. I'd mowed lawns and baby-sat and clerked at a grocery store. Nate, always in coat and tie, had interned in air-conditioned offices with his father in Evansville. I would once become angry with him for calling me his "little peasant."

But that fall I was charmed by his visits, and so was my boss. Nate was the only one in the diner who could make Jake smile. It was one of my boyfriend's principles that his circle of acquaintance could never be too wide. About the third or fourth time he came in, he went over to the counter and said to Jake's back, "Mr. Garcetti, my name's Nate Duke. I wanted to say I like your diner. It's a nice place for breakfast." Jake turned around, and I expected him to scowl or say nothing, but he put out his hand to shake. I could see as Nate took that hand that he was working some magic, that Jake's hard black eyes were softening. He was saying, "Thank you, sir," and smiling faintly, as Nate said again that he liked to come here, liked the sunlight, and the waitresses.

"Tell me," Jake said quietly to him, but loud enough for me to hear. "Is she a bad girl?"

"Very bad, Mr. Garcetti. You would not believe."

"I knew it. That's why I hired her. I could see it in her eyes. You're lucky there aren't rivals coming in every morning just like you."

"The early bird gets the worm."

"The worm!" Jake laughed, turning slowly back to the grill.

I assemble them in my mind. All boys to these eyes, but then, my most impressionable October, they wore some invisible coat of glamour. They were business school students, an athletic, high-stamina bunch that uniformly wore dress shirts and khakis to class. They gathered in university bars three or four nights a week, the usual objective being to bag "a piece of undergrad talent." The redheaded man in jeans and a T-shirt has the air of someone completely at home. He commands attention without trying. Surrounded by comrades, he leans against the bar, as a young woman sits by his side and listens.

"What's the upside?" is the challenge put to every problem, including Andy Becker's long-distance girlfriend. The lanky boy with a slouch stands beside Nate and looks at him when he talks, seeking approval.

"She's in love with me," answers Andy with irony.

The group roars with laughter.

"That's the downside."

"Nobody loves anybody from three hundred miles away," says Nate. "Cut your losses, reinvest, diversify."

"What are you going to do, e-mail her all year? She's not going to stand for that."

"Let me tell you something, Andy," Nate says, putting an arm around him. "You just got to make a decision and *do it,* tonight, before you waste more time. You think too much. Don't think. Whoever told you to *think* about women?" He smiles at me and winks.

"Take it from a goat," Tokes says. Then to me, "Or is Nate a romantic now?"

I watch my boyfriend drain his glass. The night before, he brought me roses. He seduced me into my own twin bed, pushed aside the stuffed animals, and nearly made love to me before I said no. He left me alone at midnight, kissing me wildly on my porch.

"He's got the right spark," I say.

Tokes howls. "Sparky! That's what I'm going to call you. Sparky Duke, the real estate tycoon!"

Why they loved him, why they hated him came down to the same reason. He told the truth about his friends to their faces. Or if it was not the truth, he believed it was, which had the same force.

"Tokes, you bastard, don't talk to my girlfriend. You don't know what romance is. All you want is money. You whack off to *The Wall Street Journal.*"

"Fuck you. You owe me a drink for that."

And Nate does buy his friend a drink, because he loves to buy people things, give money away, show his wealth to his peers. He's known among them as an heir, a man who has already come into a fortune.

"Just don't talk to Maggie about love," he says, handing Tokes a margarita.

"Tell me about love, Maggie? Tell me about love and Sparky."

"We don't talk much about that, actually."

"We're more into action," Nate says, biting my neck. Then he looks up at Andy. "What are you doing standing there, complaining about your girlfriend? Don't ever complain about that. Love her or leave her. And stop being so sad." He playfully punches Andy on the arm. Somehow the boy's grateful for this attention.

We spent hours and hours inside those bars. There was nothing else really worth doing. Business school was for drinking and bullshitting, at least for a certain crowd, and Nate was in the thick of it, with a preference for Jim Beam chasers. I drank Seven & Seven's. Arm-wrestling matches erupted three or four drinks into an evening. Pool games. Darts and late night basketball skirmishes played in the light of headlamps. Nate wanted me there watching.

"So you're a goat," I say to Nate that night in a moment of privacy in a backroom. There's a pool table between us.

"Who told you that?"

"Tokes always speaks the truth, doesn't he? You said that yesterday." Nate believes in the infallible honesty of only a few people I know of, one being himself, another his father, a third his friend Howard Tokes.

"That doesn't mean it's wise to listen." He takes down a cue. He sets up the rack, and I watch him break.

"It's good to know what a girl's getting herself into." I take my own cue, suddenly wanting to beat him. My first shot smoothly knocks a solid ball into a corner pocket to his surprise. The next one misses.

"Who says you're getting yourself into anything? Who says we're not just killing time? Fucking around?" He comes over and grabs the back of my hair and kisses me.

"Stop it and shoot."

He misses by a foot. I show him up, knocking two down in a row. When it's his turn, his face becomes serious. It's suddenly clear he wants to win as badly as I do. We hardly talk for twenty minutes. I make about half my shots, and so does he, and it comes down to an eight ball on the table. When it's my turn to take it, I do.

"Now tell me why you're a goat," I say.

"Let me show you."

"I'm not a conquest."

"I never thought you were. Not once. Not even the night I met you."

"Say three things you think you know about me," I say.

His smile spreads involuntarily. "One: you're going to become more beautiful every year of your life. Two: you're worth fighting for. Three: you don't lie."

He kisses my neck and says, "How'd I do?"

"Not bad."

"Your turn."

"You need people to love you," I say.

"No."

"You want to be famous."

"Yes."

"You're good. Despite yourself."

"Sparky!"

Tokes appears to pull my man into a game of fooz-ball.

I would run along a country road outside of town on the mornings I didn't work. I liked the open spaces, the gentle lift and fall of the land, how the vistas made you feel you could run a long way. I had strong legs. I ran slowly but for a long time, and the farther I ran, the freer I felt. I told Nate about this, and he said he wanted to come with me. I think he wanted to see what it was in me that came out on the road. That's how I kept winning the man over, I believe now—piquing his curiosity about what I might become.

We ran together two or three times. He, too, was a strong runner, perhaps more so than I. He would want to push the pace early on, and I had to slow him down. But as we moved away from the houses and into the mud-rutted fields where the violet light of morning spread in the sky, he would grow quiet. He would stride easily, with a peaceful expression on his face. And when he looked at the land and he looked at me, I sensed a soft respect in him for our traveling together, for our being such strong, graceful athletes as we then felt ourselves to be. As the miles passed under our feet, we picked up speed that wasn't forced but came to us naturally.

On one of those mornings, Nate waved a hand at a construction site we were passing on the edge of town. Skeletal frames of houses rose up against the cold white sky. "We're doing that in Evansville," he said. "Dad and I. We've got tracts of land. It's like gold."

"The houses?"

"And the land."

I looked at the empty wood frames. A cold breeze moved through them.

"They sell fast," he said. "We've got a bunch going up right now. Someday I'll show you."

"Someday I'll show you" was a sentence that had been coming up. His green eyes shone when he talked about the future. I recall thinking his ambition was boyish and charming, though perhaps not something you could always count on.

We stopped talking and just ran, and my legs felt sinuous, lit up with energy. I went faster, and Nate followed my lead. We looked at each other once more, then started to really go. We sprinted up the last hill into town.

I'd never gone to the trouble of placing photographs in albums, but that school year I filled up two. We were worth chronicling. I instantly felt this. Beneath the creased plastic of these albums, I pose at parties in pretty dresses, kiss him showily on the cheek. I find it hard to relate to this girl. They say that when we are traumatized as I was, you are reborn, a new person emerges. We cannot expect our new selves to live up to the demands of the old. Yet when I see this girl posing for cameras among friends and family, trying so earnestly to live a life that deserves respect and love, I am not envious. She runs faster and is quicker on her feet than I. She wears daintier clothes, has a brittle smile and glittery eyes. Her breath is sweet and does not know, as this mouth of mine knows, the taste of bourbon. Whether she is aware or not, she has already been claimed by the redheaded man. He appears in every photo with the malignant insistence of a centaur. All that fall, he drives her at breakneck pace through the dark, to far-off bars, to parties held by older men. He pulls her gradually away from her circle of friends. She sees less of Julie, the cellist in the music school, or Tracy, who dreams of working for Greenpeace. The girl I was cherishes no vivid ambitions. She believes unreasonably in Nate. She shuts her eyes to danger, stretches one arm out the window and feels the power of speed.

And Nate? What is learned from his photos? There is no gleam of treachery as he stands beside my mother in front of the family Christmas tree. There is no reason to fear this man on New Year's Eve, the day Nate came to meet my parents before driving us south to his home. He shook my father's hand, kissed my mother, left a bouquet of flowers behind. My mother quizzed him on the future and received nothing but satisfactory answers. He explained over tea how he would take over his father's real estate business, maybe he would run for office. I was so proud to present him, proud to see my parents impressed. My mother gazed on Nate as if sizing him up for a suit of clothes she wished him to try on right then. And in the kitchen she hissed into my ear, "He's a keeper. He's just lovely." Before Nate and I left, she insisted on a tree-side photograph, of me and Nate, then Nate and her. In these images, Nate beams at the camera, a suitor anxious to win everyone over.

Perhaps there is more to fear in the New Year's photo I took in his home. It's of Nate and his father in their kitchen. They're dressed exactly alike, in worn jeans and T-shirts, and each man has his hand around a can of Budweiser. They're sitting at the table, looking into the camera with force. Mr. Duke has a jowly face, folds in his neck, and he stares at you with deadpan eyes so full of confidence it's as if he's willing the shutter to wink. Nate has the same strength, only with a bit of a smile, a flare of mischief in his green eyes. The two of them sit in solidarity, drinking at noon on New Year's Day.

When he met me the evening before, Mr. Duke didn't so much shake my hand as test the sturdiness of it, finger the bones to make sure they were not easily broken. "How you taking care of Nate these days?"

"I think Nate's taking pretty good care of himself."

Mr. Duke frowned. "You need some help with the bags. Nate, help your girlfriend with her bags. Let me show you the rest of the family." He walked me through the house—a modern structure with rooms the size of hotel lobbies. The kitchen was out of a showroom, with chrome and digital appliances scrubbed shiny by maids. You could have played Frisbee in the living room. A forest of palms flourished in the corners. The walls were almost entirely blank, as if they'd yet to move in. Beside a stone fireplace, an armchair embraced a frail woman reading a magazine. This was Nate's grandmother, a widow, the only woman who lived there.

"Mom, meet Nate's girlfriend, Margaret, or you go by Meg, or Maggie. Maggie. Mom, meet Maggie."

The grandmother offered a thin smile through a lot of wrinkles. She struggled to her feet and told me she was pleased to meet "Nate's new girl."

I could see Nate's face in hers, its small, boxy frame and pugnacious chin. I watched Alice Duke carefully the few days I stayed there. She had a problem with the lighting. Her son was always flipping on lights, and she was always turning them off after he left the room. She kept her own bedroom dark, with heavy drapes drawn against the sun, and the door closed off from the noise. She used a black patch to cover her leaky eyes when she slept and stayed clear of sunbeams breaking through curtains.

That night we ate Kentucky Fried Chicken for dinner and had the same thing the next two nights. Drinking bottles of beer, we sat around the table with a paper bucket as its centerpiece. Despite the glorious kitchen, no one in the house seemed to cook. Nate's mother had been an amateur chef, but she left them thirteen years ago for Atlanta, where she started a catering business.

Later, after we were already engaged, I learned why. She'd had an affair with her future second husband, a Georgian, and afterwards Dick Duke had won custody. "She didn't really want us," Nate told me once. When visitations become a matter of choice, Nate stayed away, and she came to Indiana less frequently. Tommy, though, Nate's baby brother, didn't feel so bitter. His heart belonged to his mother. He would fly to Atlanta when he could to stay with her and the stepfather. Always good in school, Tommy had applied for early admission to Emory and had just been accepted.

Tommy appeared that night in the middle of the meal, a lanky, weed-like teen with jet black hair down to his shoulders and a Nirvana T-shirt. He mumbled hello from a safe distance, hands deep in his pockets, then tripped across the family room and hunted under newspapers for the remote. He found it, and the big TV at the end of the room split open to an interview of a movie star.

"This chicken's awfully good," said the grandmother, looking up with a little grease on her mouth. She turned to me and smiled hopefully, to see if I was happy.

Tommy changed the channel. A game show. Mr. Duke bit into breast meat. Nate wanted to get out and find his friends from high school and start New Year's Eve. We were all going to a bar to get drunk, and I was to meet everyone he grew up with. But I was in no hurry to leave. I wanted to get to know Mr. Duke.

"Your house is nice. It's very spacious," I said in his direction.

"You like it? It's new. We had it built a few years back, when my mom came to live with us."

"And your family's been here a long time?" I said, knowing the answer.

"You better believe it," said Dick, chewing. "There's a piece of land, not far from here, that my great-grandfather cleared back in the 1880s. Not many families go back that far." Pointing in his son's direction, he added, "Nate, you ought to take her out there."

"I'd like that," I said, trying to be good.

"And what about your family. What do your parents do?"

When I told him my mother worked in J.C. Penney's and my dad was an electrician, I could see the judgment in his eyes. And when he asked me what my plans were after college, I blurted out, "I'm a history major." It felt like the dumbest thing I'd ever said.

"I want to work for a newspaper," I added. "I'm a copy editor for the paper at school."

"Good. That's a good thing to want to do."

He turned toward Nate and I thought he might have given him a wink. I couldn't imagine what that meant, but it gave Nate the green light to get up and find my coat and head for the door.

I thanked the grandmother for dinner—she seemed to be the only one who would have cared—and we left. Mr. Duke didn't bother to wave from behind the next breast; the grandmother bent over a thigh, and Tommy changed the channel.

Celebrating New Year's Day with the Dukes came down to watching football and drinking beer. The grandmother amused herself with magazines in her own room. Tommy played computer chess. So it was left to Mr. Duke, his elder son, and me to monitor the Sugar and Cotton Bowls. Out of boredom and the desire to get away from his father, Nate insisted we go for a drive, which turned out to be the trip his father had suggested the night before.

He drove us into the countryside outside Evansville, through land that looked forgotten, mud fields flashing with ice. A silence sprang up between us, a new kind of excitement. He wanted to show me his world that day, his true home. He pointed to a tired house, saying, "That's where my friend Greg used to live. Now he's in the army. We'd go squirrel hunting with pellet guns. That's the barn where we'd drink the booze he stole from his dad."

The two-lane road wound through low hills. He pulled into a gravel drive that led to the gray Victorian farmhouse with dark windows.

"This is it," he said.

"Your grandparents' place."

"And their parents', too."

He got out of the car, and there was a sense of relief in his features, as he stretched and gazed across the dirt fields on either side of the house. "I spent just about half my life here."

After the divorce, his father deposited the boys with their grandparents for entire summers. I imagine it must have been idyllic then. The house wore a fresh coat of paint, the flowerbeds were full, and the house was warm with good cooking.

"How do you like it?"

The house had not been well taken care of since the grandfather died. But there was something exotic and lonely about the structure. There was almost nothing at all nearby, just one small cottage, and this particular bend in the road possessed a stillness that made you feel very much alone, held inside some secrecy. We walked across the grass up to the door. He opened it without a key, and the timbers settled around us. The house breathed cold air. We walked into a dark living room and found some furniture—a couch and pair of chairs covered in sheets, a delicate antique coffee table. On one wall hung black-and-white portraits of the grandfather, an ethnic-looking man with a heavy brow, and Alice Duke, looking young and glamorous in her gilded frame.

The sun emerged, casting light on a patch of varnished floor, and I suddenly knew. At any moment, perhaps that day, Nate would ask me to marry him and I would say yes. He would take me to this place to start a life. I knew this all at once, and the knowing was a chill that ran up my back and turned into a smile. I walked across the room and kissed Nathan. The house moaned under our feet.

Then I bolted away from him. I ran up the dark stairs, laughing breathlessly. Faced with two closed doors, I chose one, hid myself inside a room. There was a bed dressed in blankets as if still warm with life. I could hear Nate's footsteps. In an instant he would fling open the door and discover me, so I held my breath and tried to be silent.

The rain falls for a third day, and the yard is a quagmire. I am in the dining room, sifting through albums and old letters, searching for some record of another rainy afternoon. I can't find any. Not even a mention in the journal, though perhaps the proper volume is elsewhere, lost in the move, thrown away when I packed?

The truth is, I did not mention Nate by name often in my journal. I did not sit down and announce to the reader of those pages that I'd found a wonderful man named Nathan who seemed to love me. Nate was a "he" or "him," a faceless companion. I did not describe his bright green eyes. Or how it was to make love for the first time, inside his apartment, in a king-sized bed. I didn't write that afterwards I cried in a far corner of that bed and asked him to leave me alone. Or that in the morning I came to him and kissed him and made love to him again.

But I remember the events, and I remember the day it rained. At first, we had sun. We went running in the afternoon upon his insistence, and as we moved away from town, the sky purpled like a bruise. We followed our usual route until we reached the twin silos, where we normally turned around. Without a word, Nate sprinted past the silos and did not look back. There was nothing for me to do but follow. I pursued him at a dead run, and he was at a dead run, and soon I caught Nate, and we began to slow, enormous smiles on our faces. He grabbed my hand and pulled me off the road, down the gravel lane that cut into the forest and gave way to red clay. Skipping over roots down an embankment, we came to a creek. He called it a river and gave it a name.

I knew exactly what he was doing. I had prepared myself to be happy and grateful. I had anticipated how he would ask it and how I would answer, throwing my arms around his neck.

The rain began to fall, a spring downpour, cool and thrumming. Nate laughed and pushed his way past a thorny bush to reveal the picnic blanket and basket, the wine bottle and glasses.

I grabbed his hand, pulled him beneath a thick bush. A mesh of wood and leaves sheltered a floor of clay.

"Bring the basket," I said. "We'll have it here."

He left and came back, his face wet with rain. He kissed me, holding me close. "To hell with this rain," he said, laughing. "Let's have a picnic!"

He unpacked the basket before me, strawberries, blueberries, smoked salmon, cheese, and wine. The rain streamed through the branches, trickled down our backs and into the food. "Oh, Jesus," said Nate. "This is crazy. I can't wait."

He reached to the bottom of the basket and pulled out the ring. He opened the box and placed it on the palm of his hand.

"You want to marry me, Maggie Wilson?"

Almost not a question. A way of creating a new reality, ushering me through the first of many doors.

"Are you proposing? Is this a proposal?"

"Rain or shine?"

I took the ring from him and smiled and slipped it on my finger. We started laughing in each other's arms. We both had tears in our eyes. The rain started to come down harder.

Looking back, I could not say it was a baptism. I could not say I was transformed or overwhelmed or that mine is a special love story. I was appreciative that a man like him, who always knew what he wanted and took it, wanted me. That Nate had gone to the trouble to create the moment, had envisioned a picnic and found the place and made it all come to life.

Maybe I said yes because he would not tolerate less than total commitment, and nothing else in my life demanded so much. Or because I'd been raised to believe in something serious and sudden sweeping into a young woman's life, changing it forever and for the better.

Or because I had not been raised to say no.

Or because I loved him.

I know that dawn found me in the man's bed. Before Nate woke, I got up and put on one of his shirts. I walked through the still apartment, touching the tabletops and chairs. I tried to imagine myself feeling at home among these things. I thought of my own apartment and how my two roommates, students like myself, were slumbering alone in the sunlight. They would rise, unchanged by the night. I wanted to be with them, but knew I couldn't reveal my news. It was still too warm a secret, and nobody I knew had even thought about marriage. For an instant I wanted to put on my clothes, walk downstairs to the street and home. I wanted to seclude myself in my room containing rag dolls smelling of my parents' house, an afghan knit by my grandmother.

Instead, I went into the kitchen and tried to make breakfast, something as simple as eggs. I made a mess of it. While I was scraping the burnt egg onto a plate, Nate came up from behind me and grabbed my waist. He kissed my ear, spun me into his arms. He always was a man of stealth.

When you open the book, the first shot is of the two of us, just married and walking away from the altar arm-in-arm. We're caught in the light of the flash. My cheeks are bright red from the heat and makeup. He's taking a big step forward, smiling sleepily at the camera. I've turned toward him, laughing, relieved.

There are many pictures of the reception. Everyone is sunlit. We were in the backyard of a modest Indianapolis restaurant, and there was chicken for dinner and poppy-seed wedding cake, a swing band with trumpets and saxophones. There's a picture of the two of us dancing. Nate's giving me a twirl, and my free arm is outstretched, my neck tilted back so I look offbalance. People stand around us, clapping. There are empty wine bottles in the grass.

Dick Duke keeps popping up in the pictures. He's either throwing his arm around someone and pressing into the center, or moving about on the periphery, chatting up an aunt of mine. He had a way of being where the picture was. Nate's diminutive mother, with her spiky red hair, hovered inconspicuously in the shadows. When she came into contact with Nate, shame and hurt made his face soft, adolescent, and he shied away from her touch. I liked her. People said she was cold, heartless, but I saw the opposite. I saw an honest woman whose affection for her son came out in quiet, secretive moments, as when she took me aside and said, "Take good care of my son. He's going to need it."

Nate had a lot of friends there—buddies, admirers, probably a few enemies, too. Old contacts and associates from the parking lots, the vacant lots, the high school football game bleachers—the world the young Nate moved in. They all came. They brought wives, some of them, wives and children. They made their way through the crowd to slap him on the back and look into his face with innocent bafflement.

"Goddamn, Nut!"

"Goddamn, George."

"Good to see you. Congratulations!"

"George, meet my wife, Maggie Wilson Duke."

"Congratulations, Maggie Duke!"

"Thank you."

"Goddamn, Nut!"

"I know, George."

"Can you believe it?"

And then our arms would be tugged, and we would run off to another space and have another variation of the same conversation.

We were public. It was what marriage was. I was impressed with the crowds that assembled under the tent, around the tent, people I didn't know or should have recognized and once come to like were there, everyone watching us. Nate and me. Nate. Nut. Standing like a compass in a crowd of drunk, dazzled friends. He was photographed with one arm threaded through mine, the other gesturing to a fellow. We were public. You don't realize before you marry that is what you are going to become, but that is what it's all about. You face the camera, gather crowds around you, and live up to their demands.

"Meet my wife, Maggie Duke."

"Charmed to meet you."

"Likewise."

"She looks beautiful."

In the pictures, I'm drenched with sun. The white lace I wear out-shines my face, which sometimes smiles distantly, or is caught in confusion, a glance of acute, scatter-minded delight. The two of us are always arm-in-arm or mid-kiss.

He told me I looked beautiful a hundred times. "I can't get over it, Maggie!". . ."Look at you!". . . "Maggie, you're fantastic!"

I shook hands with calm, smiled with poise. I moved into the revelry with moderation in mind. Together every step of the way, Nate and I mingled well, warmly greeting every guest.

There is a picture of the car. His buddies took care of it with tubes of icing and balloons and blown-up condoms. The guests are throwing fist-fuls of birdseed. It wasn't the blue Camaro, but his father's light green Cadillac with leather seats.

We drove the car to the airport later that night. We took a highway that goes along the runways, where the planes rise over you. It was a dark road with the glare of the airport to our right, forest to our left, and a long stretch. We chatted about the wedding, and he steered with one hand on the wheel, the other rubbing my neck. He drove slower and slower. He grew quiet, then pulled the car onto the shoulder.

The memory is liquid. A night distilled, and headlights glide through it.

We moved into the backseat, where there was the scent of leather. We shared the exposure, the danger, proximity to asphalt, and the hot shriek of a truck moving past, feet away from where we kissed and clum-sily removed our clothes.

"Desire gets to you all of a sudden," I wrote in the journal.

I had hoped for something more graceful after the wedding, but the night fell out of our hands and into our hands. The cars kept going by, and it was all about the fear of being hit by a semi on the high-way. He said the hazard lights were blinking. I think I liked it. It didn't take long. I think an airplane took off in the middle and made me tense, but Nate said it was just an airplane. We laughed and it was okay.

Risks were going to be taken from the beginning. Semitrucks were the least of them. Airplanes. We were a bold couple. It was a good place. It was a wide seat, and we'd always remember.

At some point we got out and looked at the runway. He stretched. I leaned against his shoulder, more grateful than I'd ever been. A plane took off, a monstrous shadow, glorious and fast. Pretty soon we would be on one, flying east for the honeymoon.

There is no record of hesitation or regret.

In the hospital they would ask me why, on my twenty-third birthday, I packed a bag with a change of clothes, a toothbrush, a credit card, and drove south. I explained it to the police one day in the hospital. They recorded the interview and have kindly allowed me to copy the cassette. I listen to it now. My voice is not more than a whisper, but there is a streak of boldness in it. It's the voice of a woman who has faith all she says will be believed.

"I was pretending to sleep in the sun. The time was five, six o'clock in the morning. He is a man who gets up early. I hid under the covers, sensing him. I heard the sound of water falling off his body in the shower, there was the scent of aftershave. And then the flaps of his starched shirt and the sound of his arms in the shirt as he ties his tie. The pants, the clinking of keys, hard heels on the wood floor. I remember all of this. This time, this room, the fear in my skin as he circles me, I am sure of everything.

"This is the morning I find the bicycle. I remember that, too. After Nate left, I got up, dressed, and went to my car. It was already steamy, heat vibrated over the road. The sun shone directly on the inside wall of the garage, lighting up the snow shovel, a hoe, brooms, that greasy lawn mower, a workbench covered with rusty tools. You understand, I can see all of this clearly, I can see the sunlight falling on the hammer with the black iron head. Its handle pointed toward the back corner of the garage, to the bicycle I'd taken to Carson's house. I saw that the tires were flat and bent out of shape. He'd battered that, too.

"The rims had been hammered. Nails poked out of the tires. I eased the nails out with my fingers. They were such thin nails, something you'd hang a small picture with. Of course, he'd come out there at night after I'd gone to sleep. He might have been enraged, only the subtlety of the nails suggested a more collected man, a man with a sense of concise measures. I pictured him in his robe in the dark. He stood over the bike, holding the hammer in one hand, the nail in the other, and he tapped.

"I was comforted. I know that seems strange—that such a sight would comfort me. But as I touched the sharp tips of the nails I knew, at least, that I would not sleep there again that night. I'd made a decision."

I listen to this recording twice. The second time, I seem to be speaking with trancelike clarity. I know so well the story I'm telling.

The officer who was listening believed me. She looked up from her notes and said, "I'm sorry we have to go through this, Maggie, but thank you. You have such a good memory."

Benjamin Hodge exploded in the news one innocent day this April. Deputy County Prosecutor Mary Starr was the messenger. I'd last seen her five years ago, sitting in an office crowded with yellow-tabbed documents full of the secrets of my life. She wasn't a woman I'd ever wanted to speak with again, but that day—she'd called me by surprise and asked that I pay her a visit—I pretended to be strong.

"Good to see you again," I lied.

A mousy woman, Mary Starr assumed a morose expression of helplessness the moment I walked into her cluttered office. I remember how she refused to move her eyes off the books behind my head as she revealed that a strange man now in jail for breaking into a New Harmony woman's house had confessed to assaulting me.

"He knows a great deal about the case," Mary told me. "He knows precise details about the house, the rooms, the clothes you were wearing. It smacks of truth."

A phrase I wouldn't forget, smacking of truth. It was a shallow expression. Something that smacks of truth can't be trusted, I thought.

Mary Starr said, "We are considering asking the court to reverse Nate's conviction."

With these words, she finally looked at my face, and my eyes blinked away from hers.

"Can you explain why?" I asked.

"I can give you information. Evidence. I can show you the man's statement." The document was in a manila folder under her hands. She pushed it across the desk toward me. "You can choose to read it, you can choose not to. If you choose not to, I'll understand."

She looked at me as if I'd already lost an argument and she pitied me. I wanted to say, There is no argument, everyone already knows how it happened. I didn't open my mouth. I stared at her shrunken face and felt the same creeping nausea that had come to me in the courtroom, a sensation of nakedness before the world.

Soon after that conversation, news cameras appeared on my lawn. Female reporters in suits, scruffy cameramen hoisting their robotic eyes high on their shoulders, looking for a sign of me. I hid behind curtains, peering back at them, then slipped out the back door and escaped into the woods behind my house.

In the ravine, beneath a canopy of maples and sycamores, I ran rock to rock. At first, the forest was a blessing. I was hidden away from view, moving freely. I did not have to think about Mary Starr as I leaped from one stone to the next. Sometimes I slipped, and my foot sank into the cold spring water. But I kept on, frantic, scanning the bed for a dry stone to carry me incrementally farther downstream.

When I came to the river the creek fed, the water became too deep. There were no more stones to hold me. I had to seek refuge on land, among the thorny nettles and mud. I hiked uphill to a stump. I sat down on it and watched the current below, the shale-cool bend in the river. It was silent there. Above the ravine, there was nothing but acres of farmland spreading and no trace of trouble. Why was I hiding like a child?

Perhaps I'd had this coming all along. Perhaps I secretly knew this would happen. Why else had I moved down here a year ago? Why had I come, but to be faced with this? I recalled my husband on the threshold, waiting to strike me, his face pale and luminous against the night. He'd demanded to know where I'd been. I'd almost answered. His hand had gone up, a sudden motion to the right. There'd been something in his grip, an object I could never name. But I'd seen him. There hadn't been doubt in my voice when I'd said those things.

"There were always, we have to admit this now, Maggie, always questions about how *clear* your memory was," Mary Starr dared to say that April afternoon I visited her.

I did not, could not remind her that merely five years ago, she and all the others had believed me. I did not say that, despite what the doctors had suggested about Maggie Duke's damaged brain, the jury had been convinced.

Mary showed me a photograph of the man.

"Have you seen him before?"

"No."

"Have you ever heard the name?"

"No."

"Why are you crying?"

"I am upset by this."

"Of course you are, that is understandable, but can you tell me, honestly now, have you seen this man before?"

I had not. I have not. Ben Hodge I know only from the papers and the television I watch upon occasion, sound turned down so that I may not hear the words.

"So you have not seen him, then?"

"Never."

She nodded. She seemed to have already made a decision, though. I was no longer her witness. I recalled a question that had come up before the trial about which prosecutor would take the case. First it was Mary Starr, then briefly someone else, as the county prosecutor weighed a possible conflict. Mary had been in Nate's high school class. Hers was one of many faceless names I'd heard dropped like secrets between my husband and his friends. I remembered this as she again suggested I review Hodge's statements. She pushed the folder closer to my edge of the desk, an apologetic look in her eye, but I refused her offer.

I persisted in a strategy of disengagement from "the story" when the reporters called the day of Nate's release. No, I do not want to say anything, I told them all. I have said quite enough. I have always been a "no comment," a hole in the center of all the stories.

But time has passed. I need information. You can only be disengaged from the circumstances of your life for so long before you begin to go crazy.

Three days a week I work in the newsroom of the *Evansville Telegraph*, where I used to be employed. When I moved back here, the editors felt sorry for me and hired me on in the newspaper library. I clip up the articles, put them all in archival files, and so I've no choice but to see the news. It passes through my fingers. The day after the reporters came to my house, I saw the picture of Hodge sitting dead center, on the front page, staring up from his cell. He seemed surprised to have been found out by the camera. I rolled the paper tight in my hand and took it home.

I stored it in a safe place and have done the same with every other story about Hodge that has appeared in the local press. I've also written Mary and asked her to send me a copy of the man's statement. It arrived in the mail last week, yet another hefty transcript. Now I possess a small archive devoted to a man I'd never heard of three months before. Though I plan on reading all this material soon, I still know little about him. I've had the courage to read only one article, and that in part.

I learned little of value to me. I gathered he was an aimless youth invisible to the public, one of many young men adrift in rural acres deprived of opportunity. A New Harmony native, he'd been imprisoned in 1997 after breaking into the home of a librarian and attempting to rape her. While serving time for this crime, he came to know a Baptist pastor and was born again "as a soldier of Christ." He earned the nickname "the Apostle" for his penitential fasts and for trying to convert his fellow inmates. This past spring, shortly before he was to be released from jail, Hodge wrote a letter to Mary Starr in which he confessed to several crimes committed prior to his arrest, in the summer and fall of 1996, following his mother's death. In addition to stealing several cases of beer from the Amoco Mini-Mart, where he worked, Ben peeped into the homes of at least four different women, he claimed. He also admitted to breaking into a neighbor's house and taking some money from her purse. All this, in addition to the attack on Maggie Duke, had been on his chest for years, and it was time to seek forgiveness in the eyes of the Lord.

The photograph of Hodge accompanying the profile has the man sitting in his cell, looking malnourished, like a tent pole you could fold up. His face is a grayish-blue, and his eyes are sunk in shadowy pits. He holds a Bible in his hand. The caption reads: "God told me to confess."

This is the extent of my knowledge about him.

I don't believe what he says about me. Perhaps his confession is a way of claiming for his own a woman he once desired from a distance. Perhaps he needs attention. Perhaps he is mad. In truth, I don't know what to think about Hodge. His claim is an impossible proposition. He is like some black absence in the world, a negative image, and I am very afraid of him.

In a nightmare I had recently, he emerged from the woods behind my house to beg for food. I opened the door and left him bread and milk, then watched him take the offering away. Squatting in the woods, he made his meal on a log, a mouthful of moss, twigs for hands. Well fed, he grew roots behind my house. He rose up to the night sky, spreading his arms wide, sprouting branches of leaves and flesh-heavy blooms. I went outside and tried to murder him with an ax, but he turned the maneuver into a dance. Round and round we waltzed, while the world watched us on TV.

Although I don't believe I will ever do it, I imagine that before the summer ends I could go to where he lives and sit across from him. There will be glass or bars between us. He will sit motionless, not knowing what to say or how to act. I will ask him, How did you dream of me, and why, when I walk the streets, do I expect you are lurking in the corner of my vision? Why and how, Mr. Hodge? And I imagine he will provide answers that have nothing to do with those he gave the authorities, but will reveal a more private secret, one nobody will have heard but me.

Summer 1995

The day before I left home for good, we bought a car together—a red Chevy sedan to replace the Camaro. We found the car at the first lot we came to. Nate wasn't one for wasting time making decisions. We took it for a test drive and agreed in the car we'd take it. He bargained the salesman down three thousand dollars. The whole deal took about an hour.

"You like this car?" he said to me as we were driving away with it.

"I like it. I like the red."

"Good. We'll take this places." I can remember how he drove leaning close to the wheel, his eyes bright as he watched the road.

"How about the Grand Canyon?" I said.

"We'll go there."

"I can't believe we just bought this. Just like that."

He honked the horn twice.

The next morning, we were packed and on the road to Evansville. We drove with the windows down. I remember wishing we were going farther than we were. It only took four hours to get there, but I pretended it was a very long trip. There was no freeway, so we took a two-lane highway that curved around low hills and meandered through little towns with American Legion outposts and guns from the old battleships on display. There were valleys and villages coming out of nowhere: Bloomfield, Elnora, Spencer.

I wanted to go somewhere not on the map. Somewhere no one had ever heard of.

I had the map of Indiana spread out on my lap as Nate drove. He passed campers and tractors and didn't slow down for the curves.

"You don't think we should have shopped around?" he said.

"You knew what you wanted."

"We'll get another one next year."

50

"A new one?" I said.

"A new one every year."

"Years," I said. "I like the idea of having years to play with."

The road blazed under the wheels. It was a hot day. There hadn't been much rain that June. The sprinklers waved over the lawns in the towns we passed at fifty miles per hour.

We stopped at a Dairy Queen. It was a dirty, whitewashed shack on the side of the road, with a picnic table next to it in the dust and a trash barrel that bees buzzed over. We went up to the window. A very thin girl with blond hair and nails painted bright pink was sitting there reading a magazine, her chin in her hands.

I ordered a cone, he a banana split with nuts. I remember the nuts, because I hadn't known if he liked them on ice cream before then, and I thought that I had so much more to learn about this man I'd married.

"What town are we in?" I asked the girl.

"Petersburg."

"Thanks."

We sat on the table and looked around. Across the road was a drift of Queen Anne's lace, and the flowers bobbed, and Dairy Queen litter floated in it. It was a breezy day and the breeze made the place feel magical, or maybe it was the cold, ice cream rush crawling over my scalp. We were in a new town that didn't really exist, and I felt hidden. I wrote in my journal about feeling hidden in Petersburg with Nate, who ate his banana split in big bites and spilled strawberry sauce on his white T-shirt. And we sat on the top of the picnic table and he kissed my neck. It was early evening. While he kissed me there was the purr of an occasional car along the road, and the sound of the girl in the Dairy Queen chatting with a friend on the phone. I felt I could have lived there and been who I was meant to be, and no one would know me but Nate. That would have been fine.

I licked the strawberry sauce off his lips and said, "I want to drive."

"You want to drive?"

"The rest of the way. It's not so far."

He held on to my hips and wouldn't let go.

"Let's go," I said.

"No."

"I'm going to drive."

"Let's not drive."

"It's getting dark."

"I know," he said. "Let's drive a little and stop."

"You want to stop?"

"I want to drive a little and stop."

"Where are we going to stop?"

"It doesn't matter. Hurry, get in the car. It's dark."

"It's not quite dark," I said.

"It's dark enough," he said.

We got in. My mouth tasted sweet. I rolled the car softly over the asphalt, and the June night flowed into the car. At the edge of town we came to an overgrown baseball diamond with a rusty fence and dugouts covered with mossy shingles.

"Pull over."

There was a bottle of champagne left over from the wedding in a cooler in the trunk. We'd planned to use it to toast the new house, but Nate took it out and brought it with us. He took my hand and pulled me over the grass toward the far dugout. No one had mowed the field in a long time, and there were no bases. Clover sprouted through the dry dirt. At the back, behind the rusty fence, trees drooped in the heat, and you could smell the balmy rot of the woods.

We sat down in the cool grass behind the dugout. Nate twisted the wire on the bottle and pried out the cork. We drank straight from the bottle because there were no glasses, and the champagne spilled down our chins.

"It's a lovely place," I said, leaning my head against the cinder blocks.

"I don't know where we are."

"There are lots of lost places like this near that old house we're going to, aren't there?"

"My favorite's the river," he said. "I'll take you swimming."

"It's very private?"

"No one ever goes there."

We made love in the grass by the dugout. I remember that for the first time I felt sure of myself, my body. Emboldened by the champagne,

I stood over Nate and unzipped my dress, letting it fall to my feet like a movie star. It was a performance for him and for me. I loved the excitement of revealing myself in a new way, in the open air. I straddled him and unbuttoned his shirt. Nate rose and moved me onto the grass, throwing off clothes. His body in the hazy air seemed young and tender, his strength adolescent, on the verge of becoming something more. He came to me blushing. I smiled and guided him inside me. I liked the sound of it, the busy sucking and murmur.

I remember the next part of the story, too. How Nate insisted he drive on to the house, even though he'd had over half a bottle of champagne. He told me he'd driven in worse shape before, on roads darker and more roundabout than this. I said it was too nice a night for disaster and took the keys away from his hand. He took them back. We leaned against the car, kissing and tugging at the key ring. The chain broke in his hand, the keys fell.

"Stop it," he said. He saw my surprise, kissed my cheek. "I just mean, it's okay, really. Look, I bet I can throw this stone and hit that telephone pole."

I bet him a penny. He hit the pole. He grabbed the key, kissing me again, and promised to take me to a motel.

In the morning, he let me drive. The sunlight was in my lap all the way. The summer fields moved like water into the distance. I felt open and flexible, my life no longer a fragile thing to drop and break. There was the ease of the sun and the caress of my husband and a road. I intended to drive that car into the ground.

Nate's friend Eddie Sorewell would later talk to *The Patriot,* Evansville's afternoon paper, about the first time he came to our home for dinner. "I never saw a happier couple or a more peaceful household." He explained how Nathan had helped with the cooking, and how affectionate we'd been with each other.

I vaguely remember the night he spoke of. Seven years is a long time. A lot has happened. But late in the evening, when they were finishing the wine outside at the picnic table, I stood by the sink, washing dishes. I was listening to a moth whisper over the screen, and suddenly Nate's hands were around my waist, his lips on the nape of my neck. He told me then I was beautiful and he was very proud of me, a small gesture I would remember for its tenderness.

He wasn't a bad man in the beginning. I don't believe I am telling a story in which I do not understand the situation completely. His hands were gentle, his intentions good. I had faith in the way we began. I recall the night Eddie mentioned. We acted like lovers. Nate kept his hand on my knee as we talked with the guests about the weather.

I have a series of pictures of the house. They are from the first week there, when we were busy unpacking and sweeping away the dust. In one picture I smile sleepily, wearing a sundress. I stand in the front door of the gray house with the wide porch and decorative lattice. In the picture I look so satisfied and at home with this structure. I recall when I saw the house gleaming against the open sky that summer, I thought it to be a marvelous, American creation, scarcely real, a dreamed ornament abandoned on the landscape. There is another picture taken in the backyard, by an apple tree at the edge of the wooded ravine. I stand against the trunk, with both hands holding on to branches on either side of me. The bark looks smooth and glossy. I've turned my face coyly to the side so that the sun shines on my cheek.

"Stay still. Smile. You got to smile. This is history."

"It's history?"

"Of course it is. That's it. You're perfect. Look at you."

The house felt too big for us. There was one bedroom besides ours upstairs, and another downstairs, a large living room, a kitchen with space for a table, and a dining room, too. We left boxes still packed in the rooms for months. The house was foreign to us, though Nate had spent so much time in it as a boy. We laughed at its deficiencies, the spiders that spun webs in the corners, the mold in the bathroom, as if we could do nothing about them. We only lived there. We would leave in the fall, move on to the next town, or maybe we would die with the leaves.

That summer, one day bled into the other. We walked barefoot in the creek at the bottom of the ravine. The creek fed into a small river about a mile away, and we went there, to a deep place walled in by mossy shale and sycamore trees. Sometimes we swam and rested on the rocks. We talked about the future, making wild wishes. He wanted to build a big home, design it himself, put in a pool. I said, No, let's stay here, by the river, picking raspberries and making jam for a living. If we have to be rich, I said, if we have to own houses and property, let them be in Italy or on the coast of Maine.

Later that day, I lay in the sheets, aware of the moisture behind my knees, between my legs. He'd taken my clothes off like I was a helpless child. He was in the bathroom. The fan moved overhead, beating the room with its shadow. The very end of the afternoon. I waited for him.

"How do you feel?" he said.

"Nothing. I feel nothing. Maybe this is happiness."

"You're just tired. Too much sun. It's hot out there."

"I can't believe I'm in this house. I can't believe we're married. You know, my friends think I'm so crazy. They whisper to each other that Maggie Wilson's mad. No one gets married at twenty-one."

"Your friends don't know anything," he said, coming out of the bathroom. "They're frivolous compared to you. You're so brave, Maggie. Everyone said at the wedding how much composure you had. They all said she seems so *old.*"

"But everyone says I look older than I am. And what's frivolous about my friends? Julie's a cellist."

He didn't answer. I thought about the word "brave." It seemed wrong that he or anyone should use it to describe me simply for getting married. I worried about this word as Nate came to kiss me. I stopped him and said, "I'm not brave. I'm afraid of things. You are, too. It's better to know that."

"What are you afraid of now?"

"I'm a little afraid of this house." I laughed. "Of the ghosts in the closets!"

He told me his great-grandfather would play the fiddle in the attic every night if I was nice to him. He told me the ghosts on the Duke farm were all kind old men.

Evansville was and is a joyless town. I drive through it today, acknowledging its assets. There is the river, the lazy, silt-heavy Ohio, but the pleasure it offers is a depressive pleasure, like a bottle of bad red wine. There is the casino riverboat, but I don't go there. Downtown struggles to attract anyone after working hours with pedestrian walkways and fake antique street lamps, but every third storefront is vacant, having lost out to Wal-Mart. In a few hours, a workforce of tidy men and women will emerge from cubicles and head home in a general daze.

I've come to see Rita, one of the few people who can compel me to drive the half hour into town. Her office is my oasis, Two modern glass mosaics intimating kaleidoscopes hang over her desk. There are sandstone sculptures and African masks and turquoise trinkets from out west placed here and there on bookshelves. I always wonder where she's traveled, why she lives here, but we never discuss her past.

"What do you want to talk about?" says Rita with expectant energy.

"Last night I found a letter," I say. "A letter I wrote."

It is not so easy to talk. I've been at home for three days straight and haven't spoken with anyone but Manny. Tomorrow, I'll be grateful to return to work.

"I wrote that letter in the summer of 1995. It's dated July, just after our wedding, and addressed to my friend Julie, who then was playing cello in a symphony in Miami. An exciting life, and I wanted her to know mine was also exciting. It was, you know. We were busy setting up our house. It was all beginning. So I sat down and wrote a letter at the end of a long afternoon.

"That was the day Nate showed me his father's company in Evansville. I describe the offices to my friend. I say they're very impressive, very big, they take up two floors in the tallest building in town. I write how Nate shows up for work in a blue shirt and a gold tie and gold cufflinks and suspenders. I say my husband's office is spacious, that it has views of downtown, the Ohio River and Kentucky hills beyond. I say the brass plate on his door reads 'Senior Vice President, New Development.'"

I have to smile at this, and so does Rita. She knows where this is going.

"You read the letter last night?"

"I didn't send it."

"Do you remember why not?"

"It was dishonest. I left a lot out, you know. I left out the way Dick Duke greeted me with a hug that lasted a beat too long and said, 'Where've you been all my life?' I didn't mention the lunch. Dick and Dick's partner took Nate and me to the most expensive restaurant in town. The talk was of retail development and square footage and discount block stores. It was about some great purchase they'd just made next to a Fun Park, and the men were dropping names I'd never heard, local politicos, bankers, and real estate men. The thing that bothered me the most was that Dick never looked at me, except once, when he turned to joke, 'Now, how about my grandsons?' Even Nate sort of ignored me that day."

"How did that make you feel?"

"I felt excluded, alone. I found it hard to believe Dick Duke belonged to me, and I to him. I don't say this to complain. I'm just telling you how it was. And I remember that after our lunch, Nate had meetings, so I had to amuse myself by going shopping downtown. I wanted a new dress, but all the dresses on sale in the stores were frumpy and plaid, Little House on the Prairie stuff. The most interesting thing I could find was a pair of fishnet stockings, which I bought to be nettlesome. To kill more time, I went into an ice cream parlor. There were three girls, all about my age, talking about their cute professors, a party they'd been invited to, sorority gossip. You know, the kind of things I'd talked about not so long ago that I didn't wish I still could. When I went back to the office, Nate was on the phone and asked me to wait in the reception area. I recall sitting in there and just wanting to cry. Instead, I wrote a letter to my friend about our wonderful old house, the forest, the river we could swim in. I wrote about the wild raspberries and Nate's big office and his gold cufflinks. And I never sent the letter."

"Because you didn't believe in it."

"Right," I say. "But there was some truth in it."

She looks at me skeptically, as she does when I begin to defend my marriage, speak up for its virtues. Illusions about love, she has often said, die hard.

"I mean, you could point to that letter in some court and say, 'Maggie was happy.' And it would be a correct statement. You can point to other facts and say, 'Maggie was afraid,' and be right again. That's what bothers me so much. I want firm ground to stand on. I want to be able to say, this is how 'A' led to 'Z.'"

"You feel you need certainty," says Rita. "More than that, you need closure. And not everything you see in your past speaks so clearly to you—"

"Because you really couldn't say that summer was terrible. We were playing house as married couples do, hanging pictures and taking them down and hanging them up again. We invited couples over to show off our treasures. Reading that letter last night, I had the idea it wouldn't have ended the way it did if I hadn't done this or that. If I'd made better choices. I know it's pointless to think this. I know it's not true, or maybe it *is*. Should I blame myself? I shouldn't, but I do, and hate myself for it."

Rita gives me a long, slow-eyed look. She glances out the window at the river in the distance. "Is it so terrible if you did make mistakes, Maggie? You were only—what?—twenty years old."

Sometimes Rita says things that have the effect of a splash of ice-cold water. I start to laugh, and it's a physical relief.

"Sometimes the stakes seem very high, you know."

"All the more reason to laugh," she says.

The morning after the day that I'd discussed with Rita found me alone at home. Jobless, I had nothing to do, and the house seemed larger than ever. I cranked up the radio and tried on the fishnet stockings with a miniskirt and a sleeveless sweater. I was admiring the getup in the mirror, adding earrings and perfume, when the bell rang.

A small old man in a Reds cap stood on the porch. He held in his hands a bowl of eggs.

"Blessed angels of mercy," he said when I opened the door. "I'm Manny, who are you?"

"Maggie. Nice to meet you."

I offered my hand. He kissed it. It was somehow the most tender gesture of welcome I'd received.

"Would you like to come in?"

He took off his cap and gingerly stepped inside. He had one of those forever handsome faces, with a puckish smile twitching at the corner of his mouth. His uniformly white hair was swept across his brow in a boyish cut. He seemed shrunken by age, but still in possession of his old ease of movement.

"I just was out at the coop, and the hens, they're popping 'em out. It must be the heat, and God you look good. Where are you from? Check out these eggs. They're still warm."

He placed one in my hand. It was warm and rust-colored.

"Right out of the chicken! That's the beauty of the country."

He saw some confusion in my eyes and suddenly stopped talking.

"No, don't worry. Thank you, it's a nice gift. Do you live next door?" Nate had told me there was an old man in the ranch house nearby.

"Exactly. Manny Carter. I live next door. I keep chickens and thought you might like some eggs."

I told him thank you twice and suggested I make him an omelette. He said, no thanks, but how about some milk and cookies? Thank God, I'd gone to the market and Oreos were on hand. Soon we were snacking at the kitchen table. The first thing he said was, "How did a girl like you end up on rural route number five?"

"Is that where we are? What's wrong with it?"

"Nothing, I suppose. We don't have too many of your kind about, though—movie stars, glamour queens, people like that. What we got are small-time farmers, welfare cases, walking suicides, near-dead old folks, vigorous bachelor types like me, and a sprinkling of *U*topians . . ."

I asked him what he meant by the latter, and he reviewed the local history. In 1814, New Harmony had been settled by a kind of Christian cult, which had been done in by a regime of celibacy inspired by a direct command from Gabriel, the archangel. He appeared in all his terrifying glory before the leader of the settlers and demanded the women sleep alone, and that was that. Or so went one legend. A more enlightened group of scientist types from out east bought the land and set up a kind of university commune in the woods.

"That failed, too, but New Harmony's still a magical town."

"I've never been. I'm from Indianapolis."

"Of course, you're a city girl. I grew up in Cincinnati. Another river town, but much nicer than this Evansville, which is an unhappy and much too religious place, in my opinion."

"I was getting that feeling, too."

"People can be 'friendly,' in an ordinary way. I lived there thirty years. Taught high school for a while, then made the mistake of going into the hardware business. It was a woman that got me into the town, but that was over ages ago." He frowned into his milk. He looked up, and his brow was furrowed. "What are you doing today?"

I was doing nothing, and Manny wanted to show me the New

Harmony town museum—"an unparalleled collection of eccentric junk."
I agreed at once.

I recall wanting to be as charmed by New Harmony as I was by my
new neighbor. Around the edges, the town was just as rough and derelict
as any southern Indiana hamlet, but the center of New Harmony was
something to see with its Utopia-era cabins and dormitories and post-
modern visitors' center. The "business district" was a humble row of old-
fashioned storefronts selling paintings of covered bridges on saws, old-
fashioned soap, and handmade confections. As we walked along, Manny
linked his arm through mine "to keep up appearances," and nodded like a
gentleman at the strangers, who all stared at me.

"You'll have to forgive the locals," he said. "Fishnets here are primar-
ily for fish."

It was the museum, housed in a cavernous brick building called the
Workingman's Institute, that won me over. The three large rooms with
their creaky wooden floors held the town's most precious and banal treasures, including every arrowhead and pot ever dug up in Posey County
soil. We contemplated the one-time glory of muskets, swords, bullet cas-
ings, rolling pins, sewing machines, nineteenth-century dresses and
quilts. In the taxonomy room, we found the papery skins of northern
pike, large and small mouth bass with their mouths open. Frogs. Turtles.
Common snapper, Easter box, painted, false map turtle. And in the middle of the exhibit, like the great curator of decay, stood a skeleton of a
horse once named Old Fly.

But the greatest attraction of all was the eight-legged, two-headed
calf of Poseyville. The Siamese twin calves were born in 1900 in the barn
of Sam Bayless, according to the plaque. He showed the calves for money
at a dozen county fairs before they died eight days later. Though the
twins were complete, with separate hearts, stomachs, and brains, with
four legs and two eyes each, Bayless chose to call them by a single name:
"Daisy, the two-headed calf." We found her in a glass case. She stood
awkwardly on eight spindly legs clumped beneath her. Her neck
branched into two shrunken heads. Each mouth was sewn shut, each nose
blunted and brow caved as if some boot had stomped on the soft skulls.
Four black eyes looked up at you with wakeful and delirious blindness.

"New Harmony's oracle," whispered Manny. "If you come here at night, she'll tell you good news out of one mouth, bad news out of the other."

"What does she predict for me?"

"Unspeakable acts, I'm sure!"

Nate Duke never lost friends. Later, even after he was charged, they would go to him and offer their support. They would appear in newspaper articles, insisting on their buddy's innocence. His inherent goodness. He was an institution that way, and probably still is. The summer we moved to the farmhouse, they would come by on weekends. Some were married, but they wouldn't bring their wives. He would meet with them in the kitchen, where they would down beers like water and talk in loud voices about people they knew in town. Sometimes I would be a part of it, but more often I wouldn't. I got the feeling Nate didn't want me around. His friends were his private capital.

One was different, though. He was interested in getting to know Nate Duke's wife, and when Eric Johnson came over, I had fun. He emerged from our woods that summer, a trespasser and a friend. He interrupted a Sunday dinner with a heavy knock on the door.

"Nate Duke's one lucky sonofabitch," he said in a smoky voice when I answered his summons. "Charmed to meet you." He kissed my hand and smiled, his eyes shadowed by the frayed bill of his cap. He was skinny and tough in a muscle shirt that showed off dragon tattoos.

"That's Johnson," Nate shouted from the back of the house. "Don't let him near the silver."

"Your husband's worst enemy, at your service." He handed me a twelve-pack of beer. "Here's a bit of housewarming."

Soon we were all gathered around the kitchen table, eating some chili I'd made, drinking the beer. "So how you like living between nowhere and yesterday?" Johnson began.

"It's home now," I said.

"Nate was telling me about all the homemaking you two've been doing."

Nate told him to shut the hell up, then opened a can of beer for him.

"See, I talk, and your husband tells me to shut up, and I keep on talking," said Johnson, starting in on the chili. He ate greedily, burning his mouth and gulping the beer to cool it down. Johnson hadn't eaten a decent meal in a while and was in a bit of trouble, which was why he'd shown up at our door. The woman he was living with had changed the locks on the house and told him through a crack in the door to go to hell. Somehow, this didn't surprise me. Johnson had the dusty air of a man exhausted by travels, women, and the audacious duty of being himself. You wanted to play some small part in his misadventures.

"Can you believe that bitch?" he asked me. "You can't, can you? You're outraged a member of your own race would lock a man out of his house. Here's to your good woman."

We all clinked aluminum, and I asked Johnson what terrible thing he'd gone and done.

"It wasn't much of anything."

"He's starting to tell lies," said Nate. "You can tell from the way he's tapping his feet. All I want to know is, who was she?"

Johnson turned to me. "Your husband always assumes the worst about his buddy, but don't listen to a thing he says. What happened was, I'm living with a lovely doll of a lady named Penny, and Penny goes off for a week to visit her folks. During which time one lady by the name of Angela Stopher—"

Nate leaned his head back and laughed out loud.

"—who, by the way," Johnson continued, "was Nate's girl way back when she had the best chest in the school district. One year or another, she came on to me, and your man here broke my nose."

I shot a wondering look at Nate, who shrugged, smiling.

"Well, this Angie, she's a single mother of two now, and desperate for attention. She jumps my bones one night in Mary's and I do her the Christian service of making honest love to her in my car. The bitch turns around and blabs to Penny, and I've been locked out of my own house ever since. I was picking raspberries two fields over when I thought of walking to your place."

"And hitting me up for a bed," Nate groused.

I told Johnson he could have a bed for as long as he wanted and a shower. I brought him a towel and soap and showed him into the bathroom, a gesture Nate found cause to complain about. "Now he'll want to stay all week."

"That's all right. I kind of like him."

"Women usually do."

Nate decided he'd present Johnson with a hundred dollars to pay for a motel room. I tried to argue, but Johnson was so pleased with the cash that my concern seemed pointless.

Before he left, though, the two played basketball in the driveway. Nate, much shorter, was also quicker. But what gave him the real advantage was his voracious style of play. He hounded Johnson from the hoop and again and again stole the ball away. The big man was drenched in sweat and gasping for air by the end of the game. I recall how he lumbered off the driveway and waved at me. "You're married to an animal," Johnson said. My husband spun the ball in his hands and sent it sailing through the net.

On the way to the interview, Nate tried to calm me down.

"Tell them you can type fast," he said. "That's all they'll care about. You can type fast and you never make mistakes."

"I make mistakes all the time."

"Lie through your teeth," he said. "And smile."

"Okay."

"Smile real pretty. You look good."

I was sweating in the black pantsuit I'd bought at the mall in Evansville. It seemed to fit in the store mirror but turned out too big for my hips.

The interview had been arranged by Nate's father, who knew the editor of the paper, Rod Rainer. He was tall and thick-chested and wore suspenders. He walked around the office in his shirtsleeves, smiling silently at people through clenched teeth. He gave me the job that afternoon after talking to me in his office for five minutes.

"I like the way you hold yourself, Maggie. You have poise. I think you'll do fine."

Starting in July, I went to the newsroom every day to type obituaries. It wasn't as lively a place as I'd expected. Upholstered cubicles caged reporters who murmured to their sources through headsets. Thick gray carpet absorbed their footsteps as they shuffled about collecting the news. Always, there was the persistent low chatter of keystrokes, chirping phones, and easy gossip. Hanging over the newsroom seemed to be a malaise of routine, the endless taking of notes, punctuated now and then by some urgent disaster—a plane crash, drowning, or double homicide. My station was near the front of the room, between the elevators and the metro desk manned by the editors. They stared into their monitors, typing wildly, and now and then stopped to listen to the police scanner crackling with petty news of shoplifters and car wrecks.

The editor I dealt with was a boyish man named Bill Richards. He had sandy hair with a funny cowlick on top of his crown, a freckled nose, and a deep tan. His wife worked in the features section and walked around the office with a baby in her belly and pens in her hair. He would never talk to her, but concentrated on his work, trimming the news down on his screen.

That first week, people were friendly. They came by my desk to say hello and welcome. Then they stopped visiting and left me alone with my announcements to type. There was urgency to the job, a lot of copy to move and not much time. Death notices would roll through the fax machine all day long, and you had to whip through them without hesitation. You had to get the names right, the ages and funeral times. You had to say where they lived and how they died and list the survivors. It was solitary work, and I craved more contact with the reporters than it allowed. There was one who interested me, the cops reporter.

He was a tall, wiry man with a severe face that reminded me of a greyhound. He was handsome in a way you could not pin down. It had something to do with his constant, on-the-job hustle, or perhaps it was his eyes. They seemed always to be evaluating the world, searching for meaning not obvious on the surface of your face. He would arrive later than the others, dashing out of the elevator at a near jog, his sunglasses slipping down his long, thin nose, whorls of auburn hair twisting willfully into the air. He moved like he couldn't get anywhere fast enough.

"Who are you?" he said the day he first came by my desk.

"I'm Maggie."

"The new obit girl."

"I'm trying my best," I said. He took a giant bite out of a banana and stared at me, sly and detached. "And you must be the copy boy?"

He grinned. "Listen to her, the new girl. Who hired you?"

"Aren't you going to tell me who you are?"

"Carson, Phil. Read the paper—I'm on today's front page."

And before I could say another word, he left.

Every day he would come to work and hang his coat on the edge of his cubicle. Wrinkled and gray, with pockets stretched out of shape by his fists, it looked like something from a hand-me-down store. Then he'd make his rounds around the newsroom. If they weren't on the phone, he'd stop and talk to the reporters, saying, "What's on the plate?"

"I got a story about the school board vote last night. Nothing much."

"What happened? Anything good?"

"You'll see, Phil."

He'd always talk to the tiny woman with the high voice, who was said to be the best reporter on staff. She got the front-page stories, and her sources would sometimes complain because she was ruthless. She had a beautiful face, and you couldn't help liking her. I imagined Carson loved her. I hoped he did. I felt he needed someone to love.

"What's on the plate, Andrea?"

"Phil, I'll tell you—" She talked right back at him. You could tell she'd been around awhile. She had a way of hooking the phone under her ear and frantically scribbling her notes on the top of her computer console. "I got a little something about this housing project, the drug busts—"

"How many inches?"

"Twenty."

"Do twenty-five. Give us everything and we'll cut."

He loved the news. He had more sources than anyone else at the paper. He knew all the cops, could call them at home and talk to their wives if the story demanded it. He was always doing two things at once. He'd chat someone up on the phone while scrolling through the wire reports or composing a lead, all the while carrying on a conversation with the sports editor two cubicles over. He was the only reporter who liked to shout across the newsroom, but when he talked to me, he came up close and used a quiet voice.

"What's on the plate?"

"Obits."

"Nothing else?"

"Not a thing."

"Got anyone interesting?" he asked.

"Dead people, you mean? Oh, there's all sorts of interesting dead people today. It's a regular cocktail party."

"I'm glad we got someone like you cleaning up the stiffs."

"Is that what I do?"

He was gone. He stopped by every day, but never stayed long enough.

Those last weeks of summer, the sun was relentless. As I drove home, the light would give me headaches. I got in the habit of taking the back roads home, in search of undiscovered routes that would delay my return. Our life together, even then, was becoming routine.

"It's August already," I said. "Almost fall."

We were in bed with a bottle of wine to share. We'd just eaten dinner. Nathan stroked my hair, saying nothing.

"Don't be so quiet," I said. "It's scary. It makes the house seem too big."

I was afraid then of some absence between us, a lack of fervor and action. Marriage had been too easy. The courtship seemed to me as quick and sudden as the memory of a dream that comes to you midday. And here we were at the end of a peaceful summer, growing comfortable in a way that made me anxious.

"Aren't you worried about the fall?" I asked him.

"Why be worried?"

"I don't want the summer to end. I'm not ready to move on."

He frowned at me, his eyes glazed from the wine. "My grandmother used to pick apples from the tree out back and make pies. That's what you can do in the fall."

"I've never baked a pie in my life."

He reached to turn out the lamp. We were in the dark, listening to the insects, while I cast about for the right words to express what I meant about the summer ending and the fall coming and the house waiting for us to keep on.

"I hope it all works out, is all."

"The pies?"

"The pies. You don't understand anything I'm saying."

"That's because you're not making sense." He moved away from me in the bed, as if he were going to sleep, but I said chattily, "Nathan, let's go skinny-dipping."

He hadn't wanted to, but somehow I convinced him. We put on shorts and sandals and headed into the woods with a flashlight. Trees, immense and black, swayed around us as we walked gingerly down the path, our beam of light conjuring up horned nettles and tangled roots, a deep green bed of poison oak. At the bottom of the ravine, we stood on stones in the luminous stream. Nate turned off the flashlight suddenly, and we held hands, struck with blindness. Soon our eyes could make out the white limestone boulders in the creek. "There," said Nate. "Follow me."

"Did you do this when you were a kid?"

"Once. When I was running from home."

"Why were you running?"

"To get away from my dad."

I wasn't surprised to hear this. I'd always imagined his father must have been hard to live with for a child, especially one as willful as Nate. Even then, when the two men were together, it seemed Nate smarted from some permanent wound to his ego inflicted by Dick Duke's heavy hand.

"How far did you get?"

"Pretty far."

"That's not much of an answer," I said, but he didn't respond. "Why were you running?"

"He'd beat me," he said. "With a stick."

"Why did he do it?"

"I'd beat up my brother. So my dad got me worse. He took me out back and whacked me with a stick and lost control. Mom had just left, and he was pretty fucked up. Drunk, I mean."

We'd reached the place where the creek meets the river and the water runs deep. What little moon there was made the wet shale shine. Stretching across the river was a sycamore bough that looked ancient, a giant bone from the ground. Silently, Nate began to take off his clothes. I watched him, wondering if he would say more, if he'd reveal what his stern face was hiding.

"I'm sorry," I said, kissing him, "about your dad."

"It's old history. Aren't you going to strip?"

I undressed myself as he watched. Finally, we stood before each other, white and soft, nocturnal creatures, our eyes gleaming in the dark. He whispered in my ear, "Don't ask so many questions. Let's just swim."

"You get in first," I said. "I want to watch you."

He shrugged, then leaped into the water with a sharp yelp. Balancing, I walked out onto the sycamore trunk and sat down, my legs hanging over the pool. Suspended in the dark, I felt delighted and vulnerable. He swam below, diving, surfacing, disappearing again.

"Where are you?"

"I'm here," he said from a ways downstream. "Get in."

"I like watching."

He dove under again. I wasn't sure I wanted to swim in that murky water—it smelled faintly of clay.

"Come on, it was your idea."

I was thinking of Nate, the boy, running away from home. He must be fast as he hops rock-to-rock down the stream. Hidden deep in a ravine, he'll go a long way on murderous thoughts and the desire to vanish like his mom. Suddenly, I felt Nate's hands on my ankles. He pulled me down with a jerk, and I screamed with surprise. I sank a long way, until my feet touched slime. Rising to the river's surface, I felt his cold legs floating around me in an awkward embrace.

These days, I am a curiosity at the *Telegraph*. Everyone there knows about what happened to me, and a few of the reporters want to be my friend. As if my hardship merits some friendliness. And so on the odd day I sit in the library and clip up the paper, they come and ask how I am, what's new, am I still living in the country? They never know what to say after I give them their answers, and the conversations die before they even begin.

I want them to try harder. I want them to wipe their artificial smiles away and endure the awkward silences, to take the time to get inside my life and fill it up. I don't know how to ask for that. You give the world the cold shoulder for so many years, and it starts to come naturally.

One reporter has tried harder. But not out of kindness. Stanley Black works for the competition, the afternoon paper owned by the same company and housed in the same building. He's had to interview me dozens of times and has misquoted me as often. Now and then, he'll drift into the morgue, as the library's called, and ask me how I'm doing.

"It's not really your business," I'll say.

"Isn't it, though? I'm just trying to do my job."

"Go find yourself a new story, Stan. This one you've beaten to death."

When he really wants something, he calls me at home. I think he gets nervous about asking the questions his job forces him into asking, and he'd rather not be face-to-face. One day this week I pick up the phone, and it's him.

"I thought I'd check in," he says.

"You never just check in. What do you want?"

"That's what I like about you, Maggie. Right to the point. Here's the deal. We thought we might do a follow-up. You know. It's been a while. People might be interested to know."

Sometimes I almost want to smile at Stan Black, the way he talks

around things. "You'll have to do it without me," I say. "Use the file photos. Maybe you can pull that shot of me looking like I'm strung out on
heroin on the courthouse steps."

"Maggie. The editors are really pushing on me for this story."

"If you come here, I'll throw rocks. I'll call the sheriff."

"Would you do that?"

"I'd do something you wouldn't expect."

"Can I quote you?"

I hang up the phone. Three days later, the calls start again. One every
twenty-four hours. He keeps telling my machine: "My deadline's coming
up. If you could find some time to call me back, we'd be able to work this
out." As if his deadline were my problem, which on Thursday afternoon
it is because he comes to my house with notebooks and pens.

I watch him get out of his car from the window. I have always
thought he has the look of a trapped man. His eyes are nervous, they skip
over your face as he talks. He's too thin for his own good and looks lost in
his oversized clothes. As he approaches, I stand in the threshold, doing
my best to look like I might pull out a gun, and he stops halfway to the
door. He's a man who expects you to dislike him. He'd be at a loss if you
didn't.

"Will you throw your notebooks back in your car, Stan?"

"Why?"

"You can't come in otherwise."

He shrugs unhappily and tosses two notebooks on the hood, then
comes to the house empty-handed. He looks damp from the heat, abused
and hungry. I say to him, "Can I get you something to drink?" He says
no, but I don't care. I lead him into the kitchen and bring a pitcher of ice
water to the table. I put some potato chips on a plate—all I can find—
and place these things before him. I suddenly want him to like me. I
want him to drink and eat and not talk.

"This is real nice, Maggie."

"I could give you more, but I haven't been shopping in a long time.
The chips are stale. Sorry."

"Oh, no. It's fine." He chews one shamefully.

"So, what are you going to do to me?" I smile.

"I told you on your machine, so you know. We want to print something from your perspective." He always talks with the pronoun "we." He is never his own agent, only a messenger for the editors. "We want your side of the story, Maggie."

I say nothing, noticing the enormous dark patches under his arms, the sweat mottled on his forehead.

"It's an interesting side. You must have some thoughts at this stage in the game."

"I have nothing."

"For example, how have you been spending your time? Simple questions, stuff like that." He licks his lips, glancing distractedly over my shoulder, as if making a mental note of the dishes piled up in the sink, the ripped-open microwave pizza boxes left on the counter, emptied bottles of beer and wine.

"I don't talk to reporters."

"Why did you let me in, then?"

"Because you looked so thirsty."

He tries to smile at me, but he is too busy thinking of another question to ask, a sharper one that might make me bleed.

"We need to print something. We'll need to talk to people you know."

"Stan. Please don't do that. Please don't call a single person connected to me. I'm asking you."

He doesn't respond.

"I'm trying to live my life," I tell him. "I'm trying to survive and work, and I'd rather not be in the papers right now."

"Can I use that?" he says.

He is like a scavenger, all bird meat. He drinks some of the water. Over the brim of the glass, his eyes sparkle with mean intelligence.

"Leave me alone," I say. "It's not so much to ask."

Later that day it starts to rain, and as soon as it does, there's a knock on my back door. The simultaneity of the events scares me more than it should. For an instant, I panic and think of places to hide—the closet, behind the hems of old coats, the basement. But the knock comes again, a quick rhythm, and I have a feeling it's Manny.

I'm right. He's carrying a present that looks like a picture book wrapped in yellow paper and a bottle of white wine. He's just showered. His hair is parted precisely to one side, the bangs fine and shining.

"Darling," he says.

"What's this?"

"I'm here to brighten your day."

Outside, the wind is picking up, bending the corn.

"I like this weather, don't you?" He wipes his feet on the welcome mat like a gentleman. He hands me the wine and present and goes straight to the kitchen cabinet to find wineglasses. "I don't suppose you made me a cake?"

"It's your birthday, isn't it?"

He nods, his eyes bright and watery.

There's no cake to be had in my house, and hardly any food. The best I can manage on the spur of the moment is a pair of microwave lasagna dinners that come out lukewarm. Manny, gracious as always, relishes this offering and we sit down in the kitchen to drink the wine. By the time we've finished his bottle and opened one of mine, he places the gift in my hands with a little bow.

"I wanted someone to open a present on my birthday, if not me."

It's a road atlas of the United States. The paper is heavy, brightly colored and fragrant. The lines on the maps are bold, the states veined with highways and byways and railroad tracks. There are blowups of downtown districts.

Manny is staring at me with mock severity. "You like it?"

"I do. I like it."

"You know what you're supposed to do with it?"

"Tell me."

"Read it cover to cover. Every map. Find out where you want to go. Make notes. Plan something. Do it like you've got all the money in the world and nothing to worry about, like all that matters is getting to the Pacific in the most exciting way you can."

"What are you saying?"

"It's my big idea."

"This is your big idea?" I say, holding the atlas.

"Not that. The road trip. That you and I are going to take this summer."

"What are you talking about?"

"It will be a great adventure. That's what I'm talking about—*the great adventure*. You've never been to the ocean and you need to get the hell out of this goddamn town where you've got these newspaper reporters knocking on your door. And don't tell me I'm not right about *that*."

Manny has a lot of ideas. He forgets them minutes after suggesting them. But this one is bold enough to count. He takes the atlas out of my hands and flips through it to the map of the whole country.

"This is what I'm talking about, Maggie. Look. This is where we are, here, in the heart of all this America. And this is how we've got to go. Down here by Texas, through New Mexico, Arizona, Reno, Vegas, the City of Angels, boom, the Pacific. San Diego, San Francisco. Or we can go this way, up north, Wisconsin, Minnesota. Just look at all those lakes! North Dakota, Montana. Think of the mountains. You got to read this, Maggie. That's why I'm giving it to you. Happy Birthday. And don't make that sad face anymore around me."

Together, we drink the wine and breeze through the atlas, talking of places we haven't been. We are poorly traveled people, lifelong midwesterners, though as a young man in the navy, Manny saw the South Pacific. I believe he had a devastating love affair in San Francisco before he sailed, and ever since his memories of the California coast have become more and more golden. Looking at the maps, the states and all the miles of roads, opens up my eyes to a new kind of living. I imagine a Nevada sunset shimmering over the desert, the empty, dry speed turning us free.

"I'd like to go here." I point to Nevada. "I've always wondered about it."

He finds an envelope on the table and writes on the back of it with a shaky hand: NEVADA. "What else?" he says. "Montana. Do you agree?"

"Yes. Montana, on the way back."

"If we return, that is. And Colorado?"

"Okay."

"Don't forget the Grand Canyon," he says.

I imagine how that old car would travel. We bought it used from a friend of Nate's named Derek. The man was over six feet tall and obese and called Nate "Mr. Duke," though they were in the same high school class. Nate took the car from him for two-thirds his asking price. It has a hundred-some thousand miles on it now.

"I like the idea of a place like Iowa, too," says Manny. "I like the idea of floating through a state like that, taking the country roads and talking to people along the way. What do you think?"

"I think we live that life already."

"Well, not in Iowa. Iowa is a dream state. It's a little cloud nestled in the center of the country." He writes it down. The list is getting long. I look at the atlas. The destinations are like candy: bright pink and yellow and ripples of chocolate highways.

"We're not really going to do this, Manny."

"Like hell." He doesn't look up.

"For one thing, we don't have any money."

"We don't need much, and speak for yourself."

"Well, I don't have any money, and I also got a job to go to."

"They'll let you off. Just smile for them pretty."

He tells me he's got a brother who's just about to die in South Dakota, and a nephew who lives like a king in Phoenix. He knows a woman from town, maybe an old lover, who moved out to St. Louis, where we could stop and buy gas and have ourselves a spot of lunch. We'll finish our drive in August in San Francisco, he says, and the white city will gleam for us, and the blue, blue bay, and the Golden Gate Bridge catching the sun.

"But why, Manny?"

"What do you mean, why?" His hands, blue-veined and spotted, rest over the roads of Southern California. "I want to see the ocean again, that's why."

He drains his glass, yawns, and stands up unsteadily. Before he goes, he tries to kiss me on the mouth, and I let him. He smells so clean today, of Ivory soap and Chardonnay. I watch him from my door to make sure he crosses the lawn without falling.

One day I come home from work and go inside the house, and the mirror is crooked. The one in the entryway with the cherry frame carved like roses. My face floats in the glass. My first thought: Someone is in here.

The house is empty of sound. I stand in the entryway afraid to step or call out. How often does this happen to other women? They come home and discover a little something out of place, a comb or a vase, a coat hanging on the wrong hook. And suddenly the halls are alive with creaking. I imagine Nathan sitting in the chair of the living room, wearing a suit, legs crossed. His red hair is longer, his eyes are sharper. I listen for his breath and stand in the entryway, unable to move. Around the corner of the wall, I see a ray of light from the back window, the shadow of a curtain in the breeze. I suddenly throw down my bag and go into the living room, ready to run into a pair of knives, a gun barrel, the horns of something sudden and nameless. And there's nothing, of course. An empty chair. A sunny carpet. Dust hanging in the air and the house empty.

I check all the rooms, and there's no one. The mirror is still crooked. They had come and gone, men with gloves. I understand that New Harmony is more heavily populated now than it once was. The cars are fast. There are men who can pick locks. Windows are easily opened. This house is a story. It has many orifices, many ways in, and the evidence sits in the dining room. I go over the stacks. They sit in the light collecting dust. I count them, each document. I can't seem to do anything else. There are seventy-four separate documents on the table. Four boxes of material unrelated to the case. One carton of file folders. The thermometer outside reads eighty-nine degrees. The time on the microwave clock is 6:03.

There is no one in the house. I check the closets. Eleven pairs of shoes. I check under my bed and behind the coatrack and in the closet, where there are three coats and a basket of mittens. And the mirror is crooked.

The next day, I get Manny to come with me to a locksmith. I tell the man in the canvas apron I need the best kind of lock. I want something that takes five minutes to open. It can be as expensive as anything, I say. He shows me a Yale double bolt made of brass, and a chain lock, and a brass doorknob. We buy all three, and Manny says he'll install them for me.

On the way home, we can see the heat, which is getting worse every day, rising off the asphalt. We smell the faint burn of tar through open windows. Manny sits in the passenger seat, the hot wind in his hair and a paper bag full of locks on his lap.

"Manny, you didn't by any chance go inside the house yesterday?"

He glares at me. "What?"

"You didn't just run in to borrow anything? While I was out?"

"That's what these locks are about then, I guess. You think I'm getting inside your house?"

"Well, did you or didn't you?"

"I've never done a thing like that in all my life."

Manny waits for me to explain myself, and when I don't, he looks out his own window. "God almighty," he mutters to himself. "Of all the crazy things."

"Something wasn't right yesterday."

"Well?"

"The mirror was crooked. And how does a mirror do that on its own?"

"Lots of ways. Things slip. They fall apart. Break. Happens every day." He watches me driving for a long time, and I know he's thinking, What in hell's wrong with you, girl, and I wish he'd stop it.

When we get home, he sets to changing the locks. He's got a lot of tools on the porch, all of them rusty. He's glad to have a chance to use them, even if it is too hot. He struggles in the sun with a screwdriver, and now and then asks for a tool. I watch him work, hand him what he needs, and pray he knows what he's doing.

There's a message from my mother on the machine. She has received a call from the man at the paper. The man who always wants to talk to me, but who now wants to talk to her.

I ring her at work immediately. When she answers, I take a deep breath to calm myself.

"So it's me," I say.

"I thought you'd never call."

"You think I'd ignore a message like that? What did you tell him?"

"Pardon?" she stalls.

Surrounded by merchandise, racks of dresses and skirts, my mother is likely now gripping the phone with frantic devotion to my well-being. She's wheezing, having run across the floor from Accessories to catch the call. A tall woman, like me, she roams the suburban J.C. Penney offering fashion advice to middle-aged women four days a week. She has talent, being both deferential and pushy enough to persuade shoppers to buy unflattering, overpriced dresses and feel good about it. When she doesn't work, she dithers about the house, clipping out coupons and reading books about head injury, a subject she knows more about than her daughter. She is certain I'm on the verge of a nervous breakdown or a debilitating seizure, and in all our phone conversations tries to persuade me to come home, see a new doctor, or take a nap. If not all three. Worrying about me has become her obsession.

"Stan Black, Mother. What did you tell him?"

There is a long pause. She is strategizing how to tiptoe through this chat without sending me into hysterics. The last thing she wants is to upset me, she often insists, though it has become terribly easy to do so. She attributes my frequent rage to my "medical condition," as she calls it. *Head injury often results in the patient becoming uncontrollably antagonistic toward loved ones,* she has read. The latest demand to infuriate me was her request that I go to Cleveland to see a world-renowned neurologist. She has nightmares about my being killed by a seizure in the dead of night, but the truth is, a part of me likes the attacks. There's a thrill in not knowing how far the convulsions will go, or what's beyond the fractured light. I don't tell my mother such things. It would make her tear out her hair.

"You know, it was nothing really," she begins. "He's really a harmless man."

"I wish he were."

"But he is, Maggie. He's polite, quiet—"

"He's going to write an article about me, my life, for the world to read. That's *not* harmless."

This silences her for a time. "I'm sorry, I didn't mean to belittle it, only he didn't come across too smart, and—"

"That's the problem. What did you *tell* him?"

I have this habit of interrupting her. For some reason, all her speech sounds trivial to me. It's as if I'm speaking from the front line of some war and have no time for my fretting mother, who knows nothing of *my* emergency.

"He asked how you were. I told him almost nothing. I told him you were having seizures still and that you were sometimes a little— depressed, Maggie, which is true, but—I'm sorry. I'm very sorry."

Her apology doesn't touch me. I imagine her growing chatty and sentimental with the reporter, grateful to have a sympathetic ear, someone who wants to hear all her fears.

"You had no right to do that."

"I know, Maggie."

"You had no right to talk to a reporter about my life."

"I know."

"Because he's going to write in a newspaper about me—"

"Maggie, please."

"—and you are helping that parasite feed on your daughter."

I hear her groan. I want to push on with my voice, to wound her, so she knows how it is to be me. She is crying in earnest. I can picture the workplace mascara streaking down her face. Her tall, big-boned frame is tragic and stooped.

"There are people coming inside my house," I say, "and reporters calling and you calling, and I don't want any of you—"

"*Who's* inside your house?"

"No one."

"You said someone was inside the house."

"No one's inside," I say.

"What did you mean, then?"

"I was only talking about Manny."

There's a pause, and I already know what's coming before she insists I come up for a few days. She always wants me home.

"I was just there a few weeks ago," I say.

"It sounds like you could use another break, and it's a good time of year for a holiday, you know . . ." She rattles on, telling me if I come home, she'll take me to the State Fair with my little cousins, and we'll all have a fun time. But I've collapsed onto the couch, suddenly exhausted. I'm thinking there is something strange about the *Time* magazine on the coffee table, a place it doesn't belong.

"Maggie? Are you still there?"

"Yes."

"You sound tired."

"I'm fine."

"You don't sound it. You sound very far away all of a sudden."

"I am far away."

"That's not what I mean."

"I have to go," I say.

"Wait, I wanted to ask you—How are your seizures? Have you had any lately?"

I tell her no. She doesn't believe me. This always happens when we talk.

"It's okay if you tell me the truth," she cracks. "We just need to know."

Suddenly, the house settles around me, creaking all over as if someone has entered. And I wish I could only remember bringing the *Time* into this room. "Look, I think I'm going to go now."

"All right," she concedes. "But you know I didn't mean to talk to that reporter. He just kept asking questions."

"He's good at that. He never stops asking them. He'll never get the full story no matter how hard he tries."

She laughs with relief. "That's exactly how it was. That's right on the money."

First thing I do after we say good-bye is dial Stan Black's number. I've no idea what I'm going to say.

"Stan Black." His voice is like a bullet.

"Stanley," I say.

"Hello?"

"Please."

"Who's this?" he says.

"I have to ask you."

"Maggie? Is this Maggie?"

I haven't the heart for it. I know he'll fight me. I let the phone slide into its hook, turn off the ringer, and look at the road atlas on the table. I flip through the pages, thinking of New Mexico, Sioux City, Flagstaff, Arizona.

The fall unmoored us. The change in seasons set us free in an ocean of years, and we felt our lives expand in the cold. Nate took me to construction sites where beams were being lifted into place, and hammers and men's voices rang through the air. Nate stood among the carpenters like he was one of them, in plaid wool shirts and jeans. He possessed the ease of a man who, after delaying his destiny, had finally embraced it without question. He did everything with assurance.

Work consumed my husband. He had the ambition of a tycoon, the abilities of a novice. Somehow I felt this. Perhaps it was the way he talked about the future.

"I want more land, Maggie. I want space. We could build a mall by the exit ramp and next to it a hotel. It's only a matter of money. A small matter of financing."

But as he said such things, he paced his study. He had fear in his eyes.

"Relax," I told him once, trying to keep him in bed one Saturday morning. "It's only your job. It's nothing. I'm something. I want you to stay home today."

"What for?"

A cruel question, but honest. A long morning and afternoon, and what would we do with each other? Make love, and then? Movies and television were beneath us. We weren't interested in cooking extravagant meals, and restaurants made Nate jumpy. When he had free time, Nate would invite friends over and drink with them in our kitchen, visit his dad and brother, or practice shooting his gun at a target out back.

"We'll go for a drive," I tried. "To Louisville."

Nate had no time. He had too much work. He hustled from the office to the county government offices to building sites. As the fall wore on, he was at home less and less, and somehow I couldn't feel galvanized by his efforts.

It was obvious I needed to find friends. I knew few people in Evansville, but one of my favorites was Johnson. I sought him out that fall. He
made his living at a grocery store in Evansville not far from the newspaper office, and sometimes I would go there to shop. He'd take smoke
breaks with me in front of the store, wearing a red vest with cigarette
burns and his first name, *Eric,* in lazy stitch on the front.

"How's he doing?" He wouldn't want to say my husband's name
sometimes.

"He's fine."

"You got yourselves a nice setup there. With that house. The two of
you, you're like pioneers."

He had trouble speaking easily while at work, as if the job dimin-
ished him. He didn't smile so much, and his well-tanned skin looked less
radiant than overcooked.

I recall asking him about Penny, his love life, and he told me he'd
moved into his own apartment. "It's a dump, but at least I'm living free
and easy."

"And now?"

"I've got my heart set on Maggie Duke," he said, grinning slyly. I
smiled back and told him that was nice to know, and could he do me the
favor of teaching me how to smoke? He was delighted. I remember how
he treated the job with special reverence, as if I were a daughter he was
helping ride a bicycle for the first time. Speaking in a low voice, he held
the lighter close.

"Now breathe in," he said. "It hurts, but that's fine. After a few cigarettes you get used to it."

"Like sex."

"Only better."

We laughed. After coughing through the first cigarette, I took
another one and said, "A new hobby to go along with my new life."

I recall how he smiled sadly. "And how is your new life working out?"

"It's working out okay."

"Is it?"

"I think so."

I felt him watching me closely. "It's funny. I always knew Nate would
marry. I just never figured he'd pick a smart one like you."

Johnson was a natural flirt, and I felt appreciated when I was around him. But we had nothing in common besides my husband, and the talk invariably came around to him. Johnson had a bittersweet affection for Nate. He spoke of him by turns disparagingly and with great praise. Deep down, Johnson was afraid of Nate.

Once, Johnson invited me to his place after work. It was a miserable apartment in a warped wood house. A tour of the cramped rooms made me want to help him somehow. I liked his smile, his shabby chivalry, the way he brushed the dirt off one of two kitchen chairs before offering it to me. That day, as we sipped lukewarm Budweisers, he told me a story about my husband.

Nate and Johnson were fourteen at the time and had just learned how to smoke. Johnson's father's neighbor was the manager of a convenience store. Gifted with a sinister shrewdness I still recognized in Nate, my future husband persuaded Johnson to steal the store keys from the neighbor's coat pocket, thus setting the stage for their great adolescent cigarette heist.

"It's three in the morning when I meet Nate on the street corner," Johnson said. "And believe it or not, this little redhead punk comes strutting along with his dad's *pistol* in his belt. With the keys, we walk right into the store and take every carton of cigarettes in the place, just like we planned it. But afterwards, in the parking lot, Nate gets happy and starts to empty his dad's pistol at a streetlamp. I try to stop him, but he's on a high, you know, just fucking thrilled with himself for having masterminded this thing. Before we can get out of there, the cop car sirens start going a few blocks away, and we have to run. They catch me, but not little Mr. Duke, who disappears through an old lady's yard with half the cigarettes. Your uncle Johnson ends up spending the summer in juvenile detention while Mr. Duke runs around free as the Marlboro Man."

Johnson smiled bitterly. I wished he was gifted with better luck and faster feet. He was a man who deserved more from life than he took. He had a beautiful talent for losing. "You never told the police the truth?" I said.

"Tell on Nate?" Johnson sucked on the butt pinched between his fingers. "Not a chance in the world."

·   ·   ·

It was almost a dinner party. We had pears ripening in a bowl and candles burning and china on the table. We sat in the dining room, talking about houses and property values. Sam was an architect and a friend of Nate's. He was very tall and thin and had large ears that turned scarlet whenever my husband bothered to tease him. He was a dispassionate man, quietly energetic in shirtsleeves and tie, ready always to execute the duty of his husbandry with extreme competence. Janet, his wife, was short and round, and wore a full denim skirt. She ate more than he did, and dropped rice on her belly and worried over the stains with a wet paper towel in the kitchen.

Using a timer on the camera, Nate took a photograph of the four of us on the couch. The men have cigars in their mouths and sit on either side of Janet and me. I look startled and pale. Janet has a wide smile and a glowing, well-oiled face. Her hair is loose and bountiful. She is opulently pregnant.

All of us but Janet had been drinking that night—wine and then bourbon—to celebrate the imminent child. I drank more than I should have and grew silent over the course of the evening.

"How many kids you going to have?" Nate asked them, standing with his arms folded, in front of the crackling fireplace. All that night he was adding logs to the flame, pushing them about with a poker.

"As many as the little lady wants," said Sam.

"That could be a hell of a lot. I never seen you look so good, Janet," Nate teased.

"Well, *thank* you."

Sam put his long arm around her and smiled with fatherly gentility. Janet glowed with pleasure. There was something grotesque to me about the inertia of their affection—their bodies seemed to be resigned to each other.

I wanted Nate to come and sit next to me on the love seat, but he was too busy trying to talk his friend into taking a vacation to the Caribbean. "You'll be elbows up in shit and diapers in a year's time," he said. "Take a vacation before it's too late."

Janet smiled. "We're sitting tight until the little one arrives," she said, patting her belly.

"The trouble I have with children," Nate suddenly said, "is they all find their fathers disgusting."

"Really?" said Sam.

"There's always something about a father that repulses his children. Nose hair, big dicks, bellies. I hated my father for being fat. And the smell of his towels. He was foul and fat and hairy. And it's the same with all fathers."

Sam and Janet glanced at me, looking for my reaction. I held my attention on Nate. It was obvious my husband had drunk too much bourbon, and the evening should have ended then.

"So you hear much from Eric Johnson these days?" Sam said. Nate, Sam, and Johnson had all gone to the same high school.

"Oh, that kid?" laughed Nate. "What a mess. He showed up homeless one day, begging for a bed."

"He wasn't homeless and he wasn't begging," I said.

Nate turned to look at me. "I guess you don't remember. Were you there? His live-in girlfriend got tired of him. She kicked him out one day for fucking—get this, Sam—Angela Stopher."

The men laughed, and Janet, offended by Nate's language, looked at the floor.

"I like Johnson," I said.

Nate's gaze was an admonition. It seemed he didn't want me to talk at all. "He's a nice guy," I persisted. "I see him now and then at the grocery store."

"Which store?" Nate wanted to know.

"The I.G.A. near the newspaper, in Evansville. Sometimes I go there after work, and there he is at the register. But he hasn't given up. The last time I saw him he said he was applying to a community college. He wants to study graphic design."

Nate gave a sharp laugh. "Johnson's had so many schemes. Once he thought he wanted to be a policeman. He signed up for the physical tests and flunked out. Can you imagine that guy as a cop? That dope smoker? Sam, you ready for another?"

He was, and so was Nate. My husband, refusing to sit beside me, stood near the fire, entertaining Sam and Janet with talk of high school acquaintances, friends, and rivals. Marcus Miller had died in a car wreck;

Ricky Tool had found a wife from Kentucky and was selling shoes; Mary Starr had gone to law school and was working for the county prosecutor.

I was glad to see our guests clear out of the house shortly afterwards. As Sam and Janet drove away in their car, Nate went back into the kitchen to refill his glass, and I remained in the doorway. The radio had said a frost would be coming. I wanted to go on a walk in the vast night that spread away from the house. I felt an intense disappointment with the evening.

"Nate?"

We were lying in bed, on top of the covers. I was down to my slip and heels, he in his underwear.

"What?"

"Why did you say that about children? What were you *thinking?*"

He turned over quietly to stare at me, his eyes blurry. "What's with you and Johnson?"

Though this was the first time I can recall Nate's jealousy surfacing, somehow I'd suspected it was there all along. I'd chosen not to tell Nate about my meetings with Johnson. I'd never spelled out to myself why I'd kept silent, but in Nate's touch now I felt his anxiety. He put his hand around my wrist.

"I told you already. I see him at his grocery store."

"Why?"

"I like him."

He waited.

"And I'm bored. And I have no friends. And Johnson's kind of fun. He taught me how to smoke."

"He'd teach you more than that."

"Why are we having this conversation?"

He smiled. "You tell me."

I couldn't reply. I was beginning to cry, but Nate wasn't interested. He turned over in the dark and settled beside me in a posture of sleep.

The days were filled with news. I watched the stories come together before my eyes—train derailings, house fires, city council votes. Now and then there was a murderous love story that would make Bill walk twice as fast and whistle at his desk as he edited the copy. Phil Carson was always in the center of crimes. He had more on his hands than he could handle

and not enough on his hands. He piled notebooks high on his desk like a
defense against loneliness. He seemed to have few friends in the newsroom, but every morning he'd stop by my desk as if he were doing something secretive.

"How're they coming?"

The obits came the same every day. He didn't know how to talk to a
woman. I wondered if he was really a good reporter or just pretended to
be, or maybe when he was playing that role something magical happened
to his face, the sound of his voice.

"They're coming like there's no end to them," I said.

"That's good, that's good."

"What can I do for you, Carson?"

"People call me Phil."

"It's all right if I don't, isn't it?" I said.

"I think you'll do what you want."

I recall we had a cold November. There were snow flurries, and the
flakes were a reminder of a secret the world was trying to tell me about
myself. The colder it became, the more I wanted to feel beautiful. I
bought pleated skirts, snug dresses, tights, and open-neck blouses. I wore
jewelry and perfume to sustain myself. At work, I'd look up from my
screen to watch the newsroom, the complacent reporters coming and
going with their stories of the day. They chattered like smart alecks to
city hall sources, quietly typed up inches of glory for high school quarter-
backs and local CEOs. I seemed to be waiting for something to happen. I
was a married woman, twenty-two, comfortably employed and too easily
bored. I sometimes forgot myself and used my maiden name.

"You look nicer than an obit girl ought to," Carson said to me.

He chased ambulances and cop cars and looked over corpses dredged
up from the Ohio. People said he would write his stories with tears in his
eyes, his fingers pounding at the keys. He was a true believer, a chronicler
of tragedy. He would smoke packs of cigarettes at night on the loading
dock, where empty trucks waited for the morning paper. He stood in the
shadow of the building, almost hidden, gazing into the night.

"Carson."

"Yeah."

"It's me, Maggie."

"Want a smoke?"

"Okay."

He handed me a cigarette and, leaning close, lit it with his lighter. He watched me intensely, yet with detachment. He seemed skeptical and generous at the same time, like a priest looking for a confession.

"What's on the plate?"

"That's my line," he said. "I could tell you were listening. Want to hear a secret?"

"Uh-huh."

"I told the managing editor they ought to promote you. It didn't do any good. I don't pull a lot of weight."

"You write all the stories," I said.

"Not all of them."

"A lot of them. And hard stories. You have to talk to families of murder victims."

"And to the murderers. And to the mothers whose sons have been mangled in car wrecks. It's probably the worst job in the world. Who knows why I love it." His smile was ironic but gentle. It made me smile, too.

I could smell the scent of newsprint coming out of the empty trucks that stood in the lot. The streets made a vacant grid all around us as we watched traffic lights change, cars float by. I recall the frenetic curls of his hair, the wintry fire in his eyes, how he said everything with quiet tenacity. When I left him that night, I knew he'd be thinking of me.

There is one hunting picture of a lightless November morning. Nate and his father have blue hands, hold blue guns, and stand against the darkness with bone-white faces. He looks at the other's gun, the other looks at his, with solemn curiosity and disregard for me. I was wearing a robe, barefoot, my feet electrified by the cold. After taking the picture, I watched them get in the truck and drive away. I stood outside in the flurry, hoping they wouldn't find their targets that day, that I would not be faced with venison in my freezer.

Minutes before, Dick Duke had appeared like a mountain in his down jacket to pick up Nathan. We'd all sat around in the shocked stillness of a lit kitchen at four-thirty in the morning, drinking the coffee I'd made. Nate was chatty with news about the deer count being high, about the deer coming up into our yard every other night. And wouldn't there be a lot of people shooting them down in the woods?

"Sure will be," said Dick. "Maggie. More coffee if you've got it." I poured and watched him. The fat pressed around his eyes, which were slow and severe at this hour. His voice came out of him like silt.

"Promise me you won't get shot," I told them.

"Are you worried?" Dick grinned, showing crooked front teeth.

"Enough to buy me this orange hat," said Nate.

"A woman who doesn't worry isn't worth keeping."

Nate busied himself checking the bags, making sure everything was packed right. He had a way of taking over, and his father let him.

"And whatever you do, don't hit any deer," I said.

"She thinks we're going to miss," said Nate. "She's praying that we'll miss."

Mr. Duke had a knife on his belt and so did Nate. They'd packed brandy, water, apples, and ammunition. There were cartridges on the table, and I held one in my hand.

"Nate's a good shot," his father said to me.

I looked at Nate. He had been detached from me since waking—no kiss good morning, no touch. He'd been hustling around the house getting things ready, all seriousness and full of electric energy. Now he was taking the cartridges off the table and putting them into a small plastic box, counting them under his breath.

"Nate, are you a good shot?"

He looked at me. "What do you think?" Then he put a hand out for the cartridge I had.

"I don't think you're as good as your father says."

He didn't answer, and pried his fingers into mine to take the cartridge away. His face seemed to harden, as if he'd resolved to bring home a grizzly bear.

He brought home his half of the deer in pieces. It was wrapped in white butcher paper and twine, a dozen tight packages, and there they were on my table. Nate stood over it, muddy from the waist down. He had a pair of deer antlers in his hands and dirt streaked on his face.

"Take one of your pictures," he said. "Get the camera."

So I did, and we laughed, because he was drunk enough to hold the antlers up to his head and look at me with a deadpan face.

"See," he said.

"Who shot it?"

"I shot it."

"You shot it, and from how far away?"

"Miles."

"And how many sips of brandy?"

"It helps the aim," he said. "How do you like your venison?"

"Not at all. And you?"

He pulled me by the waist and brought my face to his. He gave off the smell of smoke and wet leaves. There was dirt on his fingers and cheek and a slash of scarlet on his jacket, the blood of a deer. I wanted to get at him with my hands.

"What do you think now?"

"I'm impressed. I'm impressed with all of this."

He dropped the antlers to the floor and guided us to the refrigerator.

"What are we doing?" I said.

He unzipped my skirt and moved it away from my hips so that it fell to the floor. He pushed his hands down inside my panties and looked into my eyes.

"Your hands are dirty."

"What's the problem?"

"Your hands, Nate. Go take a shower."

He pulled at the panties so they fell, too, and unzipped his jeans. There is a hand on my shoulder and he is taking me. I am suddenly confused. The confusion is massive. I've never felt so naked. I am pressed against the refrigerator as he pushes himself inside me. I swallow him, absorb him, and I can do this. I am amazed with how capable my body has become. Caught in this act, we are a spectacle to ourselves. It's over in two minutes.

Fucked, I sat down on the tile.

"What is it?"

"I didn't want you to do that."

He took a deep breath, then began to put the deer meat into the freezer, piece by piece. I got out of the way.

"Did you hear what I said?"

"I'm going to make dinner. It's going to be good. It's going to be the best venison stew you ever tasted in your life."

"You're not listening to me."

He turned his back and reached for a skillet hanging on the wall. I left the kitchen to him and took a long hot shower. I would not leave the bathroom when he called for me to come down. I made him climb the stairs and knock on the bathroom door and say, "Come on down, Maggie, it's peppery and hot." I opened the door and saw him sipping on a bottle of beer. He kissed me on the cheek and said he was sorry like he knew he'd be forgiven, like a boy used to getting in trouble and talking his way straight out. Reluctantly, I went downstairs. While he bragged about hunting the deer, I ate the stew, which was delicious, though hard to get down.

I stopped being cute that fall. Perhaps I was beautiful, but not cute. When you're cute, men look at you with eyes that are passively interested and somewhat furtive. Their glances sweep over you, or they stare with a dispassionate intensity for a short while. But when you are the way I was that fall, men—and women, too—will look at you in the face, in the eyes, with arduous curiosity, as if they need to watch you. They stare directly at you because they want to get inside you and find out what makes you move the way you move, what it is about your face that seems to them different and unaccounted for. Somehow, I was that way. I did not move down streets with the lightness of sunshine. I adopted a somber air, eyes that saw farther. I frowned at strangers.

Phil Carson noticed. I often returned to his smoking place at night before leaving.

"If it isn't Margaret—Margaret . . . what's the last name?"

I'd been working there for months with my nameplate on my desk.

"Duke," I said.

"That's your husband's. What's yours?"

"Wilson."

"Margaret Wilson," he said. "Do you like it better?"

"It is softer."

"Yes," I said.

Phil Carson could suddenly penetrate circumstance. He had Nordic eyes. Pale gray, sometimes silver, they gleamed of underground quarries.

"Cigarette?"

He always offered. "Thanks," I said.

We would stand in the same place, on the loading dock, on the edge of a field of light, and had a clear view of the stars.

Once I asked him where he was from.

"This place," he said. You had the sense he did not like talking about himself, that he held the substance of his life to be deeply personal. "Where are you from, Margaret Wilson?"

I told him I had just moved from Indianapolis with my husband. He seemed to listen as if he might be suspending judgment about me. He asked me about my husband and what he did and where we lived. He asked where I went to college and what I majored in. He asked how I felt about the weather. I began to feel he was asking questions for the sake of asking, as if he were moving around something, avoiding it, circling. He was curious, but about nothing he inquired about. He kept trying, and I didn't mind. I wasn't afraid.

"You ought to be a reporter," he said suddenly.

"Why?"

"It's the way you're looking at me. You notice things, I can tell. People spill the beans for quiet eyes like yours."

He told me then that he also lived near the Wabash, on the edge of New Harmony, the Utopian town an hour from Evansville. I asked him why.

He looked at me, and I could see he was beginning to respect me and would divulge what I was asking of him.

"I was staying there once in a bed and breakfast. And one night I went walking around and came to this baseball diamond. There was a softball game going on. Men on the field with their big mitts, their wives sipping Coke in the bleachers. Something about that summer ball game under the lights, kids running with their ice cream cones and bloody knees, the rise of fireflies and towering pop-ups and home-run hitters landing balls over the fence—it made me happy. I felt I could live there. I felt I'd be at peace in that town."

He pauses, checks to see if I'm following him, then looks away into the dark again. "I was running away. I was living with a fiancée and wanted to get out of it. I had to bust out by some magical escape, and then New Harmony appeared."

"You broke it off?"

He nodded, and I knew it was time to stop asking questions.

Most of the conversations we had on the landing dock are distant to me. They remain in snatches. I have made pieces of them up, I suppose, but I don't know which. As he came to know me and trust me, we spoke of our private lives. I asked him questions and he me, and the tacit agreement was that we would tell the truth.

"So you're not in love with anybody?"

"I suppose not," he said.

"Really?"

"I never met anyone I wanted." He spoke as if trying to keep his voice within a small sphere.

"Why not?"

"You're like a child, asking all these questions."

I smiled, my head held high, wanting him to admire me.

"You should come visit my house," he told me. "It's my one love."

He drew me a map on a page of the reporter's notebook he always kept in his back pocket. He ripped it out and handed it to me, looking the other way, as if he did not want to be implicated in the act.

A lot of nights Nate worked late or had to have dinner with people, so I'd be on my own. Returning from my job, I drove my car slowly through the empty November landscape of mud-driven fields, the dull infinity of electric wires and slate skies. New Harmony was my most frequent destination. The sky seemed to crouch low over the humble Main Street, shrinking the buildings and the lives within them. I still knew no one there, and so walked the streets as a stranger, absorbing the stares of residents, wondering about their worlds.

That fall I went there not to tour the grounds of the historical park or Utopian cabins and redbrick dormitories, but only to get out of our empty house. For a month, I made a habit of going to Jaime's, a late night diner on the square. The patrons, all men, sat like stones in denim jackets as they sipped their coffee and stole glances in my direction. All of us sat together, listening to the lanky cook fry up our orders on a grill. You could not talk to him, this cook. He only chatted in quiet tones with the waitress, to whom he was married, but they did not act like lovers. I was convinced everyone there was waiting to fall in love. Drinking the stale coffee, I wrote letters to my friend Julie the cellist, to Tracy, who was working in Washington, D.C. These letters I did send. They were all about the past, about people we would never see again, wild parties we'd held together. I tried not to mention Nate, and when I did, I wrote about his business.

I drove back with little gas in the tank, and the car creaked at chapped, windblown intersections. When I coasted home, Nate hadn't arrived. He was having dinner with Ericson, a man of vague importance. He was a banker and would lend Duke Properties money for the shopping plaza on the edge of town. Nate approached this deal, and all his business, like a thief. He met accomplices covertly in bars, made late night calls behind closed doors. Winning wasn't fair play to him. When speaking about the company's prospects, his eyes would blink with the presumption of innocence.

I hadn't eaten at the diner and, looking at the paltry options of frozen food on hand, I decided I wouldn't eat alone. I got in my car and left in the dark. Carson's map was on the dash. It took ten minutes to get there.

Why I did this no longer matters and it did not matter then. I acted according to instinct, something I try never to question. Here I was, deep in a countryside that was not mine, and I wanted someone to have dinner with. It all seems innocent when put this way, but I know full well that evening I did not drive like a woman with a clear conscience. I pushed the pedal to the floor until the wheel rattled in my hands.

Even as I did so, I defended Nathan in my thoughts, counted what blessings I could see. He was still that man who can win anyone over at once. I would rediscover his charm at parties hosted by high school friends, where Nate assumed the aura of minor celebrity. He was everyone's pal, the one they wanted to stay in touch with. He presented me with delicate pride, leading me into a room full of people, his arm light around my waist. "This is my wife, Maggie." The words leapt from him, bright and true. They were, at first, hard to believe, and it was easy to confuse the claim with devotion. "She's the best thing to happen to me," he'd say. People loved him, and, by default, me. My parents asked for pictures of the two of us, and for Christmas, I'd send everyone I knew a framed photo from the wedding.

But that night I drove to Phil Carson's red cottage on Butternut Ridge, a lane that snaked along the bottom of low hills on the edge of New Harmony. I recall the dusty porch, spun with cobwebs, the screen door squeaking as I opened it. It was like a summer place where you read paperbacks, take long naps, and dream happily.

"Is there a Mr. Phil Carson home?"

He answered the door in black jeans and a T-shirt splotched with wet. He looked lean and strong in the clothes, not athletic, but capable of strength in emergency. He was not the same man he was at the office. The atmosphere of his home subdued him, made his eyes melancholic and probing.

"You saved the map," he said.

"Of course."

"Come inside. I'm developing some photographs downstairs. You can come watch, but hurry, there's not much time left on the clock—"

He walked quickly through a dark living room, to a door. I stood still in the entryway. "Are you sure it's okay?"

"It's a perfect time, but you've got to hurry, Maggie."

We went clattering downstairs into the dark. In the back of my mind, I thought of the distance of my drive home versus the distance of Nate's commute and how to get back before him.

I was easily distracted from worry, coming into Carson's darkroom. A light hung from a beam, filling the basement with red-tinged gloom. In a sink against the wall was a row of trays filled with liquid, and all around us was corkboard covered with black-and-white prints of barns, run-down gas stations, earnest Hoosier faces. Carson stood at the sink, turning a print over in a bath with a pair of tongs. It was a picture of a woman in a flouncy hat you might wear to church. She was standing outside on a windy day, her dark hair blown in strands across a face lit harshly by the sun. She seemed perhaps attractive, but full of anxiety and vague confusion about how to behave before the camera.

"She was waiting for a bus. I saw her one day on the way to work and asked if I could take her picture."

"Why?"

"It was the way she was waiting, the slow pacing along the curb, back and forth. You got the feeling she was waiting for something that wasn't coming, but she had to wait anyway." He held the print up with the tongs. "I was kind of in love with her for a moment."

I watched him hold the print up to the light so he could see better.

"It's only a hobby, but some day maybe I'll quit my job and travel around the world with my camera." He let the print fall into a tray of water. The woman floated beneath the surface, shimmering darkly.

"Will you give her the picture?"

"You never see women again if you fall in love with them on the street. It's an unwritten law." He frowned at the print. "That's the best one I've taken, I think."

I took a look at the other portraits on the wall, some of which I recognized: Jaime from the diner in New Harmony, the man who cooks the eggs, an old woman who walks a St. Bernard.

"Are you going to ask to take my picture, Carson?"

"I was wondering how I'd go about doing that."

He quickly led me through the dark upstairs, bumping into the furniture as he went. We ended up in a small study with wooden cases of books lining the walls. A light flickered on above. The chaos of his cubicle at work was nowhere here. The oak desk was clear of all clutter but an old typewriter, a few sheets of loose paper, and a fern. In a corner stood a tripod with a camera.

"Are you sure about this?" he said.

"When I was a girl I didn't like having my picture taken because they would make me dress up frilly and smile too much."

"I want you to do what you want," he said.

"That will be nice for a change."

"What do you mean?"

"Hurry up and take your pictures before I change my mind."

I eased into a large, rolling office chair. He stood behind the tripod, leaning over the camera. A cool night draft whistled through the pane behind me.

"What will you do with my picture?"

"Let's wait to see if it does you justice."

The shutter made a soft, seductive noise as I stared straight into the camera, unsmiling. He took three more pictures, saying nothing to me. Having my photo taken by Carson was a feeling like nudity, a thrill, this exposing of film with the light from my skin. He moved the tripod closer.

"How is it going," I said. "Am I a good subject?"

"Pretend I'm not taking your picture. Here, why don't you smoke a cigarette."

He gave me one. I inhaled the smoke, closing my eyes. I'd thought Carson would just take a few shots, but he didn't stop at that. He snapped almost an entire roll, moving the camera around the room, and it seemed he was becoming absorbed in the work.

"I should go," I said.

He looked up from the camera. "Not quite yet. I could make some dinner—"

I got up right away. "I'm sorry," I said. "I've got to. I need to get home."

He frowned, placing the cap over the lens.

At the front door I told him I'd had a nice time, and he promised me a print or two. "At least this woman you'll see again," I said.

He helped me on with my coat, pausing a moment with his hands on my shoulders. Perhaps because I did not move away from him, he cleared his throat and asked me the question I did and did not want to hear. "You doing all right, Maggie?"

"I don't know."

"Why not?"

I thought of Nate's hand on my wrist, the way his voice had sounded so angry and quiet as we'd spoken of Johnson.

"I'm having a hard week," was all I said.

Carson lifted his hands off my shoulders and opened the door. He looked at me and said, "You know you can call if you need help."

I left him, feeling his eyes on my back.

The party was in mid-December. I'd decorated the house with Christmas tree trimmings and red velvet ribbons. Candles burned on tables, a fire roared in the parlor. We wore our finest—I was in a new black party dress and Nate in a camel blazer I'd helped pick out. We had fun in the hours before the guests arrived. He came up on me in the kitchen as I was basting the chicken, lifted me up all at once, and carried me to the living-room couch. He made love to me there until the corn bread in the oven set off the fire alarm. We came to the rescue and soon began dancing to the radio.

Dick Duke arrived first and alone. Tommy, Nate's brother, was still at college in Atlanta.

"Maggie, you look fantastic. I hope Nate tells you that every five minutes." My father-in-law embraced me in his fat arms and squeezed, kissing me on both cheeks. Every time our bodies touched, it felt like he was making demands, insisting on my belonging to him. "It's mistletoe, ain't it?" he said, noticing my alarm and pointing up to the leaves I'd strung from the ceiling. "Now how about a drink?"

Nate was already working on that. He had the scotch open in the dining room and the ice in the glass. His father plopped himself down in an easy chair like he owned the place, which in a way he did, and Nate delivered the drink with humorless efficiency.

"Your wife looks fine, Nate, so does the house. What's for dinner?"

"Fish sticks. Take it or leave it."

It was a family joke. After Nate's mother ran out, the Duke boys lived on fish sticks for a year. They could laugh grimly, these two men, at the old hurt, the old bitch, as Dick Duke liked to call her.

"I'll leave it," he said.

Nate, who had fixed himself a drink as well, proposed a toast. "To leaving it."

"No, to Maggie," corrected Dick.

My parents came minutes later, both of them overdressed for the occasion. They weren't dinner party people, and seemed to be aware of this from the start. My father, hands in pockets, jumped into a conversation with Dick about pickup trucks, as if seeking refuge. My mother, wearing a horrid J.C. Penney dress with purple ruffles, played a shrill and emotional mother-in-law. She couldn't decide if she should be helping me in the kitchen, or letting Nate charm her silly, or humoring our old neighbor, Manny, whom I'd invited. Not being used to parties, Manny became quickly inebriated and seemed intent on flirting with my mom.

A part of her, I could tell, just wanted to collapse on the couch and cry, for it was no small thing to see her daughter all grown-up with a house to show off.

Carson came later than the others.

Inviting him had been a dare. I wanted to know if Nate could tolerate him in my life, this stranger who had become a friend. That night he looked tired and harried in his rumpled jacket and day-old beard. He'd rushed here from the office after filing a story about a trailer park fire, he told Nate and me as we greeted him.

"Jesus, what happened?" my husband demanded.

"A couple was fighting and ran out, leaving the stove on. A toddler nearly died," Carson said. "No topic for a cocktail party."

"All right, then," Nate said. "You must be ready for a drink."

"Don't partake, thanks."

"Wine? Beer? Nothing?"

"Some water, thanks."

"Not a drinking man."

"No, sir."

I brought him some water, even as Nate poured Carson a small glass of scotch, "in case he gets thirsty for something substantial." Standing in front of the fireplace, Nate watched me introduce Carson to the other guests as my friend from the *Telegraph*.

I left them all for the kitchen, where I put the finishing touches on a golden chicken, creamed spinach, braised red cabbage, and rolls. Several bottles of white wine were on hand. I looked down at the dining-room table, the silver serving trays and fine china and the brass candelabras. All wedding presents, these possessions embarrassed me, as did the house, with its new curtains and rugs and antique furniture. My parents' house was half the size of ours.

Carson came into the kitchen to find me.

"I brought you something."

He reached into his coat pocket and pulled out a black-and-white photograph. It was eight by ten, on matte paper. Taken without a flash, the photo was slightly blurred and underexposed. My face took up the entire image, shadowed and awake to the lens. I wasn't smiling, though my mouth was open, suggesting pleasure.

"How did you do this?"

"It's half luck, half knowing what you're after. It's wonderful, isn't it?"

"It is," I say.

"It's a gift. It's yours. Put it in a frame and hang it. It's a portrait of this year that you'll always have."

I looked down at the photo again. I seemed to be leaning toward the camera, aroused, expecting something to happen. The grainy image was undeniably intimate.

Nate came into the kitchen looking for another bottle of wine.

"What's this?"

He took the picture out of my hands. I can still remember how his face became serious and callow as he gazed at that photograph. Maybe if he'd been generous at this moment, if he'd had that in him, to enjoy the picture, our future would not have unraveled as it did. But there was no chance of that, no chance my husband would not decide to hate Phil Carson immediately that night.

"That gets you just right, doesn't it, Maggie?" he said. "Who took it? You, Phil?"

"Yes."

"That's something. A hell of a photograph. Professional." He looked at Carson, then me, a smile plastered on his face. "You don't mind if we keep this, do you?"

"Not at all. I brought it as a gift," Carson said.

"Thank you. I appreciate it." He offered his hand, and Carson shook it. "We'll hang it in the bedroom, won't we, Maggie? So you two work together?"

"Not exactly. Same newsroom, but she's the obit editor, and I report."

"And how's the lady doing? Can she type fast enough?"

"She's the best obit editor we've had in years."

"Good. That's good to hear. Now, how about dinner? We all set, Margaret?"

Soon we were gathered around the table, and Nate carved the bird, dividing it among the guests. I poured the wine. A chorus of compliments arose. An awkward silence gave way to small talk about my parents' trip from Indianapolis, how remote and charming my mother thought our home to be, and wasn't this hilly corner of Indiana *awfully* scenic? Not only scenic, Manny began to explain, but historic, too, and did she know about our failed Utopias, our humble paradises gone wrong? Just then, Nate broke in to ask Carson how long he'd been at the *Telegraph.*

"Four years."

"That's a good while. I'd think a young reporter like you'd be ready to move on to a bigger paper."

"We'll see," answered Carson, who was three years older than Nate.

"You'd like that, I suspect, a bigger city, more readers, more crime. Evansville's not much of a news town."

"It's my home for now."

"Mine too, Phil. Born and raised here. You know, you ought to do a story about Duke Properties."

"That's a real story," cut in Dick Duke in his baritone voice.

"That so," said Carson.

Nate's father took command, droning on about how the company had built itself from a two-bit outfit into "the largest real estate management corporation in southern Indiana." He ticked off addresses of office buildings that Phil Carson, as a proper news man, ought to take a look at—seeing as Duke Properties was playing so prominent a role in the future of the city.

Carson didn't seem impressed with this lugubrious pitch, but he tolerated it for several minutes until Manny jumped in to say Carson ought to write a story about his chicken coop, which had been invaded by a weasel. My mother, being brought up in the city, was charmed by the very idea of a chicken coop. Manny boasted to her about his hens, now numbering two after the weasel, both of them "beautiful girls."

My father, silent up till then, turned to Nate and said, "So Maggie tells me your grandparents lived here."

"My grandparents and my great-grandparents and great-*great*-grandparents, Mr. Wilson."

"Is that so?"

"The Duke family's been here for over a hundred years." It seemed Nate was talking to the entire table, and soon all of us were listening. "William and Esther Duke came out from Louisville in 1887 and bought this property and built a small cabin and began to farm. Corn, mostly, but they also had an apple orchard. We don't know much about them, but William could play a blue streak on the fiddle. Somehow the cabin burned down around the turn of the century, and it was up to Nathan, the oldest boy, to take over the farm and build this here house. His only son, Richie Duke, was my grandfather. Gramps fought like hell in World War II and came back with a limp, got himself an education, and started investing in real estate. Business got so good he almost stopped farming, but when I was a boy, Richie and Alice still lived here with the chickens and the corn and acres and acres of strawberry fields. We'd come out in summer to pick the berries, detassel corn, and all that. He could teach a boy a lot of things. How to wrestle, hunt, fish, fight—"

"Richard Duke was a great man," boomed Dick. "He was an uncommon and great man."

Dick was proud of his son, flush with family feeling. My mother beamed at Nate, her eyes brimming with actual tears.

"And what about the Duke women?" I said. "What were they? What happened to them?"

"They stood by their families," Dick said, slightly drunk. "They knew how to do that. No matter what happened. Fires, drought, disease, war. They kept their people going."

Before I could press for more information, Nate asked me to check on the pie.

Manny declared it a splendid party as I helped him on with his coat. We wished each other loud "good-bye's" and "come again's" and "thank you so much for coming out on such a cold night." By the time I opened the door to see Carson and Manny and Dick out, the wind was blowing snow across the fields.

"Nice party," I said to Nate, sidling up to him in the kitchen. "But I still want to know all about the Duke women."

"My father told you. They were good women. They raised families. Esther was a great dancer."

"Well, that's something. What about your grandmother? Why didn't you invite her, by the way?"

He didn't seem to hear me. He was concentrating on a spot in the distance, behind me.

"I'm in love with you, you know that?"

"I know it."

"But who's that faggot reporter?"

"Don't call him that."

"I can say what I want."

He took out from his pocket the picture. He'd bent it twice in quarters. He let it fall to the counter, then pulled me to him, circling my waist with a strong arm, and tried to kiss me.

"Why did you bend the picture? You've ruined it!"

"Why does it exist, Maggie? Why did you pose for him?"

"He asked me to. It was nothing—"

"He asked you to, and you said yes."

"Stop acting like a fool."

His face hardened. "Don't make me one."

I tried to leave the room, but he grabbed my arm and yanked me toward him. He pressed his mouth against mine. "Come upstairs," he said.

"No!"

"Please."

"I'm going to clean."

"Your mother did it."

"I'm going to finish."

I spent a long time finishing, until my mother and father came down. They wanted tea. They wanted to tell me how proud they were of me and Nate, how good we were together, and that we were naturals at entertaining. "I think Nate and I are going to get along fine," my father said.

I pretended to be exhausted so they would go to bed and stop saying things that weren't true. When they finally let me alone, I did feel tired. Wind buffeted the walls of the house as I turned out all the lights. In the dark kitchen I drank the rest of a bottle of wine and unfolded the photograph Carson had given me. It really was ruined now. I didn't want my parents to see it in the morning or to ever look at it again myself, so I ripped it into four pieces and buried it in the trash.

In bed at night, I picture the floor plan of the house. I envision the dimensions of the rooms and put them into their place and try to hold the whole of the blueprint in my mind. If I can watch the house, all of it, nothing will come inside. I imagine the bolted door, the strength of steel, each and every window locked. In the bottom floor, everything is still in its heavy shadowed place, the couch, the fireplace, a blank television set, and my begonia plant hanging from the ceiling hook. The staircase is made of old wood. The stairs creak. There is a chimney rising from the living room, through the middle of the house. The roof is shingled with dark tile, and from the roof one could see the fields of corn sleeping, cooling, the leaves and the tassels gathering dew. And in the forest, there are owls I hear and the rustle of night rodents and coons and the stream that slides over slate, through debris of branches and logs, through drifts of nettles and violets marbled by the moon. I hold the forest in my mind, and the apron of grass around the house and the floor plan, the doorknobs on the door, steel double bolt and how if you shake the door it won't give.

Often, if I still can't sleep, I get up and go downstairs, into the kitchen. I look out the window to find Manny's light, which is a comfort at two or three a.m. But usually I'm on my own. I pour a glass of wine and find food. Maybe if it's cool enough I'll go outside and sit on the picnic table and look at the woods. Behind me is the buzzing, the anxiety of the house, the conspiracy of its rooms. Not to hear it requires the concentration of something like prayer and quick sipping and the quiet surrender to being hidden. My eyes gleam from the pocket of dark, and I whisper: "I'm fine, I'm fine, all right, all right, Lord, I'm fine, all right." And sometimes, often, I will notice the slight motion of a deer's long, soft neck, the glint of an eye, and then the hesitant step onto the wet grass. It moves delicately, parallel with the woods. If the wind is right, it will not notice me and will keep moving along the line of trees, stopping to look at the fields—alert, bright-eyed, poised for speed—and keep moving before going back into the forest. I am alone again but fortified by the sight, a strange cause for faith. I slip off the table and go inside, up to bed.

In the evening I'm in *The Patriot,* Evansville's p.m. daily.

I think about rows of homes, a boy on a bicycle tooling along. With a flick of his arm every ten seconds, he sends a rolled bundle flying to a doorway. Sends a picture of me to the doorways, on the front page or at least the front metro page. I think of the men in the *Patriot* offices standing around arguing about where to put me—which page, and how big, below the fold or above the fold.

I walk to Manny's. He's not on the porch when I get there. I stand watching the haze over the corn, and the hard black circling of a crow. He comes outside with the gin. His back is slightly bent, which means it's sore. He sits in his chair without looking at my face.

"How are you?" I say.

"Fine. Great. Did you see it?"

"No," I say.

"That's good."

"So don't tell me about it."

"Wasn't going to."

He turns on the radio, then moves the dial off the public station, in case the local news picks up the story.

"Single or double?" he asks.

I gaze at the blood red clouds hanging low over the corn. "Tell me what page it's on."

"Front page."

"Did they use my picture?"

"Yes. And Nate's. Do you just want to read the thing?"

"No." I look at the radio tower blinking in the summer haze. The drink I've got in my hand is strong. "I didn't tell them anything they wanted," I say.

"No need to."

We drink. The summer feels endless. We're in the middle of the middle week of July, a long month with hot day after hot day and no more holidays. There's a fall in the future, but we can't taste it, and the fields look the same as they did two weeks ago. He turns up the radio, hums between puffs of his cigarette. I can't help thinking about the paper.

"I learned something from Rita," I say.

Manny, frustrated, turns the radio off with a flip of his hand.

"Do you want to hear about it?"

"We should be talking about the Cleveland Indians or playing badminton. Do you want to play badminton, Maggie?"

"Sure."

"Don't give me that," he says. "I'm a great shuttlecock—"

"He's coming," I say.

"I'll shuttlecock you from here to the Wabash."

"He's coming to Evansville, next week."

"I don't give a damn and hope to God you don't, either." He rattles the ice in his glass, then turns the radio back on. "Another drink?"

I'm not going to have another. I can't sit still this evening. I finish my first drink and tell him I have to go. I lean over and kiss him on the top of his head and walk off the porch, across the grass. I hurry my step and think of the car keys being in my purse and the time being eight-forty-five, and I'm wondering where I could get what I want at this hour of the day.

I'm in my car. The limit is forty. I'm going sixty. It may be hard to find a copy this late. I realize after I've passed the stop sign I could have asked Manny for his, but I wouldn't have wanted to. I'm glad to be out in the twilight with an empty road before me.

The sky is crimson and cloud-swept, the landscape scattered with silhouettes of barns and lone oak trees. In New Harmony by my diner there is a drugstore with magazines and newspapers. It will be closed, but there will be boxes, and maybe one of them will have a copy, and if not, there will be copies to steal from people's doorsteps.

In town, the streetlights are on, every corner is starkly lit. I walk fast around the square, looking. I find a box, but it's empty, and the stores are closed. I keep walking around the park, where two boys play basketball, their laughter high and soft in the trees. I find no boxes up the streets, no open stores. I come across the diner, which is open, as always, and two men sit at the counter. They turn to look when I walk inside. There, on a far table, a newspaper, wrinkled, used. Unfurled by an empty coffee cup.

I sit down, turn it over in my hands. The headline, stained with coffee, below the fold: EXONERATED, DUKE REBUILDS LIFE. There's a color picture. He's wearing a blue suit and tie, unsmiling, looking out a window. There's a smaller, black-and-white picture: me, a head shot, my mouth a sour smear of dots.

The story is saying he's *spiffily dressed, upbeat for work in a sixteenth-floor office.* He's *high on the future, gainfully employed,* the story is saying. He works for Midwest Consulting, Inc. *founded by business school friend Howard Tokes.* There is Tokes calling Nate Duke *in good spirits, ready to work,* calling it *all a disgrace.* There's Richard Duke, unable to decide if he's happy or furious, being *too mad to spit and too happy to spit,* and *thank God for the truth,* the story is saying.

I read fast. This is only newsprint, only ink. Telling me of Nate Duke, who is *trying not to think of it,* it being too hard to think of after *six years of thinking of nothing but it,* it and her, thinking of *why and how,* and if she was *honest.* He is hopeful that she may *live at peace with herself because God knows,* says the article, he is *too bloody mad for peace and too tired for forgiveness.*

The picture is there: he's bearded, looking young, in a suit by the window. The eyes are blurred by the printing. The pink dots of his skin mix with the whites of his eyes and the green iris, which is a dull smudge. I'm a no comment, and my mother is worried: Maggie is *not right, still plagued with epilepsy and depression.* All in all, fifteen inches, including a pulled quote in bold, large type, the words of a man I made love to: *It was a living hell.* The story ends abruptly. *Shaking his head, he mutters, "I don't understand."*

I close the paper and roll it tight in my fist. The men sitting at the counter are watching me. I don't want them to know I'm upset. I carefully walk out the door. In the dark street I see a trash can and place the paper inside it. It unrolls, and Nate is there, thoughtfully staring out the window. He is handsome still. This astonishes me. I had not expected his face could make me weak. Sick to my stomach, I turn the paper over and go looking for my car.

·   ·   ·   ·

The fields shimmer with heat. I'm driving, listing the things I know.

What I was wearing that night: a white nightgown.

What I did: drank sherry.

What I wanted: safety, resolution.

What I did not take but could have: Phil Carson.

The temperature: upper nineties.

I think about the sound of the car door, a soft slap in the dark signaling my relief. I wondered why I hadn't heard the familiar crunch of tires on gravel. I saw the dull sheen of the doorknob, and the door was opening. Onto blackness, onto Nate standing in the light of the lamp, an object in his hand.

Around the house, dark trees hang in the humid air. The eaves, the rooflines are humble etchings on the evening, the windows vacant. When I first saw it, the stained glass, the ornate lattice and smart shutters, had made the house dreamlike. And now, still, the house is a dream, only darkened, yet durable, as the summer moves on.

I am trying to get over my fear. No one has come inside. Nathan is in Louisville doing well for himself, remaking his name. He will earn a lot of money, probably find a new wife. He will make something new and desirable of himself, and I won't ever see him again.

I enter and find the gun in the closet. It feels comfortable to me now. I hold it in one hand and walk through rooms. The rooms are unreal—vaults of dusk and air and almost-truth. I can walk through them, and through them. I can look under the couch and the love seat and behind the curtains. I can walk up the stairs and open a closet in a scared rush to find nothing but harmless sheets and pillows. I can stand in the bedroom, watching the light play on the mirror. I can listen to the maddening silence.

There isn't anyone here. I almost wish there were.

Nate sat close to me, but his eyes were on the woman across the table. Her name was Karen Walters and she worked for his father as a secretary. She was from out west, but had married a no-good mechanic from Evansville, whom she'd just divorced after a year of hell, and now she was stuck in Indiana. She wore a tight purple sweater with sequins, a leather skirt, and too much mascara. She was garish, but beautiful. Her black hair hung heavily to the small of her back, and her eyes gleamed at you with hard rock sophistication that made you wonder what life had done to her.

Beside Karen, his arm around her shoulders, sat Eddie Sorewell, one of Nate's political friends, a republican adviser to the mayor. We were in Timothy's, an upscale bar with lots of mahogany and expensive martinis. Nate liked to meet Eddie there that spring, smoke cigars, and act like fatter cats than they were. Nate began to bring his dad's secretary, too, and Eddie had managed to sweet-talk his way into her bed. He was handsome in a conventional way, like a man in a fifties ad, with lofty cheeks and feathered blond hair. He considered himself a charmer of women. He sought their smiles, even mine, especially Karen's. She didn't offer it often.

"Don't fuck around with city council seats," Eddie was saying. "If you want to throw in your hat, run for state senate and don't look back."

"I could do it. I could do it this summer." He looked up at Karen, eyes bright with vanity. "What do you think? Would I make a good candidate?"

"He asked me that on our first date," I told her.

A chain smoker, Karen exhaled over the table. "How did you answer?"

"I told him what he wanted to hear, if I recall correctly."

"Always a mistake. Lying, I mean."

I wanted to take her hand, leave my husband and his friend behind, and go somewhere. I wanted to find out what she knew. Nate was sitting up straighter, reaching for her with his eyes.

"What's your answer?" he said to her. "Are you voting for me or who?"

She shrugged. "What have you done for me?"

"How about gave you a job?"

"How about a raise?"

Eddie guffawed, squeezed her like she wasn't twice the person he was. His laugh suggested privilege. He belonged to country clubs, invitation lists, gated communities. "Go ahead. Vote for Nate. He's my buddy."

"What do you think?" Karen asked me. "Do you want him to run?"

I was instinctively against the idea. He would become too engrossed in the game, just as he was with his work. He was too vain and too young to be a leader. He would be swallowed up by the glory of his name.

I shrugged off the question. "If he wants to."

Nothing I did that spring felt honest. Not even sitting beside my husband with his arm around me.

I excused myself for the bathroom, but a pay phone stopped me. On instinct, I picked up the receiver and dialed, keeping my eyes on the back of Nate's head. He was leaning over the table, joking with Karen about what his slogan should be. "How about, 'Live large, vote Duke'?" he asked.

Phil Carson answered the phone.

"It's me."

"Where are you?" As if I were in some emergency and might need assistance. He lived in a constant state of alertness.

"A bar, and there is too much smoke, and I'd like to leave." I could hear him typing fast. "What are you doing?"

"Finishing a piece of shit article so I can meet you somewhere you'd rather be."

I looked at Karen. Nathan was asking her about Arizona, where she was from, and if she liked to ride horses.

"I can't, you know."

She said something witty about riding bareback. Nate's laugh rang out, encircled her. He sat on the edge of his chair and admired that woman's breasts.

"I'm with Nate."

"Do what you want," said Carson.

I laughed bitterly, and my husband turned, his face suddenly stripped of social nicety.

"Not right now," I said into the phone.

"How about Saturday?"

Nate would be playing basketball with friends that afternoon. Carson and I agreed to go on a bicycle ride in the country. After hanging up, I slipped inside the restroom. I felt the thrill of a teenage girl who's just made a date with a crush. I felt fear and nausea at what I was doing. Sitting down in the stall, I covered my face with my hands.

Karen came in. I saw her red heels. She was standing before the mirror, spraying musk perfume that drifted in the air, mingling with the scent of urine. When I came out, she was carefully applying lipstick.

"I was ready for a break myself," she confided.

I looked at the two of us in the mirror, comparing her curvaceous figure with my slender body. She was a rare, spectacular woman, with the taste of a harlequin, the manner of royalty. I would have been jealous had I not liked her instantly. I imagined she only obeyed her own desires, took what she wanted from men. She would fuck Eddie Sorewell until she was tired of him, then say good-bye without a tear in her eye.

"Nate says Eddie's a kind of wolf," I told her, taking a chance.

She smiled. "It's good to have your own set of fangs. Nate's no lamb either, I'd guess."

We returned to the table, and Eddie declared us more beautiful than when we'd left them.

My husband asked me who I'd called.

"A friend at work." Knowing I'd be grilled later.

I sat in silence, nursing my gin. Nate and Eddie barraged Karen with reasons Nate would make a hell of a senator: he never lied, looked good on TV, had a loud voice, knew how to box, and could arm-wrestle anyone.

"Even me?"

Glasses were moved, cigarettes put out. Karen stripped down to her tank top, stunning the men. Her arm was long and molded with the muscles of an ex-waitress. Eddie stood up, placed his hand over theirs, and shouted go. Nate made a joke about getting to kiss her after he won. But Karen withstood him, her face full of poise. After some time of stalemate, his smile faded and Eddie snickered. Finally, Nate's arm wavered. He let out a gasp. Karen pushed his fist down to the table.

The surprise on my husband's face was tender and unaware. I remembered how it was to fall in love with this cocky, foolhardy prince. I reached out for his hand, but his eyes were still on Karen.

We left on our bicycles. Mine was the silver and rusted three-speed Manny had found for me in his garage. Phil Carson's was black and fast and made an insectlike buzz on the road. In a backpack he carried our cameras and sandwiches. He wanted to photograph the country; I wanted to lose myself in it and listen to him talk.

"Shout if you see a picture," he told me.

"What is a picture?"

"Anything you want to make more beautiful than it is."

Our tires hissed through puddles. There was no one else to be seen, not on that morning, in the still-cold time of March. It was like being on a lake, adrift in currents, and far ashore trees stood bare, holding remnants of winter in their limbs.

Our gears clicked as we went up a grade, and then coasted down through trees, brittle sunlight. We came upon a lumpy pasture, cows standing in a circle near the edge of the road. Carson slowed his bicycle, I followed, and the animals suddenly turned, lumbered a short distance, then looked our way. Their faces were bleached-white, the color of bone; you could imagine the skulls behind them. The cows stood in a staid formation and watched us with emergency in their red-rimmed eyes.

"A Greek chorus," I said.

Carson laughed. "They are going to tell us what will happen next in the play."

We took out our cameras and photographed the cows, and they all groaned balefully.

"What does it mean?" he said.

"Someone is going to tear out her eyes."

We turned off the road onto one that was narrow and meandering and seemed to have no destination. A sign warned of a village up ahead, but the village never came. Carson stopped occasionally to take pictures. We were secretive with our cameras, silent but for his quiet advice and the furtive whiz of our tires on the road as we slipped by sleeping homes and trailers. We came into a field where there was a rusted oil drill bobbing. Beside it, an old barn tilted like a rhombus, slatted and shot through with sun. The wood was chapped and whitened with age.

"Let's go there," I said.

"Where?"

"Inside the barn. We'll take the pictures inside-out."

The door moaned on its hinge, and the whole barn creaked. Inside, the darkness was churchlike, alive with the mystery of long-abandoned places. A rusted pitchfork leaned against a ladder, a faded cap hung on a nail. Beams of light fell through cracks in the walls and made delicate etchings on the dirt floor. The wood smelled like it could combust into flame if you said the wrong thing. Carson knelt in the doorway and shot upward at the vaulted space, the ceiling rising to its apex.

"It's a ruin," I said. "It's beautiful."

"It's about to fall down around us."

We took a lot of pictures inside that barn, and I felt powerful to square away the darkness in the lens.

In the afternoon we came to the banks of the Wabash, south of New Harmony. We got off our bicycles and walked down to the water. Sitting on flat rocks, we ate sandwiches and watched the wide river carry limbs torn down by the previous night's storm.

I took a picture of Carson. In the photograph, which I somehow still have, he is scowling, and his whorls of auburn hair frizz upward. His legs and arms are in generous repose across the stone. He looks as if he could have traveled a long way, painstakingly. He has been made weary and a little holy by his travels.

"What is it?" I said.

"What is what?"

"You have a way of looking at me."

"What do you expect?" he said. "Do you want me to shut my eyes to you?"

"No, it's fine. Why don't you even take a picture of me—by the water?"

He took out his camera. I saw through the dark lens. I felt tender and bold as he released the shutter.

"You're so relaxed," he said. "You're acting like some kind of star."

"Do I look like one?"

He wouldn't say. I leaned back on my arms, taking the clip out of my hair so it fell heavily around my shoulders. He paused for a moment with the camera, and then released the shutter a few more times. He put it away, and we sat still, cautious in the full, foaming sound of the river.

"You should ask me whatever it is you've been wanting to ask me," I said.

"All right. Are you happy?"

"That must be what everyone wants to know. It's the question no one asks me."

"But will you answer?"

"Don't you already know?"

I would save the pictures I took with his camera. To look at them now, they do not seem like much. They are all of plain dull country, a flat morning in March. Many are out of focus or overexposed. The post office in the town is nothing but an ugly building in a parking lot. The interior of the barn is a lightless mistake. You would wonder what it was I was trying to photograph, what I was trying to capture in the lens. It was the silence and the cold; it was spring and fear.

On the loading deck, smoking, Phil Carson spoke to me about the beauty of disaster.

"You can't question grief. Skepticism has no use," he was saying. "Witnessing grief shocks me every time—I turn the corner and there it is, giant as a mountain."

He was on his way out to report a story. A man had skidded into a wall on his motorcycle in the early evening.

"I remember the mothers, especially their bodies. They are like sculptures. There was a round young woman. Her son had electrocuted himself in the bath, and when I got there, she'd come outside onto the grass in front of the house. I remember she wore a robe and was wet all over from the bathwater. She doubled over on her knees, like she'd been knocked down, and sobbed into the grass. Everyone was watching her do this, the whole neighborhood. It was like theater. It was terrible and beautiful, and there was nothing we could do."

He spoke to me with the intensity of a confession. I'd figured out by then he had no one else in town, no real confidants other than me. That night was so warm, almost like summer, and he was excited for it and for my company. I was on my way home but realized I didn't want to leave.

"Can I come with you?"

"Of course."

"You wouldn't mind if I watched?"

He frowned in his cloud of smoke and shook his head.

Nate stands outside our house and sees that my car is gone. He begins immediately to suspect, and the suspicion is like knowledge. The house is abandoned, only still rooms and no note left behind. He calls my desk at the newspaper and gets no answer. He calls his secretary to see if I've left word, but I haven't. Walking through the rooms in the diminishing light, he opens doors, slams them closed, expecting to find something that will confirm what he suspects.

The house is in disarray. His wife is no housekeeper. Standing in the kitchen, he observes the dishes piled in the sink, the dirty plates on the table. In the living room, in a corner, are three boxes she still hasn't unpacked. They are wedding presents, probably all useless and valuable. To see them now infuriates him. Why hasn't she taken care of this in the past eight months? What has she been doing with her precious self? He picks up the top box and drops it on the floor. Something breaks inside. In the kitchen he finds a cheese knife and uses it to cut the tape on the box. Inside, a set of place mats, untouched. He throws them on the couch. A Bible. A set of drinking glasses, a ceramic salad bowl, now shattered. He kicks the box to the side and takes the next one down and then the next. He cuts the tape with the knife and starts to throw out the contents: a toaster, bed sheets, champagne flutes, stationery with their names in gold, a tool kit, some old textbooks of mine from college, monogrammed towels, a green linen tablecloth. When he's done, the floor is covered with gifts. He stands in the middle of it and pauses, listening to the silence. He looks at the door. She is still gone. She is far, far gone from him, and he knows it.

We are headed toward the accident, which may or may not have been fatal. Carson is explaining everything to me.

"It's good to stay calm. It's good to talk like this, like you aren't as excited and bloodthirsty as the men with the TV cameras are. It's important to remember that these are lives on the asphalt. This is a man who just a few minutes ago was conscious of a million things—the taste of wine, an afternoon at the beach, the shape of his lover's body. There is no rush, only a deadline, but that is no good reason to hurry."

"I've never seen you so relaxed," I say. "It is like I'm talking to a masseur, a Zen master. You are the Zen master of cops reporters."

"It isn't exotic. Look. He's got a blanket over him."

We come up to the intersection and a ring of observers. We're in a leafy neighborhood of sprawling, dilapidated homes. Through the crowd I can see a blue blanket over a shapeless form. There's a crumpled motorcycle and the brick wall of a pawnshop. The police car lights flash over the arena, on the faces of those who have come to see.

Soon I'm circling the periphery of the accident. Carson is standing at the yellow tape, only a few yards away from the victim, talking to an officer. He looks rumpled and tired. He is a man who can go anywhere and not be noticed, learn everything, and then disappear.

I walk among the neighbors who have come out of their homes. The houses are old, wooden elephants with crooked angles, cluttered porches. Children circulate through the crowd, excited and lost. A boy walking his puppy looks up at me with severe little eyes, like he has seen me before and is still resentful of something I once said. There are fathers with fearful, bloated faces in the flashing siren lights. They stand on the curb muttering to each other. There are three teenagers with a basketball bouncing between them on the corner. They say, "Motherfucker was going too fast . . . How fast you think he was going? . . . I don't know, fast enough."

Phil Carson has slipped out of sight. As I walk slowly among the people, I hear the story being pieced together. Someone somewhere knows who he is, a man, definitely a man, and his name is, was Travis.

There was a fight. There was a girlfriend. He was going too fast, skidded and hit that pawnshop wall. There weren't any other cars, he just tried to make that turn too fast. Was he drunk? Nobody knows.

The people relay these rumors to newcomers. They will all have forgotten it by dinner, but still, they stay, they watch, wanting something else to happen. The police are trying to talk to someone under a tree on the corner. In the shadows we can hear the voice of a woman.

She is wailing. The sound is high and animal, full of breath and strength, disbelief and acceptance. We can hear it, but for the shadows of the tree we cannot see the source. Another voice joins in, also female, higher, younger, and now a third begins. Who knows how many women there are? It is a clan hidden inside the tree's shadow. The voices are brave and presumptuous, and each one is distinct, yet part of a whole. The spectators stand struck, listening. They watch as the ambulance people lift the body up, slide it in, close the doors shut. The detective shouts at the crowd to leave, but the people stay, hypnotized by the sound of the wailing.

I have walked all the way around the intersection, and now I take a side street to get away from the crowd. It is such a warm, serene evening. Children are out with dogs and hula hoops. The elderly stare at each other on the porches, as if to say, Did you hear something? I thought I heard something? Mothers call out from inside houses. Dinner is ready. Perhaps these are happy homes.

A boy as tall as my waist, a candy bar in one fist, comes running after me to deliver the news. "Did you hear what happened? Did you hear?" he wheezes.

"No."

"Travis Green got caught *screwing* a girl that lives right there in that *blue* house and got kicked out by her dad and went off on his motorcycle and crashed himself with it right down there at the end of the street."

Before I can respond, he runs off to tell a little girl on her porch. I spot the blue house. Carson stands on the porch with a young man with red eyes and a flushed face. The young man is speaking quickly while leaning close to Carson, as if relaying an urgent secret. I walk past without making myself known and turn a corner. I suddenly feel the urge to walk. There is a whole city spread out before me. I could slip away, and

Carson would have to hunt for me, too. Like my husband, if he is looking for me at all.

It was on a day such as this that I'd said yes. When he proposed, it felt less like a question than a statement, one I could only confirm, or so it seemed at the time.

Behind me I can hear the ambulance siren, and beneath it the high, soaring wail of the women.

"Her name is Amanda," says Carson. We are in his car again, on the way back to the office. "Her brother showed me a picture of her. Looked like she might be twelve years old, though she's seventeen. So was Travis. They were sweethearts, you might say. So tonight they get a little out of control on the couch, right in the living room, when the father walks in. He throws the kid out of the house and Travis rides off on the bike, wrecks it about thirty seconds after. Amanda was missing for a long time, but then someone found her in the basement, crying in an old refrigerator box."

I say nothing. He asks me what I'm thinking.

"I don't feel so well."

"I'm sorry," he says.

"This is your living?"

"Yes."

"It's monstrous."

Carson drives slowly, his eyes considering the road. He is made solemn by the public and its dramas.

In the office parking lot we say good-bye. I lean against the door of my car, and he stands before me not knowing what to do with his long hands sticking too far out of his coat. "I'm sorry," he says.

"Don't be ridiculous. I asked for it. I wasn't anxious to go home."

"Why not?"

I shrug, look away from him, and hope my eyes don't well up with tears. "I don't know. I'm kind of bored sometimes. I need more stimulation, you know, and your work seems interesting."

He considers this for a time, watching my face closely. I can feel the pressure of his concern. He's leaning toward me, wanting to say more than he does: "Mindy will go on maternity leave soon, and they'll need a warm body to work the copy desk nights. I could set it up so you'd be trained and promoted—if you wanted it."

"I think that would be good."

"You could write headlines."

"Rendezvous ends in fatal crash," I say.

"Not bad."

"I'm a natural."

He kisses me. There's no reason for him not to, and I put my arms around his neck. He kisses me softly, then hungrily, his hands caressing my face. This kiss smells like cigarettes, and I can imagine a different way to live. It's a moment of intense possibility followed by fear that someone from the office will see. There are windows above us, the loading dock, the late night printing crew.

I pull myself away.

"What do you want?" he asks.

"I'm going home."

"Do you *want* to go home?"

I take out my keys and unlock my car as Carson stares at me. "I'm sorry," I say.

"Don't ever say you're sorry, Maggie. You don't have to be sorry for what you want. Do you know that?"

"Yes."

"Then go home and be careful."

There is only one road leading me back. There will be no turning, no meandering or getting lost. I will hit the pedal hard and drive fast into the night.

On my way out of town, I pass the bus station. What would it be like to be inside a dark bus, floating cool and slow over the plains? I could do it now. I have money enough in my pocket to disappear into the web of American roads.

I pass by at fifty miles an hour. I drive through the last stoplight and up the ramp onto the highway, which narrows to two dark lanes and leaves the city behind. I am going home. I am certain only of that. I am going home, and my husband will be there waiting, wondering, asking with his eyes, *What have you been doing*? I will run to him and press his hand into mine and lead him upstairs to our bed. I will kiss him with new conviction and make the suspicion go away.

You're only just beginning, I think. Not even a year. Nathan needs you, loves you, and you love him. At your wedding his mother said, "Take good care of my son."

He isn't home when I arrive. I find wedding presents strewn across the living room floor. I walk over the shards from the broken salad bowl and champagne flutes, imagining Nathan's tantrum. I am frightened by all this, but not surprised.

Once I make sure he's not here, I begin to find places for the unbroken gifts. The work is like penance. I put away linen and tablecloths, stray forks and spoons, then go for the broom and dustpan to sweep up the broken glass. I complete these tasks with energy and hustle, not fully believing in my reasons for doing them.

I fall asleep on the couch and wake at the kitchen door slamming shut and Johnson's voice.

"He's drunk, Maggie."

"Shut up, Johnson." Nate is wavering in the dark. I cannot make out his face.

"We went out drinking, Maggie. We got pretty fucked up. So I took him home. Here's your bastard."

"Where did you go?" I say.

"Mary's."

He means the old bar off Highway 66, not far from New Harmony. The wood shack, tucked away behind a stand of trees, is marked only by a small tin plaque that reads in appropriately tiny letters, *Mary's Hideaway.* Nate began going there back when he was a teenager living with his grandparents for the summer. He doesn't go often now, but the regulars know him, as when he does show up he usually gets soused on whiskey and makes a lot of noise.

"I picked up some guy's wife," says Nate. Johnson shakes his head at me. "Some guy's wife. Like picking up a dime."

"You ought to shut up and sleep, man. You're about to fall over."

"This, this," he says, picking up a cheese knife from the counter. "Nearly cut my finger off opening up the boxes." He turns to Johnson and points the knife at him. "Go home."

"Nate, *stop* it," I say.

"Forget it," says Johnson. "I'm going." He waves his big paw and ducks through the doorway, disappearing into the night.

Nate holds that little knife low down by his leg, loosely between his fingers. I ask him what he is doing. I think Johnson is gone—I cannot see his car, though I am not sure if I've heard the motor. The knife falls to the floor.

"You have something to tell me," he says.

"I've been cleaning up. I put away the gifts, or those that weren't broken. I put them in the kitchen cupboards and your grandmother's cedar chest. Funny how much empty storage there is in this house, and here we are with so many keepsakes. Your books I put away, too. They're in your study now."

"They aren't my books," he says.

"You want to know where I was? A reporter took me to do a story about a motorcycle accident. It'll be in the paper tomorrow. Do you want to hear the story?"

"No."

"A boy was caught screwing a girl and got chased out by her father—"

"I don't want to hear it. I don't want you to do . . . anything."

"—and then wrecked his bike in the street and died."

"I don't want to hear about your boyfriend."

"He's not."

"*Who* is he?"

He cannot hold this pose of a jealous husband much longer. The shame of it is making his eyes glassy and hard. He steps toward me and reaches for my hair.

How do we look? Like lovers, could you see us through the window. His body is molded to mine as he kisses my neck and pulls gently on my hair.

"You should have called."

"I know it."

"What do you think you're doing?"

"I'm sorry."

I'm aware of the night outside the window, the expanse of dark acres between here and Phil Carson, smoking alone on his porch. I believe he is thinking of me. Somehow the talk comes around to this:

He's after you. He's not. I can tell he is, and I can tell you like it from the way you lie to me. I'm telling the truth. Why don't I believe it? Because you're afraid. I'm afraid of nothing, he says, then kisses me. Look at you, Maggie. What? Stop crying. What? Stop crying. Don't pull, I say. Stop crying like that. I'm sorry, stop pulling my hair, it hurts. You have to stop it, he says. What do you mean? I say. You'll stop it with him. I say okay, all right, because his fist is pulling my hair so hard and his body is pressed against mine. He is drunk and does not know what he is asking. All right, I say, all right, can we go to bed? All right, you'll stop, you'll stop seeing that man. All right, I'll stop. Then we'll go to bed, he says.

As he guides me up the stairs, his hand is on the small of my back.

In bed as he sleeps I pull my own hair. I think of that kiss, my lies, and pull harder than Nate.

Part Two

The importance of angles is obvious. In the mug shot he has glazed, unseeing eyes, he shows nothing of himself. Ben Hodge walking to the courthouse wears a scowling face. He is pale and starved and sleepless. And in the high school yearbook he is a shy boy with a soft, ruddy smile and girlish eyes. He is a prince in that picture. He could almost be in movies, were it not for the large ears and crooked nose.

He was famously inconspicuous, this man New Harmonians knew intimately yet never seemed to notice. He would pass by your house once a week at least, no more striking than the shadow of an hour falling. Reading the articles about him—the reporters were so thorough—I can imagine his daily routine. He awakes in his mother's home on Carnation Street, a cramped house of sagging wood incapable of right angles. Inside, the mother, old and sick, lives in her bed while the six cats doze on the furniture, kitchen counters, the bathroom sink. From birth onward, Hodge has grown up with his mother and the stray animals she loves to save. Having achieved adulthood, he stayed out of inertia or a lack of options in such a small town. A long time ago, a father left the state, and then his older brother found his own place, so Hodge is now the man of the house.

He dresses himself in tight black jeans, Amoco shirt, and polished cowboy boots. His profile sharp as a jackknife, mirror shades throwing back the world, Ben walks hard into town. No one sees him pass. The sky over his head seems to hide the man. He is New Harmony's secret messiah. A small apocalypse lives in his limbs.

At Jaime's Diner he talks to no one. He sits in his booth and smokes three cigarettes, drinks coffee, and eats his eggs. A man of routine. The waitress needn't even ask what he'd like, just tells the cook Ben is here. From Jaime's, he walks to the downtown library, where he reads old paperbacks, now and then gazing at the patrons as if they are guests to his dream. He watches most closely the young librarian, whose house he will break into a few months after I'm hurt. He'll be jailed for that crime, but on the morning I imagine him, he is free. Does he have a tenderness for romance? Once had? I think I can see it in the high school photo—a delicate gleam in his eyes, a precious forehead. Of course, he was an altar boy. He served the seven a.m. mass for three years before he stole a statue of the Virgin Mary and hid it in his closet, the paper says. A man equally talented in obedience and transgression, as if both derive from the same instinctive sorrow. So it is with the Amoco. He walks there at four and spends eight hours selling gas, beer, tampons, and chips. The only store open past six in town, the Amoco is a nightly stop for many, and for years Ben Hodge ("the most steadfast employee I ever had . . .") has been the one they hardly notice behind the register. But local women will tell reporters how he *was* a bit odd, come to think of it. He *did* sort of stare at you a beat too long when he rang up your goods, like it was his secret privilege and he had something on you.

I take out the copies of the crime scene Polaroids. They took them early that morning when the sun was just up. I was long gone, and so was everyone else but the state police. The bloodied guestroom, rendered in a grainy black-and-white, looks small through the Polaroid lens, like the room of a doll. A frontal view of the house shows a heavy gray sky, the house transformed into a ruin. I try to imagine Hodge moving through these images, standing in the doorway, inside the bedroom, but he is too large for the miniature world of the photos.

It's two a.m. now, and I'm looking at Manny's atlas. Here's Colorado, resplendent green, sprinkled with secret lakes. I could get us good and lost in a state so big and rich in peaks. The map of Montana has the expanse of the cosmos. We'd never cross it if we dared to try. I imagine endless roads and small decisions of no consequence as we race through valleys, in search of nothing more than speed.

Maybe, soon, I'll leave this place. I'll drive away, and the house will go on creaking in the wind as if I'd never lived inside it.

Now it's time to do what I've been avoiding. It's no good pretending the manila folder from Mary Starr's office isn't right here in the center of my story. I take it with me to the backyard with a candle and a drink. The forest smells sweet tonight, invitingly so, but this man demands my attention. Sitting down at the picnic table, I finally open the deposition.

It's Mary Starr lobbing question after question for him to swat back. The whole business is typed up double-spaced and has the heft of a novel in my hands. On the last page is the man's awkward signature and a stamp from the court.

She starts from the beginning:

When did you first see Maggie Duke?

In the diner. Sometime in the fall of 1995. I saw her there, drinking coffee alone and not looking at anyone. I sat and watched her until she left, and when she'd gone I asked the waitress, Who was that? And the waitress said, Maggie Duke, Nate Duke's wife, lives out at the Duke farm. That was the first time I saw her.

Why did you ask the waitress about her?

I thought she was pretty.

When did you next see her?

Few months later. It's about Christmas. I'm working at the Amoco six days a week. I've got the night shift, one to ten, and just when I'm shutting up the place, just before I lock up, she comes in. She walks down the aisles like she doesn't know what she wants, like she just wants to buy something and it doesn't matter what that happens to be. She comes back with hot chocolate mix and asks for a pack of cigarettes. After she's gone, I get in my truck and follow her home.

Mary asks him why. He says it's not something he'd ever done before, follow a woman, but that night it seemed like the right thing to do. He didn't think twice. He just got in his truck and followed me to the Duke farm, where he paused on the side of the road to watch me get out of my car.

And no one ever asked me if I saw that truck by the road. No one asked me if I noticed a man staring at me in the diner. It's his right to do all these things, and my right to remain silent.

What did you see, Ben?

I see her get out. I see her smoke a cigarette on the front porch. She's there smoking in the dark, and I'm hidden on the road. When she goes inside, I just drive away.

There were nights I know of when I smoked on the porch. That is possible. A man in the shadows watching is possible.

But I don't remember. I have no recollection of this man. Nor can I imagine ever stopping at the Amoco to buy hot chocolate, something I never drink. It doesn't smack of truth, but a story is a powerful thing. All it takes is the telling and the lies form grooves in the mind. They become almost true.

I look up from the transcript and am surprised by the darkness surrounding the candle flame. This small, fuzzy circle of light I inhabit is in danger of being overwhelmed. The forest beyond emits a chorus of noise—the rattling of coons and crickets, an owl's moan beating deep within. With some effort, I see the ink-black holes between trunks, and I think I'd like to break out of this dim light, away from this storyteller, and enter my own kind of tale, told not in words but by the patter of sprinting feet. Story is motion, a deer escaping a hunter, a hunter tracking a deer. But Hodge has more to say.

Did you return to her house?

Every night for two weeks.

Why?

I got hooked on her. Can't say why, I just wanted to see the woman every night. Was like I had to. It got to be necessary. I'd drive to the house, park my truck, and walk up to the back window. I'd look in and see her there, having a drink, making dinner, talking on the phone. Once I saw her crying her eyes out at the kitchen sink. That made me want her more. The husband never seemed to be around.

Mary Starr will not accept that answer as complete. She asks him, *What were you trying to do, Ben?*

All this is happening before God touches me. Before I enter the fellowship of Christ. I'm just drifting sin to sin, trying to burn up time while my mother dies.

What was wrong with your mother?

She was real sick. Heart problems, bronchitis, high blood pressure—everything. I wanted to get out. I needed a life of my own.

There's Mary's justification. One simple, slow-footed motivation as dead as a rabbit run over on the road. He began to stalk Maggie Duke to escape his mother and take revenge for his shitty life. It's too simple. It has nothing to do with me, with how I recall the event. I opened the door and saw my husband. His hand went up to the right and came down on me. I remember everything vividly, the quality of the light, the near smirk on his lips. Give me oils and I'll paint the gleam in his eyes, the shade of night, the way the air moves as the violence begins.

But the questions and answers won't stop. There's nothing to do but read on as I sit in this candlelight. I am only a third of the way through.

Summer 1996

Sometimes I know a seizure is coming. I can feel that I am unsettled inside. My body's equilibrium is unsustainable, and I walk about waiting for it all to begin. The world offers up small happenings that could trigger the inevitable reckoning—a crow flapping too close overhead, a door slamming, a car's headlights floating over my eyes. And suddenly the night will begin to spin, and I'll fall off the wire my body has been treading so lightly.

This anticipation—I'd call it dread were it not so familiar—excites in me the need to move, to run into vast distance, or work steadily without thought. I want to throw myself into some endless, savage effort. Doing so will not stop the seizure. It will only bring it on all the sooner and more terribly; but knowing this doesn't curb the need.

That last summer with Nate, I was no epileptic, but felt the same tremulous fear and thirst for action. We shared an uneasy peace that June as we tried to be pleased with each other. For a time, he came home early to have dinner with me, and we'd work in the yard as the sun went down, pulling up weeds in the flowerbeds, planting impatiens and rose bushes around the house. This common effort made me anxious. Every day had become a chance to hold off disaster, and the more successful we were at being married, the more frightening marriage became.

One day Nate said to me, "Why should we drive into the city in separate cars? I can take you to the newspaper and pick you up."

"You could," I said.

"Is that okay? What's wrong with that?"

"Nothing. But you finish an hour or two after me. I'd have nothing to do."

"You'll see," said Nate. "I'll be there on time."

Nate was always on time. He showed up at the newspaper at five-thirty sharp. He did not wait in the parking lot, but came up the eleva-

130

tor and into the newsroom and stood over me as I finished the obits. On the way home, I would sit in the passenger seat, looking out the window at empty roads stretching to the horizon. I would wonder what Carson thought of me, as he smoked alone on the loading dock.

"This is working out," Nate said as he drove. "It makes more sense."

"Sometimes you'll need to stay late, and then what would happen with me?" I complained. "And anyway you shouldn't do this at all, Nate, because I know why you're doing it."

"What do you want? You want to drive your own car?"

"Yes."

He stopped at a crossroads and stared at me. I would not turn my eyes to him.

"Fuck it. Drive yourself."

So I began again to take myself to and from work, but did not go to Carson as Nate feared I would, at least not at first. Carson would come to my desk and ask me to visit him during his cigarette breaks, but I'd tell him I had to get home.

Which was true. I had projects. So many very important projects.

From that summer there is only one entry in my journal: A list of things to buy for the house. Dried flowers, Russian dolls, a Persian rug, a new dresser, scented candles, potpourri, an Amish rocker, a portrait of a woman, a painting of a river, more flowers, bluebells and violets and ivy plants, a kitten, a dog, maybe some geese.

I would make that house a home. I became mildly obsessed with the idea. I returned from work with my car full of decorative items: guest soaps, wicker baskets, an actual Amish rocker for the porch, bottles of furniture polish. I bought a print of a Hopper painting, a lone girl in an Automat, sitting at a table with her cup of tea. I had it framed and hung it over the parlor couch. One day, Nate and I redecorated the guestroom, rearranging furniture, touching up cracks in the paint and hanging new pictures. As we labored together in that sunlit room, I thought to myself, *This can work.* That afternoon was what I had imagined our marriage would become, a quiet and earnest effort in the name of an expansive future. In near silence, we hustled to perfect the room. I hung up in one corner the wedding photos of Alice and Richard Duke. He checked to make sure they were straight, then helped me put up his grandfather's painting. We centered the canvas over the bed, then stepped back to admire the picturesque gray house set against a forest. The room was complete.

It terrified me. I didn't want anything to be finished.

"I'm going to polish the dining-room table," I said.

"No, you're not." He circled his arm around my waist. He led me to the bed. "Someone's got to use this room."

"Let's not."

"Why?"

"I don't know. It's too hot. There's so much more work to do."

He pushed me gently onto the bed and began to kiss me. He moved my protesting hands away and casually unzipped my shorts. The movement was too deft. He tore off his shirt, revealing his pale muscled chest.

Something snapped inside me. All my energy and fear became focused, a hard beam of light. I grabbed his head in my hands and kissed it. I kissed his mouth and cheeks and neck. I pulled him down to me and reached into his clothes with animal quickness. I pictured in my mind a dark tunnel, one course of action, one route out. I'd never done it that way, with such manic intent. He grunted in my arms, overcome, then began to fight back. He pressed my arms to the mattress, raised his head high and stared down at me. Our eyes locked, expressing mutual confusion—a rare instant of honesty.

"What was that?" he said, panting, when it was over.

What you wanted, I almost said. But it wasn't at all what he wanted.

"You're like a stone these days. You know that?"

I was not like a stone. I wished I was.

"Let go of my arms," I said.

He did, then kissed me. "You're crazy," he said. "I didn't know you had that in you."

"You don't know much about me." I got off the bed and began to look for my clothes.

"Where are you going?"

"How do you know I'm going anywhere?"

"I just know about you."

"Then you don't have to ask."

I went outside to the garage and found the bicycle. I took it out onto the road and pedaled hard. The fields would not ever end. You could struggle against the wind, standing high on the pedals, and not reach any destination for hours. That was what I thought I needed then.

By the beginning of August, Carson had stopped coming by my desk at all. After several days of silence, I watched him go outside for his smoke break, then got up from my chair and followed him.

"At long last," he said.

He looked exhausted, unshaven. A man in the throes of some drama. Carson offered me a cigarette, and I took it.

"I'm working on a great story," he confided. "But first tell me about you."

"What do you want to know?"

"Everything."

"I've been fixing up our home. That house, it's practically a B&B now. We could open up for business." I tried to laugh.

He said nothing.

"I could use more sleep, I suppose. I always seem to be tired. Maybe it's the heat. Our house, you know, we only have the window units, and they make the air stale, which Nate doesn't like, so nights can be fitful. I dream like wild. Carson, you need to light my cigarette."

He leaned close to me to do this, positioning his body and his arm in such a way as to suggest an embrace.

"Do you want to talk about it?"

"What?"

"The dreams. Why you're so nervous. Everything on your mind, Maggie."

"I want to hear about the story you're working on."

"You tell me nothing. Why is that?"

"It's what happens when you marry. It's not good to talk about what goes on with outsiders, especially ones who like to kiss you. And anyway, there's not much to tell."

He flicked his cigarette to the pavement. "The other day the sports-writers voted you the most mysterious woman in the newsroom, and they're right. Though you don't lie very well." He took a deep breath and checked his watch. "What are you doing right now? Because I have to go somewhere to interview a twenty-year-old girl in trouble. You might be able to help if you wanted to come."

I knew at once I was going to. I didn't need to ask where or why or how. I looked the other way, squinting into the sun. "Fine," I said. "Let's go, then."

Phil Carson drove me over the Ohio. The wide, dark river opened up beneath us, and suddenly we were in a small town called Henderson, Kentucky. The whole time I was thinking of Nathan, of promising to stop it with Carson, stop it with Carson, all right, all right, I'd said. And I listened to Carson explain.

A couple days before, the police chief's son had beaten up his live-in girlfriend and was caught by two officers when the neighbors called. The girl, named Tammy Cox, was sent to a hospital, but the boy was let off the hook. His father ordered that the report of the incident be "ripped to pieces," according to reliable sources. A front-page story, sure to make waves if only Carson could get the thing into print. All he needed was the girl.

"I talked to the brother. Says she's scared witless. She's hiding out in Kentucky with a cousin—he told me where—and isn't answering the phone. Hence we're going to find her, to sweet-talk her face-to-face."

Carson had been working on this for thirty hours straight, conferencing with cops at three-thirty in the morning, hunting down the girl's family. Now, in his fatigue, he'd never looked so vibrant, with his auburn hair whorled up high and eyes bright with excitement. "When a story demands you take a long trip through counties and across rivers to find it, you know it's worth telling," he said.

"Thanks for letting me tag along."

He looked at me a beat too long and swerved the car. "You're not tagging along, you're part of the story. You'll have to help."

"You're just flirting."

He fell silent for a while. "Well, I look kind of scary right now. It might be helpful if you just talked to her first, tell her who we are."

The town of Henderson was long gone. We were headed into expansive hills, and the country, darkening, was heavy with summer. You could smell the corn and the rot, sweet and nutty in your mouth. The farther we drove away from Evansville, the more certain I felt I was making a grave mistake.

"Why are we going so far?"

"It only seems like it. We're not so far from the river now."

Still, my heart was pounding when he slowed and peered down a gravel drive. The trailer sat in the shadow of a hill, on cinder blocks, like a ruin sinking into the ground. Its windows were covered with curtains, but you could see, in the television light, a body's shadow moving across the room.

When I rang the bell, a pudgy white face appeared in the dark behind the screen door. The woman it belonged to stood mutely in the doorway for a moment as I told her my name, that we were looking for Tammy Cox. Her eyes widened, but she said nothing still, and I wondered if she could hear or understand me, as if we had entered another country where our English would do no good. Suddenly, a slight blond girl in a white robe pushed her way in front of the woman and opened the screen.

"Go back inside," she said quietly to the woman. "And shut the door."

Without a word, the woman obeyed, and the girl stepped out onto the small cement stoop with me, nearly close enough to kiss.

"What do you want?" she said in a flat Kentucky accent.

"Just to talk to you a little. My name's Maggie and this is Phil. We're with the newspaper in Evansville, the *Telegraph.* You're Tammy, right?"

She stared at me with a wounded expression in her eyes. Carson had told me she was twenty, but her face had the raw delicacy of a sixteen-year-old beauty. A jagged row of black stitches arced over a lazy eye that gazed steadily at me.

"See, we're reporters and we're working on a story that has to do with your boyfriend."

"I don't got a boyfriend," she said hardly loud enough to hear.

"I can imagine," I said, "after all that's happened."

She watched me, her body tense like a cat waiting for its attacker to strike. "Who's he?" she murmured, without looking his way.

"Phil Carson, reporter for the *Telegraph.* Nice to meet you, Tammy." He stepped forward with a worried wave of his hand.

"Who says I'm Tammy?"

We were all silent for a beat, and it seemed possible we had the wrong trailer. "Well, your brother told us we could find you here," Carson cut in. "I talked to him this morning."

"My brother? You talked to my brother? What the hell's going on here?" Her eyes suddenly welled up with tears.

"Let me explain." Carson stepped closer to the porch. "Some police officers told me about what happened between you and John the other night. They said there was a report describing it all, but somehow that report got destroyed on account of John's family connections. Now that's something we got to write about if it's true, and that's why we drove down here tonight."

Tears rolled down her broken-china-doll face.

"Tammy?" said Carson.

"Stop calling me that."

"I know it's hard—"

"Nothing's hard. I got nothing to do with it."

"We only want to know how you feel about what's happened, so we can hear all sides of the story."

She looked up at the starry sky. There was something eloquent about her silence. She seemed to have arrived in this Kentucky night like a child waking up from a nightmare, too full of fright to speak. I wanted to mother her, to tell her not to worry, we're going to leave and let you be, now go back to bed and get your rest.

But Carson persisted. "Maybe you could just answer a few easy questions for us, a few easy questions. For example, how long had you and John been living together?"

She looked at me. I didn't know what to tell her.

"I already got this here head busted open."

"I know," said Carson.

"And I don't want no one knowing where I'm at. My cousin put me up, and I don't want no one to know about that."

"We won't have to say where you are," said Carson. "I promise your location will never be in the newspaper."

She considered, her lazy eye settling on my face. "Why don't you ask a question?" she said.

"I'm listening to you."

"What's your name?"

"Maggie. What's yours?"

"That's a secret."

"Why is that?"

"A name's a good secret to keep when there's men that want to bust open your head. I think I'm going inside now."

"Tammy, please," said Carson.

She turned to the door, put her hand on the latch. "You got the wrong girl," she said. Then she opened the screen and disappeared inside, kicking the front door shut. We heard the door lock twice.

"We have to knock again," said Carson.

"We're going."

"We've got to try harder."

"She wants to be left alone."

"She doesn't know the full story," he said. But he didn't resist as I pulled him away from the trailer.

We stood by our car and looked back. We could see her shadow move against the wall inside. She was a waif of a girl. I would have liked to walk with her somewhere, just the two of us. She had a kind of strength I wanted, a girl who could disappear.

"What did you think of her?" Carson asked as we were driving back.

"I liked her as much as anyone I know."

"What was it?"

"She seemed good. She seemed honest," I said.

"She lied to us."

"I know."

The cool night streamed through the windows as Carson drove, saying nothing for miles. I shut my eyes and thought of the girl. After a while, he pulled onto the shoulder and reached back for a tissue. I turned my face away.

"Look at me."

"No."

"Look, Maggie."

"Why don't you drive?"

He waited for me. Finally, I turned around. He tried to hand me a tissue, but I refused.

"What is it?" he said.

"Nothing."

"You should talk to me. You should tell me."

"I don't want to talk to anyone."

We began to kiss then, and we kissed for a long, dense time by the side of the road. It made all the sense in the world. I felt myself becoming honest again, tasting the smoke of him.

"Are you all right?"

I nodded. I didn't know if I was all right, but I was sure of myself in a new kind of way. I was inside a sin and felt comfortable there.

We took a long time by the side of the road, then drove over the river.

"Where are we going?" he said.

"Go home if you want."

"What did you say?"

"Just go where you want."

We drove up through the city lights, not stopping at the office. Remembering my car in the lot, I asked him how I'd get home, but he didn't answer. He kept driving. He hit the dark of the country and pushed on the pedal, hitting the curves like a drunk. I thought to myself, Tell him to stop, but I said nothing, only held on to the door. I let the car take us. We sailed through New Harmony, down Butternut Ridge, where his red house waited.

He guided me through the dark rooms to his bed, and some new confidence took hold of me. I can do this, I thought, I am as strong as this. I couldn't have known that is the approach one must take—not weakness but strength, not temptation but power. I undress myself as he does. We kneel on the bed, clinging to each other. He is reverential toward me, amazed to have discovered my body. He covers my belly with kisses, eager to please. I throw myself upon him, placing my ear to his chest to hear the thrum of his heart. I claw at his arms and pull him inside me. I can say that in darkness and quiet like this, when you are busy with tasks such as these, you are like a buried woman. Buried in your sin, nameless and delighted. I stretch myself beside him, wrap my legs around him. It is so humid here, and we are soaking ourselves in the hot, easy sliding and the clutch of our hands.

Why did you do this? lawyers would ask me much later. I was spared

the humiliation of answering. Had I responded, I would have said there
was no choice. I was not weighing options. I moved into his arms and did
not think for hours. We made love three times, so deep and quiet a time
in his bed. I didn't pause to scold myself. Only after we ceased all movement and lay tangled in the sheets, dozing, exhausted by our own heat,
did the consequences come crashing around my ears.

"Oh, Carson," I said.

"Whatever you do next, don't crucify yourself," he said.

The real question they should have asked me was, why didn't I stay?
I could have. I could have called Nate to say, I've a lover and have to leave
you, and you will have to let me go. This would have been the forthright
thing to do. But I imagined that my husband was on the way. There
would be violence, punches, and I would be ashamed. I sat up in Carson's
bed.

"We have to go to my car," I said.

"Why?"

"It's late. Look at the time. It's nearly three in the morning." I
crawled out of bed and began to dress.

"I want you to stay."

"Get dressed, Carson."

"You want to stay, too."

"I don't," I said. "I have a very bad feeling about this."

"About what?"

"Use your journalist's intuition."

"My intuition is you should stay here."

I ignored him, and he obeyed in silence, stung by the rejection. On
the road, he drove at breakneck speed, and as we approached the office, he
put his hand on my knee. "You don't need to go back, you know," he
instructed me. "You don't need to if you don't want—"

"It isn't about what I *want*."

We said nothing else until we reached my car. I kissed him good-bye,
and he held my wrist and kissed me longer than I wanted.

"Don't worry about me."

"I'll be worrying all night. Call if you need me."

As I drove home, the fields gave off vulgar scents: humid earth,
melon, dung. Our house smelled of fire-prone timber. Going inside, I

heard Nate's voice, Eddie's. They were drinking in the kitchen. I went toward them, stepping like a thief.

Eddie sat at the table in a posture of luxury and disregard, looking up at Nate, who talked feverishly. He seemed not to notice my entrance, but Eddie gave me a wink, then looked back at Nate, who was saying, "I will get her fucking picture and prove it to you." He left the room, his stride made brutally fast by the rum they were sharing. Eddie rose, all gallantry and smiles, and kissed me on the cheek.

"How are you, Maggie?"

"I'm fine."

"Nate's worried, we're all worried, about where you've been."

"Working." The lie woke me up like cold water.

"I bet you're tired, want some rum?"

"I would love some." He handed me his glass. And it was strange to drink the rum with his eyes on my face, daring me to misbehave. I drained the rum from the glass like a street urchin greedy for milk.

"There you go," said Eddie.

"Get away from my wife," Nate said, coming between us suddenly. "I found the photo, here it is."

He held up for Eddie a Polaroid of a girl caught unaware, holding a sleeping bag against her naked chest. Nate's face was frozen in incredulous surprise in the corner of the picture. "Halloween, 1994. Emily Parker. Best lay I *ever* had," he said, making sure I could see the picture. "Arnold came in on us in the middle of everything with his camera."

Eddie turned to me. "You married a real son of a bitch, didn't you?"

Nate spun the picture onto the table. He leaned with two hands against a chair, his back to us. "Time for you to get out of here, Sorewell," he said.

Eddie took his navy blazer off a chair. He winked at me for a second time as he went. I heard each one of his footsteps.

Listen now to how well I lie:

"You wouldn't believe the night I had," I say.

"Tell me. Tell me."

"You're drunk, aren't you, Nate? I don't think you drank so much when I met you."

"Tell me."

"They wanted me to work the copy desk tonight because this woman was sick, and so I did, I wrote headlines all night. I did such a good job they might promote me."

"Headlines."

We are in the kitchen, the place where these sorts of things happen. Where husbands waiting for wives are likely to drink. The place where fights often break out. Perhaps it is the location of the liquor. Or food, or knives.

"So many headlines. You'd be amazed how many stories there are. What did you and Eddie do, get drunk all night?"

"Yes."

"I don't like him."

"I don't give a shit."

Leaning on the back of a chair with his hands, he has the look of a man on the verge of throwing up. Nate Duke is nauseated with suspicion. He despises himself. He waits, staring balefully at my legs, as I cross the room to the cupboard for a glass. I fill it with the rest of the rum and sip.

"You like that?"

"It's okay."

"You like that rum?"

"What?"

"You like to lie?"

"I like the rum."

"What? You like to lie?"

He's called the office and knows everything about me, Nate says. Knows what? I say. He opens his mouth, but can't speak. He has no talent for jealousy. It steals away his voice. He advances, eyes widening, hand rising into something like a greeting. He slaps me against the side of the head.

My face whipped, I stare at the curtains I have just hung. I stare vacantly at them, ears buzzing, until the next blow comes.

How I end up is on my back, legs cocked, head knocked against a wood chair leg. I am down, upside down and breathless before I know how. There are his shoes, gleaming darkly. I would not forget them. Nor the vibrating sting of tile to cheek, or the nakedness of being floored. His face came down to me, sweat-glazed and confused.

"What happened?" he says.

"I don't know."

And I watch his shoes, their dark gleam. I watch his rising legs. And I won't forget how he stands, helpless and stupid, waiting for his wife to get up.

"You hurt yourself," he's saying.

"You hit me."

"I didn't mean to."

His mouth seems to be moving, trying to find some words to make me disappear. Don't speak, I think, please, don't say anything else or do anything, leave me alone to crawl into my car and drive away. But I say nothing. Hearing the buzz in my head, I stare at his mouth.

He grabs me by the shoulders and, with a grunt, pulls me to my feet like a rag doll. His hard body pressed close to mine, he leads me to the couch in the living room and eases me down.

And what is learned? That it could happen and did. That it's a danger to have precious hopes about love. It does not matter when he reappears with a glass of water. I hide my face in the couch pillows.

Drink the water. I don't want the water. Drink the water. Nate, you hit me. I hardly touched you. I can see you doing it. I waited all night. I know. I waited all night. So what? So what am I going to do while you, while you, you bitch, come home a lying bitch? What do you want to know, I'll tell you everything as true as you knocked me down, as true as that. I hardly touched you. You knocked me down. Drink the water. You knocked me down. Just drink the goddamn water, please.

He throws it against the wall above the couch, and the glass rains down.

He leaves the bed to me and spends the night downstairs. I sink my teeth into my arm as I think of what I did in that other house, with that other man. I've got the smoke of his hair high on my mind. I see the image of a girl with a broken face. A name's a good secret to keep when there's men that want to bust open your eyes, and I am starting to have an idea.

I sleep not at all. At some point Nate appears in the doorway and looks at my body under the sheet. Shutting my eyes, I lie motionless and listen to the sound of him dressing in the bathroom. I stifle my sobs as I smell his aftershave, the floating scent of my husband going to work on any regular day.

Alone in the house, I let myself cry, but only for a while. I've a job to do, an office to report to, and for this small certainty, I feel grateful. I dress in the bathroom behind a locked door. I try to put on makeup, then look in the mirror, feel the bump on my head, and begin to cry. I skip the makeup and put a Band-Aid on my elbow, where the glass left a scab.

Later, outside, I walk to the garage. In the far corner, the bicycle I took out with Carson leans against the wall, shining in the sunlight. Something is wrong about the wheels, I see that right away. They are bent, twisted out of shape. There's a hammer on the workbench next to the bike. I see all that happened. How he came down here drunk late last night, how he found the hammer and did his work in secret. I come closer and see that several nails are embedded in the tires. I bend to touch them and pull two out. They give easily. I was knocked down by my husband. It was real, though I didn't see it coming. The bike is useless. It was a hit or a punch. I put the nails in my pocket and feel sick to my stomach. There is someone behind me.

"Darling."

It's only Manny.

"Yes."

"Good morning."

"Yes. Good morning."

"What's the matter?"

"I'm late for work."

"Sure you are. I always go pale as a ghost when I'm late."

"It's the heat," I say.

"The heat." He nods and looks at what is in my hand, and then at the bike behind me, and says nothing.

"I'm thinking of taking a trip," I say.

"Where to?"

"I'm not sure yet. Maybe Kentucky."

"I got road maps. Like one?"

I tell him yes, I would, my heart pounding at the thought of escape.

I'm letting the house slide. Roaches are making inroads. Flies, too. The garbage under the sink is foul. Dust gathers in clumps in the corners, and spiders reign. I move through the filth like a resentful guest.

Late at night, I hole up in the dining room and turn the pages of the transcript, the gospel according to Hodge. I imagine I can hear his voice as I read. It's rough and low, has the texture of bark. His eyes, in the *Telegraph* color photos, seem to be green like Nate's.

And back in the summer of 1996, New Harmony is burning up. A heat wave's on. The corn is wilting all over the county. The Wabash runs low and tepid, its shoals scalding hot to sit on. Some people are dying in their homes.

Some old folks, I recall. Some old folks passed away then.

He's starting to repeat himself as he gets closer to the tender center of his story.

One night I come home from work and she's not so well, he tells Mary Starr.

What was wrong with his mother? He can't say. He says it was worse than usual. What *it* was isn't clear. At one point he mentions the flu, but later it's bronchitis. Whatever she suffered from, Meredith Hodge asked her son to find some cough syrup for her the night before my birthday in August.

I'm finding it necessary to hold some picture of these lives in my mind. As I imagine it, the house is small and usually dark. They keep the curtains drawn tight against the heat. Inside, a small woman wastes away in bed, watching a snowy TV, and talking to her cats. Her thin body, naked but for panties, is covered by a single cotton sheet. She breathes weakly, her head knocked back, mouth open and drooling. The remote for the television is in her lap and one hand is loosely curved around it.

The door opens, and her youngest son enters. He passes her bed-

144

room, but doesn't look in. She rubs her eyes and blinks. Through her open door she can see him sitting at the table, pouring himself beer from a two-liter bottle. He drinks deeply from the glass. Though his back is to her, it makes her proud to see him do this in the same way it once made her proud to watch her boys eat. Ben has a good strong back, broad good shoulders. She has the urge to call out his name, but he is such a private and prickly man these days. He always liked his peace and quiet, but now he can be downright hostile if you say the wrong thing. Maybe it's the heat.

We didn't talk much, she and I. We was sort of on our own, but together, and that was the trouble. That night she says to me, Benny, I'm seeing black spots. I'm seeing clouds. And I says back to her, What can I do about it? Buy me some cough syrup. Cough syrup won't help. It's better than nothing. So I say fuck it, I'll go. So I get back in my truck.

He doesn't forget to bring the beer with him. Driving drunk, he says in the transcript, is as common for him as driving sober. He swings onto the road in the pickup, and all of Posey County is asleep but for him. I can imagine him coasting through fields, taking roads slowly, unafraid of driving into the weeds. The bottle is upright between his skinny thighs, and one hand is on the wheel.

He is not the boy at the Amoco anymore. No one knows who he is. He is invisible. He could drive all night and not once be seen.

I wanted to find Maggie then.

Why?

Don't know.

Try to answer the question.

She was the big thing happening then.

It isn't right. The countryside is too large. There's too much room for secret admirers harboring ill intentions. I can imagine the truck growling as it comes up the grade to my house: porch light on, windows grand and dark. She is in there. It must be nice inside, he thinks. The night is long and peaceful in a strong house. She might be alone in the day.

In the secret passing of a moment, an idea is born in his mind. He is taken by it, stops the car completely. He doesn't see the idea for what it is.

I wanted to get in there, you know. I wanted the night to amount to something.

There is something new about his world. He has the desire to disrupt a life. But what was it he needed to do? What was that one, unnameable thing that was pressing from inside him, against his ribs and eyes? He stares at the dark windows, the lone porch light. He begins to drive faster. Emptying the bottle with a long swallow, he swerves off the road, swerves back, grazing a mailbox and running over some marigolds. It would only be a matter of stepping up to the door and knocking. Only a matter of speeding up the county grid. And finally doing something to her.

Next morning, his mother is alone. She is five feet tall and less than a hundred pounds. She is enveloped by the sheets of her bed, and lies next to a fan that spins slowly, sending a draft of air in her direction.

It is most likely his bladder that wakes Ben. Not the mother's television on the other side of the wall, nor the faint rustle of her gown, the creaking in her ankles as she crosses the house with much consternation. Not the sound of her high, wavering voice as she talks to the cats that come out from under the furniture to greet her. No, he does not hear his mother stir this morning.

How does he find out?

He will later say that he made a guess. Certain observations fell into place and pointed to a conclusion. The sound of her voice the night before, the sweat mottled on her forehead and cheeks. Perhaps a news story he'd read in the paper about the heat and what it was doing to the elderly.

The late morning quiet and sunshine. The innocent *thump* of a cat jumping off her bed.

He said he "found her." As if she had been lost before. She was hidden in covers, asleep, only her face showing. Found, as if she had disappeared. There had been a complication over the night as her son had gone out looking for cough syrup. Perhaps if he had found some? No, it was heat stroke. They told him this on the lawn of his house with the neighbors standing around. They hadn't seen her in weeks. She was carried away with her face hidden, put in the ambulance and driven away.

Hodge was a practical man.

I called the hospital, emergency room. They came out and told me what I already knew. So I call up my boss to say I need a day off, then call up my brother

and leave the message. I just say, Come on over, Mom's sick, meet us at the hospi-
tal, 'cause I don't want him finding out on the machine. I knew he wouldn't get
the message till that night, so it was up to me to take care of matters.

What sort of matters did you take care of?

Funeral sort. Got it done for not much. Whatever I had in the bank, which
turned out to be all right. And then the obit came in that ways.

He knew my name. He'd seen it in the paper. Margaret Duke,
Obituary Page Editor.

I drove it in myself.

Drove what in?

The obit. She did the page. I'd seen her name in the paper.

A sudden feeling of helplessness causes me to stop reading.
Something here is familiar. The vague memory of a man approaching the
desk. A tall, very skinny man with tinted glasses, stooped, with a slip of
paper in his hand. Looming over my desk, waiting for me to look up.

She's typing on her computer when I walk in the office. I tell her I want to file
this report. About my mother. And she just hands me a form like she don't care at
all, like she gets orphans walking in every day. And so I fill out the form and
hand it back to her. She says, I can't read this, do it again. I say, Do you recog-
nize me?

And I say, no.

And she says, no.

And he says, I'm Ben Hodge.

My stomach is turning. Something here is real. I recall a tall, thin
man with the stench of animal looming over me. I tried not to look up.

I fill it out again and give it to her, and she says, What did she die from?

Heat, I say.

What? she says.

H-E-A-T.

I typed it up. I heard that man. He was standing before me. I recall
the way he spelled that word slowly, as if trying to impart some secret
between the letters, and the way I ducked my head to hide my eyes. I
nodded and typed and did not look up. After a time, he left. One small
but sinister encounter I was able to forget.

I hear a noise now, a car in the road, rare for this time of night. The
gun's in the closet. The doors are locked, windows open. I walk to the

entryway and peer outside to see a car turning around in the drive. The headlights flash across my face, and I think the driver may have seen me. Maybe he's lost, or maybe my house was his destination. The car hesitantly rolls away now, as if he might be staring inside the windows for another glimpse.

I go to the phone and pick up the receiver, determined to speak with a human being. The man who comes to mind is Phil Carson.

I don't even have his number now. Remembering the end of our relationship makes me wince. Before his move to Chicago, while I was still in Indianapolis recovering and having grand mal seizures daily, he'd visit me on weekends. We'd sit in the yard and drink lemonade like some awkwardly courting couple.

"How was your week?" he'd ask me.

"The same," I'd say.

"You can do better than that."

I'd shake my head in reply. I didn't want to let him or anyone else into my life. I'd been reborn a loner, one who kept her own counsel and never talked to strangers. I hardly spoke to my parents in those early months after the incident. And when Phil Carson came to visit, I always felt ugly and broken.

"Can't you talk to me?"

"Can't you see I'm not the same girl?"

"I only see that you're angry, Maggie."

"Then why visit me at all?"

"Maybe I still love you."

I wouldn't let him love me, though. I received his kindness, his humble bouquets and gifts of photographs with cruel coldness. "You loved me," I said. "Loved. Now I'm sick. Now I live here and you live there." And when I looked at Carson, my eyes were hard and dark. I felt them slowly turning to stone. With every seizure that drove me down into the earth, I wished all the more to sever myself from the past. Eventually he stopped his visits, and I tried to feel relieved. Then came the letter, announcing he had moved to Chicago to take a job with the Associated Press. Shortly after that, he wrote he was planning to marry. I never heard from him again.

And so the number one man in my life is now the septuagenarian living next door. I pick up the receiver and call him.

"I don't want any," Manny says.

"What are you talking about?"

"Women."

"Were you sleeping? Were you dreaming of a pretty girl?"

"That's all I dream about," he says.

"Manny."

"What is it, my darling?"

"Do you think I'm nice to look at?"

"Of course," he says. "You're beautiful."

We are quiet for a moment, and a rain begins. It falls heavy and full in the trees.

"Have you ever wanted to disappear?"

"What are you talking about?" I hear him sitting up in his bed.

"Disappearing," I say. "Never mind."

Manny clears his throat. "Remember what I said a while back, Margaret? Do you remember what I said about all that? Forget about it. It's history. Let it all go by in the wind. Let it disappear. Don't you listen?"

"I'm going to go now."

"Look. Do you want to play a game of blackjack?"

"No. I'm going to go."

"Don't."

"I'm going."

After we hang up, I finish my glass of bourbon, then curl up on the couch, hoping sleep will come. But before I go completely under, a seizure jolts me to my senses. I hold on to the couch, mash my face into the pillow as the night pulses behind my eyes. The spells have been more frequent, probably because of the drinking. This one begins as subtly as a dancing moth, then accelerates, turns savage, corkscrews into my head, pinning it down against my will.

It doesn't last long, but afterwards I feel too disturbed for sleep. I go into the kitchen to take some extra pills with water, noticing on the windowsill a cornhusk doll with a burlap apron. She tilts to the side, as if knocked offbalance, and has a gaping mouth of smeared red paint and mad black dots for eyes. I'm struck by an irrational fear that the seizure has left me speechless, and so I test my voice, addressing this humble ornament before me:

"Doll," I say. "Woman."

I say it once again, louder and with false authority, though there is only me to hear myself.

Rita knows I've had something to drink. I saw the knowledge flicker through her expression the moment I sat down in the chair. She must be accustomed to reading the signs, the uncertain step and skittish eyes.

"So, what would you like to talk about?"

It's the typical manner. She acts as if I am interrupting her day, but that because she is such an old friend she will stop and listen to me speak my mind. The informality is purposeful. Usually, it sets me at ease.

"Nothing, actually."

"That's unusual. Why did you come?" She smiles at me with her brown eyes.

"I come in every Tuesday. I have an appointment, and so I'm here."

"Talk to me," she commands, folding her arms.

"I'm not in the mood today. I've been drinking. You probably know that. I don't usually drink anything in the afternoon, just at night, and then only when I really can't get to sleep, but today. Today I somehow didn't want to leave my house. I somehow—"

"Go on, Maggie."

"I didn't want to show my face."

I shut my eyes, and feel the room spin.

"I didn't know you'd been drinking, Maggie. What I did notice is that you look very tired and a bit gaunt. Have you been eating?"

"Yes."

"What?"

"I eat whatever there is. There isn't much. I don't go to the store. I don't need to because I'm hardly ever hungry. When I do go, I buy chips and frozen chicken patties and maybe some apples. The last time I went, some woman at the register said she knew me. She told me my name like she had a right to it. Then she said I needed the saving grace of Jesus and handed me a New Testament. I opened the booklet in the parking lot, and the first page read in bold red letters, **The Day of the Lord Will Come Like a Thief.** The day of the Lord has already come, and if it comes again, I don't know what I will do. Rita, what do you want to talk about? I came here because I had an appointment. I had such a bad night. I never sleep anymore. When I get close, I have a seizure or hear some sound in the house that makes me leap out of bed and wander around with the rifle. I'm a fool, Rita."

Rita is unimpressed. She watches me. "What do you do at night?" she asks. "What do you do when you can't sleep?"

The sun moves from behind the clouds. It shines through the window and onto my face. A sharp pain shoots through my head, making me flinch. "I've been reading. I've been reading all about him."

"Who?"

"Ben Hodge, the one in the papers."

"I know who he is," says Rita.

"Of course you do. Everyone does. Everyone knows his name and mine. Do you think you have some aspirin?"

She tells me she does and leaves the room. She quickly returns with a tall glass of water and two tablets in her palm. I swallow these down and sit in the chair, holding on to the glass.

"So you are reading about him. And what are you learning?"

I sip the water and stare at a sandstone carving of a phoenix on her shelf.

"Do you want to talk about it?"

"I'm learning that he's very persuasive and that Mary Starr believes him. I'm learning to hate him and that he is full of lies. And sometimes he speaks the truth."

"About what?"

I stand up and walk to the window so that my back is to Rita. We are on the second floor of this building, so I can look down at the street and concentrate on the shape of a tall, thin man walking along the road. He shimmers darkly in the heat.

"Last night I wanted to disappear," I say.

"How did you want to disappear, Maggie?"

"I might go on a trip," I say.

"That's very different from 'disappearing,' isn't it?"

"Maybe."

The shadow man is persisting through the heat. He squints at the sky. He walks with a faltering rhythm that makes me think he's homeless.

"Maggie, why won't you sit down and tell me what you mean."

The pain comes back, shooting through my head. I see faint ink spots bleed in the sun. My hand lets go of the glass.

"Don't worry about it, Maggie."

All around my feet are shards and water.

"I'm so sorry. I'm so awful."

"No, you're not. Don't be silly. It's nothing," says Rita.

"I dropped your glass."

"It's nothing at all, a cheap lousy glass. Go sit, and I'll take care of everything."

She goes to look for a broom. I bend over, feeling like I'm about to cry, but I bite my tongue and focus on the job of picking up big pieces of glass. Rita comes back and crouches next to me with a hand broom and dustpan, into which I drop the fragments I've collected. Her dark hair hangs low to the floor, smelling faintly of flowers. She begins to sweep, then stops.

"Maggie, dear girl." She takes my hand and turns it. There on the base of my palm, a fine cut from the glass. "I'm going to get our first-aid kit. You sit down in this chair and take some deep breaths, okay?" She puts her arm around me. "Are we having fun yet?" she says, grinning.

I could take care of myself, I think, but Rita rummages in her desk for a white tin box. She bends next to me and takes out a bandage, a cloth, a tube of ointment. She daubs my palm with the cloth so it soaks up the blood.

"I'm going to put this on, and you'll be fine, though I'm going to want you to rest here before you leave. I don't want you to have trouble getting home."

She bites the cap off the tube and squeezes some clear gel onto the cut. She rubs it about so it stings, then puts on the bandage. This act of kindness makes me sorry I felt so resentful toward her, but I want to be alone all the more.

"Thank you," I say. "I think I'd like to go to the bathroom for a moment."

She directs me down the hall. I close the bathroom door and lock it and stare in the mirror. I've never seen myself look so drained. I splash water over my face and suddenly know what I'm about to do. It's a decision I don't take time to question. I hear her chair squeaking as I open the bathroom door and hurry through the beige lobby and the glass doors of her office.

Before she knows it, I'm in the parking lot. The afternoon is humid and monstrous. Walking across the burning asphalt, I see the tall man I'd spied from the office, glaring at me from a bus stop. I run to my car. As soon as I start the engine, I wish I were still with Rita.

I drive out of the lot, my eyes stinging with sweat, and hit the highway that leads out of town. I don't want to leave yet. I want something more to happen, to hold me back from home. A phone booth at a corner gas station catches my eye, and I pull over.

Inside the glass booth, the heat is unbearable, the phone itself almost too hot to touch. Why am I here? Who do I want to reach? I know so few people in this town. There is the receptionist at the newspaper who once invited me to her Methodist church. There is Stan Black. There is or was an Eric Johnson. There is Mary Starr. I drop the change into the slot and dial the number I once memorized and have failed to forget.

Waiting for the ring, I shut my eyes. The ink spots bloom again in the dark. I know something terrible will come from this call.

The receptionist tells me Mary Starr isn't in, but would I like to talk to her voice mail? I say yes, please, holding on to the phone, mesmerized by the electric motion of the cars.

Hello, this is Mary Starr. I'm afraid I can't come to the phone, but please do leave a message and I will get back to you as soon as possible.

The tone goes off, and I gape into the silence. I say, "This is Maggie Wilson. Maybe I'm ready to talk now." I hang up the phone and fall back against the glass.

I sat with the sensation that I could not be touched. I blocked out the business of the newsroom, the phones and reporters passing my desk. My goal that morning and afternoon was to type as quickly as possible, get the names right, then leave. Because he might call and say not sorry, no, but Can we have dinner, lovely? Can we have dinner tonight, Maggie? Happy Birthday, Maggie. Not an apology but as close to one as he'd get. He'd be bright and charming, and I'd want to say yes, to forgive and be forgiven. Even that morning, with the carpenter nails in my pocket and the ache in my head from where it had hit the chair leg, I felt vaguely sick and false for simply packing my bag.

If he'd called earlier, I would have given in. If he'd caught me, I would not have taken the trip. I know it as well as I know my own name. Yes, dinner, I would have said. I'm sorry.

I had brought the map from the car. It was under the keyboard on my desk, and every now and then I would slip it into view so I could look at the tangle of black lines south of Evansville. I could cross the Ohio, then west and south, and stop, and then? I could make up my mind as I went. Running away wasn't something you planned. It would only succeed according to instinct. Even a map seemed burdensome.

I remember there were more notices than usual, and that I had to force myself to concentrate on my typing. I had a job to do. I was swamped with announcements from the fax and the phone. Perhaps there were visitors at the desk that day, too, but I don't remember their faces.

Carson walked past my cubicle several times. What now, what now? his eyes seemed to say. How can you sit there like that when I'm in love with you? How can you be so stoic?

That afternoon when I pushed open the loading dock door and saw him there smoking, he did not turn around to greet me, but stood motionless, as if in fear of a snake coiled at his feet. His face was unshaven and gnarled with fatigue.

"Did you get the story in?" I meant the one about Tammy Cox.

"I don't want to talk about that," he said. "Did you get home in time last night?"

"You sound bitter. Home in time for what?"

"I'm only worried, and, yes, angry—the way we said good-bye, like you felt the whole thing was a mistake. Home in time to escape persecution."

"It was a mistake."

"Go to hell."

I started to walk back to the door, but he grabbed my wrist. "I'm sorry," he said. "Don't go."

"You can't talk to me like that. I can't fight with you, too."

"I just want to know what happened."

"Maybe you don't need to know."

I looked at the ground as his eyes examined me. His hands, like those of a priest blessing a child, rose and touched the bump on my head.

"Dear Lord, Maggie."

I moved away.

"Come here."

He took me in his arms, and I surrendered to his embrace, hiding my face against his chest. I tried to say, "It was an accident," or, "He didn't mean it." I tried to utter some nonsense to dispel his concern, but I didn't want to open my mouth and break into tears. To do so would admit too much, and I didn't want to be compromised more than I already was. Still, he whispered promises into my ear; he'd take me home, give me a room in his house if I wanted it. He'd fix my meals and keep me company while I worked things out. "You've got to get away from him," he said. "I don't know what's going on, not really, but I know you can't trust him now."

"I think I'm going to vanish for a few days."

"Where?"

"I don't know, someplace—"

"Tell me."

"I don't know. Kentucky, maybe. Somewhere south. Somewhere I can have a rest." I felt like I was failing him with every word.

"You need help. He might come after you."

"He won't know where to go."

Phil Carson wouldn't let me go easily. He was too strong-willed for it. He tried every argument he could think of to keep me close. He said he'd known cases like mine, "domestic abuse situations" in which the wife runs away, then returns to an enraged husband waiting to pounce. Hearing him talk about my life this way made me sick. I remembered the night before—the sight of Nate's legs rising above me as I caught my breath, his sweat-glazed face looming in the dark. And here was Carson, pledging to protect me. At the very least, he said, he'd put me in touch with a woman's shelter in Evansville, a place he'd written articles about. In the end, I rejected his offers, insisting I needed to be alone.

"It's your birthday," he pleaded. "You deserve more than this."

He reached inside his blazer and pulled out a gift wrapped in newspaper. It was a framed photo I'd taken with him in March. It was one of the shots of the inside of the barn: vaulted space beneath a slatted roof, with the sun leaking through it. We'd taken many pictures from many angles. I remember how he'd stopped what he was doing for a time to watch me work. The camera had felt cold and powerful in my hands.

"You took it. You took that picture."

"What's your point, Carson?"

"The point is it's beautiful."

"It's nice."

"It's more than nice," he said. "Can't you see anything?"

I looked at Carson's face. He had the eyes of a zealot, this man who would save me.

"Don't love me, Carson."

"Don't tell me what to do."

I kissed him on the mouth, and he cleaved to me. I gently pulled away and walked back to the office.

I went to the restroom to change into a pair of black jeans, white T-shirt, boots. I looked strong, tightly outfitted. It was good to be rid of all those cotton dresses. I tied my hair up and washed my face with cold water and gave myself a look in the mirror. Just for now, I told myself, believe in what you are about to do.

I left at five. I had in my wallet about eighty dollars Nate had given me a week ago (he controlled the banking) and a credit card in my maiden name from my college days. The traffic moved slowly. My car idled at an intersection, and there I resisted the urge to turn right and head home. To call my own bluff. It would have been an easy thing to do. The light turned and I drove forward. Ahead was a gas station gleaming in the sun, and the heat rippled off the chrome pumps.

My husband would have been at work then. Three blocks to the right, six blocks back, building on the left, first floor, end of the hall. He would have been talking to Eddie Sorewell or some other man.

Perspiring in the car, I tried not to consider my options. I hadn't seen it coming last night—a slap or a punch? Or was it only a push? Don't wander off your purpose, Maggie. Don't think it will be all right back home, don't think he'll stop drinking. That's a fool's trap. As I drove, I took from my pocket the nails from the tires. I rolled them between my fingers.

Why did I leave town? They would ask me this later when I was in the hospital, unsure of everything.

I left because my husband, over the past eighteen months, had sabotaged our lives. Because his voice was not the voice of a man I'd wanted to marry, and he did not wish to win me over any longer.

Because Phil Carson was in love with me. Because I was guilty, we all knew this to be true, and I wanted to evade the knowing by means of stealth.

A light changed. The road opened up and I bolted. The city eased off. I rattled onto the bridge, the first of two crossings. My car was well prepared, lubricated, gassed. I had unreasonable faith in it. It was like a pure white dream of prosperity now rusted and degenerate, but still capable. It took me over the Ohio. The river lazed. It died in its own silt. It was coiled and dark, a careless sprawl over the land.

I emptied my mind of everything but travel: turn signal, change lanes, slow down, accelerate. I soaked my shirt in sweat, but my eyes were dry. And so going slowly, not cautiously but with strong, vacant intentions, I drove.

The road undulated southwest, released me into an expansive twilight. Out of a bronze horizon rose cooling shades of blue. I'd passed through

Corydon, Waverly, St. Vincent, Kentucky. The towns were hardly noticed.

If I drove all night, stopped before dawn, then slept, I'd be nowhere. This seemed like a plan. I thought of Alabama. Mobile, the Gulf of Mexico. "Mexico?" I said the word out loud. The possibility, once I heard it croaked in my car, was a lie to myself so that I might feel freer than I was.

If I'd turned around I could have been back by morning, even before midnight. He might not have missed me.

But then he might have. And then what would I have done? He have done?

I could have convinced him, maybe. Held his face in my hands and kissed him like I did when I was still single and sure of our love. It takes getting used to, marriage does. It takes strategies of influence I don't have yet, but maybe could learn. There was some good to Nate Duke. Think of before we moved here, think of Bloomington, how scrubbed clean and gallant he'd been those mornings in the diner. Think of the night in the baseball diamond, in the grass, his strong back under my hands.

The cattle faces rose from the grass to salute my passing. An outsider, I drifted at my own risk through a foreign economy: wood traded for feed, traded for crude oil, for beef, for car parts for sheet metal, for rust. In the distance I saw the trace of a parallel road, and the headlights moved softly along it. At a crossroads on the crest of a low hill, I came upon a horse and buggy headed the opposite direction. There was a bearded driver and a little girl with a squint beside him. The horse was enormous and glossy. It pulled them slowly, clopping, insistent, pulled them upward to the top and then forward, down. They watched me. The man smiled slightly, nodded, as if to say, Please do not run over me and my little girl. Her mouth was scornful, showing large gaps in her teeth and a soft red cavity. She had many freckles and fair skin and wisps of brown hair under her bonnet. The horse accelerated, clipping, fast staccato steps, the gaudy gloss of it withering.

My heart was beating quickly. It'd been a fright and a relief to be seen like that. My car had stalled. I turned the key again, afraid I might be stranded.

Turn back now, I thought, when the car started.

But I went on. I headed southwest on Highway 60. At Morganfield I continued straight on state road 56. The town fell away, and I came into fields bearing lush crops.

There was half a tank left.

There is in all this testimony a terrible absence—the humanity of Hodge's mother. She does not completely exist. She is only an accident, a failure. He refers to his mother not as such but as "her" or "she," as if naming her long ago became irrelevant. I want to lift her up in my hands, breathe some life into Mrs. Hodge. She falls over limply. She won't stand up straight or speak a word.

Only her older son mourns her properly.

Attached to the statement made by Ben is a shorter tale told by Rick. Rick, the brother who escaped the squalor of that home and made some good of himself. He explains that he rents farmland and works hard enough to own a small trailer of his own.

While Ben was in Evansville filing the obit, Rick arrived at the hospital to learn of his mother's death from a nurse. It is known that from there, he went straight to his childhood home with the intention of finding Ben.

It is also known the two brothers had been estranged for years, over Ben's failure to care properly for their mother, whose health and spirits had been declining due to the neglect of the younger son, or so says Rick. And now, after hearing the news, Rick wanted, he says here in the transcript, to hurt his brother, but Ben was nowhere to be found. The house was empty and locked.

What did you do next?

I ripped the back door open. I didn't have a key, and the wood around the lock was pretty rotten.

And once you were inside?

It was grief in motion. He destroyed what he saw. Tore down curtains, kicked in a TV, overturned furniture, shattered plates and cups, and ripped Ben's centerfolds down from the bedroom wall. He was ruthless. I understand him. I understand this urge to make waste of these lives. Once he'd spent himself, he drove to Wal-Mart and bought a box of trash bags, drove back to the matchbox home, and began to fill them up. He worked ceaselessly from five p.m. till midnight, he says, hesitating at nothing. Clothing went into the bags; silverware and appliances and radios and a CD collection. Whatever books could be found. Even old heirlooms, a wedding ring once worn by his mother, who'd been long divorced. An incomplete set of crystal goblets passed down from a grand-parent, quilts and bedding and underwear, dead plants and cat litter. Everything he could get his hands on that came loose from the floor went into Rick's bags, and when he was finished, he started in on the furniture. A big man, he heaved chairs and tables, even the couch out the front door and into the back of his truck.

He says he did it all out of respect. He wouldn't let Ben live in a dead woman's house. It had to be purged of everything.

When his little brother finally showed up, Rick had broom in hand and was sweeping the living room floor.

I didn't, couldn't say a word to him.

Ben walked right past Rick into his own room. The two brothers shared the strangely empty house in silence for a time, pretending that the other was not even there.

I saw him, says Rick. *I saw he was shaking. He was so angry at me for doing what I'd done, and I was so angry at him, neither of us could talk.*

Until finally Rick threw down his useless broom with a clatter and charged into Ben's bedroom. He pushed his little brother against the wall and demanded to know what had happened.

He wouldn't tell me. He would only say, It was the heat, it was the heat. And I said, Jesus Christ, you should have been watching her, keeping the woman cool, and he said, I was busy. With what? He wouldn't say.

Rick couldn't take any more. He told Ben he had to get out. This would be the last night he could spend in that house. *I'm putting the place up for sale tomorrow.* And Ben began to cry.

He was still a baby. He was a ten-year-old boy living in a man's body.

Mary, always searching for motive where there is none, asks Ben:

You spent the night in the house?

Yes, ma'am.

How were you feeling?

I wanted to bust something open. I wanted to kill Rick. I was so angry I couldn't see straight. I just started to punch the wall, you know. At a weak point in the plaster, and I got my hand through, and it hurt so bad, but I didn't care

'cause my mother was gone and the house was gone, or most of it was, so I just sent
my hand into the wall again and again.

In the trial, much would be made of the earrings Nate purchased on his
lunch hour the day I fled. My birthday gift had to be pricey after he
knocked me over in his kitchen. Diamonds, it seemed, would do the
trick. The price tag still attached ($439), the earrings were offered to the
jury as evidence of Nate's devotion to his wife.

He bought them before he failed to reach me. That afternoon he
called the newsroom and our home several times, only to discover I'd
"vanished into thin air," a development that inspired him to seek out the
company of Karen Walters, his father's secretary.

She was a witness at the trial, called by Mary Starr to discredit my
husband and hint at infidelity. She appeared in the courtroom in leather
pants and a black silk blouse that matched her hair and eyes. She walked
to the stand with regal authority, comfortable with a grand entrance, the
turning of heads. Everyone listened as she spoke in her smoky voice.

Nate Duke was an acquaintance who wanted to be something more.

And when did that become apparent to you?

The day his wife disappeared.

She agreed to go with him to Timothy's. After work, they sat in a
booth and drank.

How did he seem to you?

Very rattled. He kept looking out the window and at the door like he was
worried about being caught.

Caught at what?

Talking with me, I suppose.

Or perhaps he was just losing control and knew it.

In the hour he spent at that bar, Nate made two calls from the pay
phone. The first to the newsroom, the second to our house. He would say
at the trial that he couldn't stop thinking about the night before. He was
trying to remember every detail, how he'd said, *You like to lie?* and she, *I*
like the rum. And he, *I know all about you,* and she, *What do you know?* How
then his arm had moved in a flash. And then, again, he'd reached back,
hit her. Had he meant to strike her that second time? And why hadn't she
admitted her wrong, shown that she was *sorry?* He couldn't get his mind

around any of it, he would say at the trial. He couldn't remember how he'd knocked his wife down.

He picked up the receiver and dialed my work number. He was going to ask me out for dinner. Somewhere nice to make up. But the receptionist thought she'd left.

"Did she or didn't she?"

"I *think* she did, but I don't know."

"Did she or didn't she?

"Excuse me?"

"Tell her her husband called and wants to have dinner with her."

And so the receptionist wrote on a pink message slip: *Nate called, is pissed, says something about dinner.*

Nate used his last quarter to call home, where he got the machine.

"Maggie? Maggie? Are you there?"

Then slammed the phone down.

As soon as he returned to the table, he ordered and drank a shot of Jim Beam, Karen would remember. He leaned over the table, not so close that they were touching, but close enough for him to think it was immediately possible.

What did you talk about?

Mostly he wanted to know about my love life.

She told him about the small Arizona town she was from, the lovers she'd had there. She told him about her ex-husband, who'd nearly ruined her. She revealed that Eddie, with whom she'd broken up, had been a fine man to know and after a short while boring. He was at bottom, she said, greedy. But then, she had not really known many men who were not, and in so saying she smiled and stared into Nate's eyes.

"How is Maggie, by the way?"

"I don't want to talk about it."

She watched him and waited.

"She wasn't home," he admitted, looking blindly at her hands.

He told her then he thought his marriage was over, according to Karen. According to Nate, he never said that at all, and if he had, it was out of drunkenness and spite and jealousy.

He said he wasn't going to talk about Maggie ever again and that life was beginning anew that evening, with me, and he put his hand on mine.

What did you do?

I wasn't about to go down that road. I worked for his dad. I needed the job. I had no intention of busting up a marriage, especially after I'd met Maggie, who I sort of liked.

She turned her wrist, noticed the time.

"I'm going to leave now. What are you going to do?"

Nate stared past her.

"Don't ask me."

My motel room was small, compressed by the lamp's thin light. The bed looked low and tired. No more speed, no more road, only this sour room, and knowing I was in a place I didn't belong. I locked the door behind me and lay on the bed with an opened can of beer I'd bought at a gas station. I saw the phone and wanted to use it.

Calls made home in the early morning hours never fail to scare my mother speechless. She was in bed, sitting up, bracing herself for the worst kind of news.

"Don't worry," I said. "It's not so bad."

"It doesn't sound good, either. What's the matter?"

It isn't easy, never has been, to talk to my mother about personal matters. I always cry as soon as I approach a confession. I told her then, a bit melodramatically, that I was a failure. She asked me what I could possibly mean by that word, and I admitted Nate and I were having problems.

"Problems, I can manage, as long as no one's dead. What's going on then?"

I knew I couldn't tell her the whole truth, not about Carson or Nate's hitting me. All that was too sordid to reveal, and this lack of honesty was perhaps my biggest mistake. The entire time we spoke, trembling in my throat were the words, *He hit me.*

"You remember my friend from the paper?"

"The reporter? What's his name?"

"Phil Carson. We've become—friends, and Nate's jealous now."

"Does he have a reason to be?"

I held my tongue.

"I see. Or maybe I don't." I heard some hint of judgment in her voice.

"I ran away."

"Where to?"

"Kentucky."

"Why in the world didn't you come home?"

A question I hadn't asked myself. It would have been easy to drive home and sleep in a familiar bed, but Nate would have found me there. "I don't know," I said. "I just wanted to get away. It made sense at the time. Nate was so angry—"

"Why can't you talk to him?"

"He's been drinking a lot."

This registered with her. So did the fear in my voice. She said, "I don't know the whole story, Maggie, but I know this: running away's not an answer. It solves nothing. You'll feel better if you face the problem, whatever it is, look your husband in the eye and tell him the honest-to-God truth. You'll both sleep better then, no matter what comes out of your mouth."

We both considered what she'd said. "He'll listen to you. I know one thing, or at least I think I do. That Nate's a good man."

"You think so?"

"Don't you?"

I didn't answer.

"Look, maybe you *should* get in your car and come here. First thing in the morning, Maggie. You can wait until he cools off and wants to have a sober conversation," she said. "You know, I've a lot of faith in you two. You could talk sense into Nate if you wanted. You could calm him down and make it work. You're only beginning, you know."

My mother has always been of the till-death-do-us-part school. Divorce isn't an option. Disappearing isn't. You stick it out, and somehow love prevails. Or in her case, it stubbornly hangs on, fades into something that resembles resentment more than anything.

I promised her I'd think about coming to Indianapolis, but she rightly didn't believe me. We said good-bye sooner than she wanted to, and after hanging up the phone I stared at myself in the mirror, disgusted with what I saw. Some fugitive exhaustion hung all around my body. I had the slouch of a coward.

I went into the bathroom and stripped off all my clothes before the mirror, discovering an enormous bruise on the back of my leg from my fall the night before. I felt the need to take a bath, as if doing so might cleanse my body of all traces of abuse. I made the water so hot it hurt to ease into it. I soaked a long time in that steamy cell. Hovering between sleep and wakefulness, I rummaged about for an idea of what to do, where to go, how to act once I got there. Though I didn't have the cash on hand to even make it that far, I fantasized about inventing a new life in New Orleans. I'd find a job doing something unpredictable like dog-walking. I'd keep no men, but keep them all hoping. I'd grow old and rich and occasionally have amorous adventures that went nowhere.

"You'll never do it," I said out loud.

I stared at the white bathroom walls, and imagined what was just beyond them—dark fields stretching for miles, farms and forest and country towns—a vast territory empty of a soul who knew me. What was I doing there? My mother, for all her faults, was right. Running away was too easy an escape, one that resolved nothing. I could go back, take hold of my husband's hand and say, what? How would I calm him? I didn't have any idea, but maybe the words and actions would come out of necessity.

I awoke in the early afternoon of the next day unsure of where I was, but relieved to know I was going home. I wished to go back by a way I hadn't come. It was not that I craved adventure or a scenic drive. I just felt the need to return in a way that was true to my desires, which were then confused and secret to me. I would come like a whisper, by the back roads, and suddenly appear to him.

I took Manny's map into the motel lobby with me. There was a young man at the desk then. I asked him to show me where I was, and he smiled and pointed to Union City, Tennessee, in the far western side of the state, just south of the Kentucky border. I might as well have been in Oklahoma, it would have made as much sense. I had no idea how I came to be where I was, and the mystery made me only more anxious to navigate a sound route home.

That afternoon, after I'd still failed to appear, Nate resorted to Mary's Hideaway. While there, he had at least five drinks. This according to Kayla McPherson, a voluptuous barmaid with whom he made lengthy conversation about rigorous physical exercise and his own sexual history. He told her that yes, he was married, but that tonight would mark the end of that marriage, and that no, he was not upset about that at all. He told her he'd always preferred women with full figures and loud mouths and high tolerance for drink, and would it please her to pour two gimlets, one for him and one for herself? She did so. They drank those, and soon after two more.

Time passed and they were left alone in the bar with a large farmer named Stiles, known for being a member of the Ku Klux Klan. Stiles entertained Nate and Kayla with a wide variety of racist jokes. Nate laughed, but the laughter wasn't really about the jokes, or so it seemed to Kayla. The laugh was reckless with some craziness running through it that made this woman afraid of who she was dealing with.

After one joke, Nate held on to the bar, as if to keep himself from falling, and laughed wildly when everyone else had stopped. With an effort, he silenced himself and went to the boys' room.

I knew something was wrong with him then—the way he all of a sudden went into hysterics, then hid himself away like that, Kayla would later say. *And then we heard the sound of glass breaking.*

When he came out, he had a bloody fist and bits of mirror embedded in the knuckles. After he threw a crimson-stained twenty on the bar to pay for the damage, Kayla decided to be generous with him, taking him into the back room where she washed the hand, dabbed it with disinfectant, and bandaged it with a cloth from a first-aid kit. *He was silent as a mouse the whole time I worked on the hand. He wouldn't even say sorry for breaking the mirror. It was just kind of strange.*

She called a cab for him, but he left on his own, ignoring her gesture. He was likely to have a wreck, the barmaid thought, but she let him go. *I thought he'd hit me if I tried to stop him. Honest to God, I had that feeling.*

Much later, Nate would say he was not so drunk. He hadn't had so many drinks as Kayla seemed to remember serving him. No, he was of sound mind, in control of all faculties when he pulled away from the Hideaway. On his agenda, he would say during the trial, was paying a visit to Phil Carson.

On Butternut Ridge Road, the windows were bright with worry. Phil Carson was up, waiting for me. He was hoping I'd return, which explains why he appeared on the porch the moment he heard the car.

"What can I do for you, Nate?" he said, disappointed and maybe a little afraid to see my husband walking toward the house.

"I'm looking for Maggie."

It couldn't have been easy to get that out, a clear admission of failure. "She's not here."

Nate stepped onto the porch. "When was the last time you saw her?"

"Yesterday afternoon. At work."

"What'd she say to you exactly?"

Every question pained Nate, forced him to bite his tongue. Before Carson's answer he already knew what he was going to do, where he was going to strike. He could see the tall man buckling.

"Not your business, to be honest," says Carson.

Nate swung at him as though to hit Carson in the face was the most natural, expected act. *It was all I could do under the circumstances.* He just stepped toward the man and let the punch fly, caught him on the chin. Nate did it again as soon as Carson stood straight. He hit him in the nose, a good honest crack.

Carson tried to put up a fight, but the attack stunned him. He couldn't pull himself together before Nate exploded again. *He came at me like a wildcat, with both fists and both feet.*

I can picture my husband's furious hustle, his quick, efficient jabs, one after another, beating Carson down until he's floored. Nate was smaller, but angrier. He didn't bother to get an answer to his question. He stormed off the porch as soon as he'd done enough damage, got in his car, and drove away.

I went straight to the Old Dam.

Shoals. A quiet place by the river, limestone peeping up above the current. A hangout for drunks, lovers, packs of teens. It was empty that night. Just Nate, the river, and the forest. He sat on the rocks, he said, and thought about what to do. He could go home and wait for me, find Johnson, or stay there and sleep a few hours, leaning against a tree. The latter option chose him, he said in court. He didn't wake up until full dawn.

The only witness was the moon. Nate Duke would have no alibi.

•   •   •

Driving toward Illinois, I wanted to believe he had the strength to keep
me. I wanted even more to believe I had the strength to be kept. I
wouldn't allow myself to dwell on the wire nails still in my pocket. I simply drove fast with the radio blaring. North, through Kentucky in the
early evening, past horse farms and dynastic homes: ornate and expansive,
they hovered on the land like vaulted dreams, peopled with children, old
women, and the ghosts of soldiers.

It was not until I reached the Ohio that I began to be afraid.

I took a road I had not taken, Highway 91 up through Marion,
Kentucky. The road goes all the way to the river's edge, then onto a flat-
boat ferry that floats you and the car across to Illinois Highway 1. You
drive up to a gate in front of the water and wait for the ferry to come.
Because I'd slept late that morning and had taken roundabout roads, it
was already nine-thirty in the evening when all this happened. The sky
was swollen with heat and the murmuring of insects. The river curled
slowly, darkly in the haze as the ferry eased up to the bank. A man in the
glass cab pushed on a lever so that a ramp slid from the boat up to the
road.

When I drove aboard, the ferry gave a little. The man nodded at me,
and it seemed from his dark eyes and withdrawn face that he had been forever subdued by the mood of the river at dusk. The smoldering day eased
into night. Watching the waves lap the ferry's side, I ached all over. It
would have been nice to get inside the river, to drift in the current. Closing
my eyes, I saw Carson's hands holding his camera, showing me how to photograph the Wabash. I thought of the other night—a slap, a punch, my
husband's gleaming shoes. I wanted the ride to last longer than it did. I
couldn't ask the ferryman to take me back again. The ramp eased onto the
road and made a clang, and the gate went up. I was free to go.

Nate is in transit, and so am I. We dash through the country, held to the
west by the pitch-black stain of the Wabash and to the south by the
Ohio, and in the angle of those rivers is our destination: this house.

How I approached it: Seated upright, leaning over the wheel, I
floated the car slowly. I was nervous, but relieved to be driving that
familiar way. There was then a bit of rain. It was well past dark. I didn't
know the time.

The black rooflines and panes merged with the sky behind. As I drove into the gravel drive, my car lighted up the impatiens in the front, the brass doorknob and eagle knocker gleaming on the door.

What I did then is well known. I went inside and called for Nate to make sure he was not there. Then turned on lights, fans, opened windows to cool the house. I lay down on the couch for a moment to listen to the rain. I went into the dining room and looked in a cabinet where Nate kept the liquor. I found a bottle of sherry and drank nearly half of it while trying to watch the TV.

When I decided to go to bed, Nate still had not come back. It was after midnight then, shortly after my husband supposedly left the Hideaway. I couldn't decide if I was relieved he wasn't home, or fearful of the delay and what might follow his return. Above all, I was anxious for reconciliation between us. But I grew too tired to stay awake for him, and finally changed into a white nightgown I used to wear in college. I cried in bed for a time, trying to calm myself. The rain stopped. I slept. Until I awoke at two with a headache.

Long ago, Rita told me it might be a good idea to take up drawing or painting. "It could free up your mind, help you relax and give you power," she told me, revealing that she'd once relied on that sort of thing herself. I dismissed the idea—it seemed to have nothing to do with me, as I'd never done anything artistic. But last night I began to doodle in the margin of a transcript. I drew an odd, abstract image of a doorway and a man inside it. You could not tell it was Nate, though I knew that's who it was, and you could not know that was the moment he struck me down, though I knew. I wanted to make the picture bigger. I drew it on the back of a page in large, aggressive lines with a ballpoint, and the exercise galvanized me. In the morning, I went to an art supply store and bought a sketchpad and some black charcoal crayons.

I have these before me now. I sit at the picnic table. Dawn is not far off, though for the moment a lantern is necessary. I open the pack of charcoal. The thick, black bar is satisfyingly heavy in my hand. You feel at once capable of creation. The paper, too, is pleasing. It's the size of a small table, a window. A world can fit inside its boundaries.

I begin, and the doorway leaps onto the page, an awkward rectangle rising from the bottom. Inside, a circle appears. It is inadequate, amateur. Of course, I don't know what I'm doing, but I shut my eyes and draw. The eyes should be admonishing and starkly lit by the porch light. They should be green, though I've only black. There is a mouth, too, always on the verge of opening and articulating sound. I draw these features in bold lines. I dig into the paper, wanting the charcoal to act like paint, like blood. I can't make the marks deep enough. I don't worry about details like eyebrows and shadows. I am stripping it down to the essential reality of the memory. The door, the night, the face, the eyes. There is also the body, but principally his arm, rising from the right.

There is something he's holding, but now that doesn't matter. It's the motion I want to capture.

Rita said this would make me calm. It doesn't at all. I am more excited with every blind stroke I make.

I open my eyes. Before me is a senseless flailing in white space, hardly recognizable. Better not to look, I think. Just turn the page and begin again. Draw it another time. Not to do it "better," but to throw yourself into the motion. Again, there is the door, the oval inside the door that is Nate's face, the circles inside that are his eyes, the imminent violence of his arm. The hysteria of charcoal that is my fear. This effort, too, is a disaster, looks nothing like anything, yet I want to try again.

I draw it four times, and each sketch brings me closer to an unreachable goal—precision of memory, knowledge like granite. I look up from the pad. The sky over the corn field to the right is blue along the tassels and full night above. Soon, the sun will be an abrasion in the sky.

I close the pad and put away the charcoal. I am procrastinating out here, delaying the inevitable. I go inside and take one more glass of whiskey, a small one, for I am not feeling so well. I take the folder Mary Starr gave me and climb the stairs to my bedroom, shut the door, and begin to read.

According to his statement, Hodge reported at the Amoco at two p.m. on August 10. You never would have known his mother had just passed away. He strolled in and gave his customary good morning to Mrs. Dillon, the owner, and the old man drinking his coffee by the window.

"How's everyone doing?" he said.

It is known he fixed himself a cup of coffee, sweetened it with cocoa powder and milk as usual, and positioned himself behind the counter at two sharp.

"All right, Ben, you sure you're all set now?" said Mrs. Dillon.

"Sure as sure," said Ben.

And it is known that just before she left the store in his hands, he opened up that day's *Evansville Telegraph* to discover his mother's name misspelled and her death mistakenly attributed to "natural causes." It is believed that he found this "amusing" (his word) and that he picked up the phone at the store and called the newspaper office. He asked for me. I was not there, so he left a message that Ben *Hodg* had called.

After closing up the station at ten p.m., Hodge allegedly got inside his silver pickup and drove to the Duke farm.

You could propose he simply wanted a place to go to. A man in his position would need that, a friendless man, an essentially homeless man, suffering from (perhaps) grief and (maybe) guilt. A man like that would need something to do. And maybe, too, a man of his age and circumstance needed another person to get close to.

It was a crush. Or maybe he was upset with me for misspelling the name. Or because he'd been driving by my house so often, he felt he had some right to Maggie Duke. Or because he was curious. He was not curious, but lustful. He was not lustful, but wanted to be. His mother was dead, and he was free. He had nowhere else to go. He wanted to drive.

Having drifted far from town, he finds himself approaching his brother's trailer. Slowing, he sees Rick's shape in a window. A barking Doberman streaks through the grass toward the truck. Ben hurls an empty forty-ounce bottle at the dog, misses, and guns the gas. Driving on, he turns south, into New Harmony, past the courthouse, around the remnants of the Utopian village. He disposes of another bottle by pitching it at a nineteenth-century cabin. Glass shatters on the step. Clocking sixty, seventy, past the library, the church, the Amoco Mini-Mart. Rattling and swerving, the pickup takes its leave via Highway 66 into dark country.

I feel trapped inside this drama. There's some dreadful rhythm beating within it, a quiet rumble of intent. Mary Starr is forming her thesis, outlining the man's grief, his frustrations and desires in broad sweeps of question and answer. There's a caricature of a man standing before me in the pages.

Had you ever done anything violent before, Mr. Hodge?

I blew up a cat once. A kitten.

When was that?

I was twelve. The cat was ours. I used firecrackers.

It doesn't matter if he is not a man I've ever touched or smelled or seen. He still exists. He was a child once, trying to grow up fatherless in a poor county. He lights the match—I can smell the sulfur—sets the fuse burning. He owns the kitten by remembering it, and so he owns me. All a lie needs is the telling. Truth starts to form rapidly, like ice on a lake during a cold night. Soon, the watery surface turns to glass, strong enough to walk on, opaque enough to hide what lies beneath.

Any man can tell a story about you.

Mary asks him, *Had you ever planned to break into someone's house?*

Not before that night. I left the Amoco with some beer and hit the road with some strong idea of what I had to do.

Had to do?

I had to do something.

I know how it feels to have decided carelessness is necessary for survival, to be willing to take any wild chance at salvation that will present itself. And so maybe he will come. He says he did. He says he drove and parked the car across the road from my house.

I don't remember the time. But I remember it'd just rained. Not much of a rain. Just a kind of sprinkle.

And what did you do when you arrived at the Duke residence?

I sat there. Actually, I waited. I looked at the house. It was all dark, but her car was in the drive.

He got out. He went around to piss in the fields, and while doing this he spied a stone. He thought he might need it.

In case something happened. Something like a dog, or Nate Duke, or who knows.

In his telling of the story, he was to be inside only briefly and do nothing more than look around, take some silver, a vase, a fancy plate. He only wanted to stand in her living room, breathe in her air, and listen to the sound of timbers, the creak of a bed frame upstairs when she turned over in her sleep. He might watch her in the bed. He might, if there was no one home, come away with a bottle of perfume, a pair of panties. It was to be an innocent caper, and she was to sleep through it, he says.

He hasn't the courage to say the word. Rape was on his mind. It's bleeding through the lines of these pages.

I put on the gloves and walk up in clear view. First, I look through the front window. There's no one there. So I walk to the door. I just take the knob in hand and turn, and it's unlocked, just like she's expecting me. It's an entryway, all

*dark. There's a mirror on the wall, their jackets hanging on a hall tree. And then
I hear this creaking, the sound of a footstep. And suddenly it's her.*

Who?

Maggie.

What do you remember about how she looked?

She's wearing white, a nightgown. And she's holding a glass of something.

The statement stops me cold. It's too close to the truth.

She just stands there at first, totally frozen.

He doesn't try to run. He waits for me in the entryway like a guest.

"Maggie, it's me."

"Yes, I see you, Nate. I know it's you. I've been waiting a long time.
It's nearly three in the morning. Where have you been?"

"Don't worry, don't worry, everything will be okay . . ."

The conversation I almost remember. In that version, Nate makes
everything okay not with a kiss, but with the swing of his arm.

Something sort of snapped in me. All my cool. I saw her—

I moved into the horns of the moment as if in sleep. I was not fully
awake. It all comes into focus, though, the moment the door is opened
and I see Nate in the dark.

Is it light enough to recognize her?

Yes.

*Are you sure it's Maggie Duke, the woman you saw in the Amoco and the
diner and the newsroom?*

It's her. She's smaller than before. She's quiet and soft in a nightgown.

Does she see you?

*She looks me in the eye, and I can see her mouth opening, like she's about to
scream, and then the scream starts. If it weren't for that scream, if she'd just
turned away and run or if she'd only said, Hello, what do you want? I would
have kept my cool. I would have just run. I might have done nothing at all. But I
wanted to shut her up. I wanted to silence that scream, 'cause someone might hear.*

What did you do, Ben?

I stop reading, look out the window. Dawn's ghostly gray is rising.
It's time to stop. I promised to get to the bottom of the lie, but there is
no such place. At the end of the night, I had three wounds, a fractured
skull. The doctors tell me I'm lucky to have survived.

I read how he slapped his hand over my mouth. How my voice

escaped and my glass dropped. Shards of glass and juice. *I pushed her down. Her legs cut on the glass.* My blood spilled. I'm reading this, how he pushed me on top of the glass. *Somehow she got up to run. Ran clear down the hall, into some bedroom.* A room I was proud of, with its fine painting on the wall, a likeness of home. *She's trying to open the window when I come. Screaming still, and I'm scared out of my mind. She's going to get free, run off and tell somebody.* That I'd seen a face I can't remember. He says he was there. He says he found a stone in the yard. *A big one, heavy.* And you can feel the weight of it. *I raise it up and bring it down. Meant to do it softly, but there was a loud crack.*

I would wake up with three wounds.

I bent down and looked. It was her. I turned on the lights and saw her clear. She was out cold, bleeding, and her foot. It started banging the bed.

I, too, can remember seeing my body on its side, dreaming beneath a painting of a gray house.

What do you remember about the room? Mary Starr thought to ask.

There's a bed, with posts, and a painting hanging over it. It's of a house. Looks like their house, gray with some red in it, and the green grass and trees out back and a blue sky.

I push the transcript away. The pages scatter. Ben Hodge saw the painting.

I want a seizure to come and stop this terror. I want this conspiracy of rooms and men and all their motives to end. But a seizure won't come, not now. Too much medicine will make you stronger than you are.

I run to the bathroom, grab the medicine, and open the bottle. I pour every last pink pill into the toilet, then watch as they swirl and are swallowed with a gulp.

For an instant I stare at the mirror, frozen in panic. I have to move. I hurry downstairs, throw open the always-locked front door, and run outside. Dawn glares through the trees, crows reel. I walk barefoot through wet dandelions to the side of the house, as Hodge could have and probably did. I stand at the guestroom window, with my back to the road, and stare through the pane. I can see the spot where hung the painting of our perfect home, the lie that started all the lies.

I want to chase Hodge into the open air, place my hands around his neck, and throttle him until the confession dribbles out of his mouth. He never touched me. He saw it through a window—the painting, my body, the white gown and blood. I can see that skinny man crouched beside the lighted glass, absorbing every lurid detail.

A small stone appears at my feet. I seize it and hurl it, and the glass cracks into a web. Still, the sky damns me.

Part Three

They brought small offerings. A sweater that was mine and one that was his, so I could feel the wool, smell our scents, and be enchanted into consciousness. They brought a stuffed bear with one eye, an old childhood companion. Its fur is ragged and drool-soaked. Put it on her chest, rub it against her cheek. Does she feel it? Yes, she can feel it. Say the name, say Herman the Bear, Maggie.

Maggie?

It hasn't been proven that bringing familiar objects to head-injured patients helps bring them back. Still, doctors will suggest it as an option. To do so also gives family members a sense of purpose while they wait.

Here is a photo album. See? Here you are in your apartment in Bloomington, Indiana, with your girlfriends Julie and Tracy. See. There is Julie, who was your best friend. She's coming up tomorrow to visit and she's going to bring some of your favorite CDs so you can listen to music while you sleep. And here are the two of you in McCormick's Creek State Park. Remember how you splashed each other under the waterfall?

Here is Nate on New Year's Eve, the winter after you first met. And here we all are, with Nate, and here's Nate and you, and Nate and the house. The beautiful gray house. Here's Nate in the house.

Maggie?

Maggie, it's Nate. He's come to talk to you.

Here is my hand. Can you feel it? Touch my fingers. Do you know me now? Don't you know me?

And here we are in Maine. Do you remember Maine? You loved it there. You'd never seen the sea. You found this shell and took it home. Can you feel it now? The outside is ridged and curved. The inside is pink like flesh. Can you feel how smooth it is right there? And now can you hear? It's the sound of the sea. Can you hear the sea roaring, Maggie?

•   •   •

First there is light and it is lurid, and there are shadows dappled over a field.

This is a new world I'm creating. Pain is the clay, and I'm in the clay. From a distance, I can see the world taking form. It is in danger of falling apart. The shifting light flickers around it, threatening its cohesion.

These are my knees under sheets.

Sharp pain needles my crown, etching a design. Inside my skull, it bursts into hysteria and races down my spine.

Right to left, a pulse jolts through me. I am slammed, as by the crush of feather and light. The violence comes from a long ways off, then tunnels inside me. I fall into endless space, jerking. The light annihilates miles of nothing. Black shapes bloom, crack apart, encroach, and I fall.

Right side is blind, faces doubled, sight falling away according to fissures. They are talking.

Maggie?

Trop arm.

How are you feeling?

Trop, torp, tr—

What are you saying?

Sur—surr—

Can you say what this is?

Surrr—

Can you say, It's a Teddy?

Rising out of the coma, a severe seizure took hold of me. It thrashed me awake, shocked the speech out of me. I could not talk with my family afterwards, yet I understood exactly what it was they were saying. Those early hours of consciousness were a strange dream. My body was like granite. My tongue was a fool's toy, shedding sound with no consequence. My ears received the speech of others, but I could not respond. I had an idea of getting up and running away, but my legs were stone-cold and massive.

What is this, Maggie?

Sur—strop.

What I'm holding.

Ga—groat—

Somebody help us?

Another seizure rose up in me. It took me into the darkness again, and only after I awoke, sticky with my own vomit, did language come back to me, a sudden and natural gift.

"Mom?"

Her face was close, exhausted with worry. Her blue eyes were brimming with tears. "I'm here," she whispered, kissing me. "You're going to be fine now, everything is going to be fine."

"Do you think so?"

"You're going to be beautiful," she insisted.

There were many people in the room, a doctor, two nurses, my father suddenly at my side. I felt their hands on me, their hushed voices in my ear. They were telling me I was a beautiful girl, a good girl, and thank God I was awake.

Dr. Stanzcik was fatigued and energetic, giant and hairless. His hands smelled of peppermint. He was not there at all and then suddenly at my side, leaning over, looking into my face with fierce eyes. "Maggie, how are you?" he would whisper hoarsely, as if my name were fragile. He said everything with a sense of deep confidentiality.

He inspired faith in my parents. He was a modest superhero because he'd rescued me. When they took me to the hospital I was suffering from a cerebral concussion, a closed-brain injury—the layers between bone and brain were not broken but whatever had happened to me had caused a blood clot on the surface of the brain. At the hospital Dr. Stanzcik had ordered a CAT scan and then operated immediately to remove the clot from the left side. He frequently told me I was an excellent patient, a remarkable girl, as if my recovery was due more to my own strength of character than anything he had done. Still, knowing that his hands had touched the inside of me made me afraid of him. When he walked in the room, a cold tremor would move in my bowels up along my spine. When he touched my wrist or face, the nerves in my teeth would freeze. But everyone said he was a very good doctor, the best in Evansville.

Despite all he did, I often had seizures. In every attack was the possibility I might not recover. The possibility the spasms and the flickering static would overtake me. This danger was a thrill I began to crave.

When the seizures grew violent, and I felt my vision churn into a kalei-doscopic confusion, my neck and arms begin to twitch, then I would become afraid and ring for a nurse. By the time she arrived I would be unconscious, twitching in the bedding. Hours later, I'd awake with a headache and a sandy thirst in my throat.

The hospital sheets always smelled like sawdust, a dry clean sharp-ness in my mind. They were a brilliant white in the sun, and the sun was the smell of pain. I worried that if I moved my head, I would upset a bal-ance that had been placed on me. There were times when the pain reliever had worn off that there was nothing but pain, and my body did not belong to me. It became like a fossil in a rock.

Not having seen myself for days, I wondered what I looked like. I was fearful of the next time that was to happen. My head, I thought, must have been three times as large. I imagined my face had become swollen and distorted. I imagined a pronounced fissure across my crown, as though I was made of ill-fitting parts. At least my hands and arms were whole. It was a pleasure to stroke them and feel the warm sun on my skin.

When I was a girl, I once kissed the back of my hand so I could know what it might feel like to kiss a boy. One day in the hospital I did the same thing so I could know how I tasted. I put whole fingers inside my mouth. I lapped my tongue over the back of my hand, and between my fingers. At first, I tasted nothing. Then there was a faint bitterness, a saltiness. I tasted like the color yellow, like light. I was in pain and assaulted with sun, but I could taste myself, and there was strange com-fort in this. When alone, I would now and then taste my arm and hand as if doing something perverse. One day, a nurse came in the room as I was licking the back of my wrist. I hid my hand and blushed, feeling tears rush to my eyes. I wanted to disappear, to die. I'd never felt so ashamed in my life.

The questions began the day I awoke.

"What happened to you, Maggie?"

"I can't say."

"Why not?"

"I don't know."

My ignorance was a secret, a quickening shame. I could remember making love to Carson and running away to Kentucky. I could remember coming home to an empty house and waiting for Nate to return. But what had happened that night, in the dark hours, was a great void inside me I did not want to admit to. I was guilty of escaping and guilty of forgetting, and the two failures seemed one and the same.

"Nate's coming to see you, Maggie." My mother's voice held some hint of warning.

"I don't want to see him."

"Are you sure?"

I nodded.

"Because he wants to see you."

"I *don't*."

"He's your husband," said my father.

"I *don't want him*."

My father asked me why. I curled up in bed and began to sob. I hid my face when my mother came close.

"Keep him away from me."

When Nate came, my father took care of it. I could hear their voices from the other side of the lobby. My father said he had to respect his daughter's wishes and not let Nate come inside. I heard my husband raise his voice against my father, but eventually he went away.

I was allowed to sleep in peace, but the next day, my mother began to pepper me with her tearful questions. Did he hurt you, Maggie? What happened when you came back from Kentucky? I wouldn't answer her. I turned around in my bed and looked at the wall. Leave me alone, I'd say, I'm too tired to talk.

The cop did better. She was handsome and strong and stockily built. She had eyes that saw far into mine. She sat on one side of my bed, a notepad on her knee, while my mother held my hand.

"Can you remember, Maggie, what happened when you returned home from Kentucky?"

"Yes."

"What?"

"I was alone. Nate hadn't arrived. So I waited for him. I drank a lot of wine—sherry—and ate a little. I was nervous because I thought he would be angry, and he wasn't home, and I didn't know what he was doing."

"And what else did you do?"

"I went to bed."

"And then?"

"At some point I woke up. I remember turning over and seeing the clock. I remember thinking it was not as late as I'd thought it was. And I remember his side of the bed being cold, and the house being quiet, and that I was still alone."

"And did you go downstairs?"

I didn't know. I didn't know if I'd gone downstairs, or if I'd gone into the kitchen, or if I'd poured myself juice. I didn't know if the doorbell had been rung, or if someone had knocked. I did not remember anything the cop asked me about that time. These questions seemed terribly personal. They circled around some secret about myself, and not knowing the answers was a conspicuous flaw, a kind of nakedness.

It's fine, the lady cop told me, not to worry, in due time it will all come back. When she got up to leave, I wanted to say, Wait, don't go, you're giving up too soon.

At some point Nate became a suspect and a news story. I'm not sure how this happened, only that it did, and with cruel swiftness. My refusal to see him, his failure to provide a substantial alibi provoked the attention of police. He was questioned at length and someone leaked to a reporter that Dick Duke's son was suspected of assaulting his wife. The story broke loudly, with a page-one headline, one day that August while I was still in the hospital. I never read the article, nor was I interviewed for it, but I do know that after reading the story, Nate appeared in my hospital room.

My parents, worried this might happen, had set up a kind of watch in the room, but my father had gone outside for a smoke when Nate slipped in late that night. I was asleep at the time, so he threw on the lights.

"Wake up, Maggie. Wake up. It's me."

He was pacing the room with the anxiety of a fugitive. His eyes were bloodshot, hair standing up. Somehow, I felt calm.

"Sit down, Nate."

"Did you see the papers?"

I shook my head.

"They're accusing me. They're saying I did this." He couldn't express the enormity of what he'd been accused of—he flung his arms out as if to embrace a world. "We've got to talk about what happened to you."

He stood next to the bed, close enough to choke me. "You should leave. My father's coming—"

"*Damn* your father. Tell me what happened."

"I don't know how."

"It isn't *possible* not to know."

His hands were grasping at the blankets of my bed as if he didn't know what to do with his body. Suddenly, he kissed me—an angry, desperate kiss—and I received it as one would a blow to the lips. "Why are you doing this," he cried, "locking me out of your room, your own husband, forcing me to sneak in here? What are you doing to us?"

"There is no us. There is only me."

"There *is* us, and you have to help me now!"

The claim in his voice is familiar and true. It silences me. Fear rises up inside my gut. A sharp pain pulses through my temple.

"Don't you know how you were hurt?"

I didn't want to say that I could not remember. I wanted my husband to leave me alone. "I'm trying, Nate."

He sat on the bed and put his hands around my face. They felt hot, clammy, his body was wet with sweat. He touched my cheeks and forehead, as if he wanted to recognize who I'd become. He saw I was a different woman. My eyes were deeper, and cruel.

"I was looking for you. All that night. I was looking in the office and at the house and with Johnson and Carson and everywhere I was looking, and you weren't anywhere. You'd run away completely."

His panic was infecting me. Some fit of hysteria was twitching in the corner of my vision. "This is only beginning, Nate. I have a feeling. I have a feeling, in my bones and nerves, that all this—is only beginning."

He asked me what I meant. He asked me twice, three times, but the seizure was already galloping through me. I was still for a time, staring straight ahead like a blind woman, and then suddenly it jerked me away from him. He took hold of my hands and squeezed. He leaned over me, wearing that same expression of bewilderment he'd worn the night he knocked me down inside our own kitchen. I went under then.

When I recovered, Nate was gone. My father was there, beside me, and so was a nurse.

"You awake, Maggie?" My father looked exhausted, as if he'd been through the seizure and not his daughter.

"Nate was here."

"I know, but he's gone now."

I could see my father, a big man, placing a hand on my husband's arm, asking him to leave. The thought embarrassed me. I was now someone to protect and worry over, and my husband was a menace. Or was he? I remembered him looking down at me as the seizure began, his hand on my forehead. He'd said something then—"Don't go yet," I think it was.

Later, on the hospital-room TV, I saw a short news segment. Nate had not consented to an interview, but a reporter had found him on his way to work. The footage showed my husband moving down a street, trying to outrun a camera's eye, and then turning awkwardly to say, "Leave me alone." His voice was loud and shrill. A guilty flush on his face, he disappeared inside an office building, lurching through a revolving door. I turned the TV off at once.

They came to my side and sat down with notepads and tape recorders and began, shyly, quietly, to ask small questions about my marriage. About the way things had been.

I hated them all—my parents, the police, the hospital psychiatrist. I hated the pity leaking out of their eyes as they sat beside me, trying to find a way in. They kept asking me about the door, where they'd found all the broken glass and blood, where the attack surely must have happened. I did not know anything about the door. I felt no association with it. As they questioned me, my memory would dwell in the dark places: Carson's bedroom, his lean strong body in my hands. Falling to the tiles, the sting of the slap, looking up to see Nate's confused face. I would not reveal most of these things. They were shameful and private, and I did not understand the end of the story. How could I begin to tell it?

Always, the questions would come around to what happened after I woke up in the empty house, in the empty bed. The queries made my head throb, my bones sore. My ignorance was a stone pressing down on my chest. Soon I stopped talking. That's when my parents hired Rita.

She assumed intimacy at once, offering a warm overhand shake, gazing into my eyes like a soulmate. She had a kind of Gypsy face. There was wisdom in her cheekbones and long dark hair. From the beginning, I was willing to obey Rita.

"You have put up with a lot of questioning."

"It's awful," I said.

"I know. Like an inquisition."

I nodded.

"That's all right. It's normal. Everyone forgets things."

I turned the TV off.

"You're going to be fine," she said.

When she began to ask me questions, I did not feel as if I were being challenged, or that my understanding was under attack. I felt comfortable and a little vain. She sat in her bedside chair with her hands in her lap, her head cocked to the side as if she were hearing a very intriguing story. She really wanted to hear what I had to say, however it came out.

That day, for the first time, I explained the circumstances. I had not told the police or even my parents about how Nate had treated me, only that we'd been having some problems, causing me to drive away for a while. But with Rita in the room, I spoke more bluntly and truthfully than I'd dared to before. About how Carson had taken me to see the woman in Kentucky, and Nate had knocked me down. How the following morning I had discovered he'd mangled the bicycle in the garage, hammered nails into the tires. And as I told the story to Rita, the facts became more real to me. I remembered again, in a way I had not before, the sensation of being emptied by my husband's blows. The vacuum in my gut as I stared at his gleaming shoes. I told her of the sun on the bicycle and paint cans. The quiet of the garage. I spoke of all these things without emotion, feeling strangely entranced by the story. I wanted to push on, and make it full. I wanted to offer up all the details that mattered.

"I trust you, Maggie."

"You trust me?"

It had become almost dark in the room. She hadn't bothered to interrupt me to turn on the lights. I was afraid to look at her after all I'd said.

"I'd sure like a cigarette," she told me.

"Me, too."

"Could we get away with it?"

"It doesn't matter. I'll tell them it was my idea."

She opened the window, and we sat on the sill. We lit up in the hospital room and grinned at each other.

"You're good at this, Maggie. What are you going to tell me next?"

I said nothing.

"You probably want to finish the story, don't you? You can feel in your gut how you want to finish it."

I nodded.

"Then it will come," she promised. "Relax and sleep and let it come."

That night, after I talked to Rita, a limping nurse with overlong bangs and a soft red mouth came with needles and pills. She gave me drugs and ushered me into my dreams, where I cast about for some answer.

Nate and I are walking across a baseball diamond at night when a boy runs to us. The boy takes hold of my hand and glances up at the stars, as if to read them and my palm at the same time.

"That's a short life you have!" says the boy.

"Don't tell me that."

"But it's true."

I'm very afraid, but Nate says I'll be fine. He leaves me alone in a field. I am a Utopian now, farming the Wabash Valley. And *soon, soon, soon* rings in my ears. Go home, it is almost night, walk along the black river. Your house is a cottage, up high on a hill. It is white and surrounded with flowers. There is a view of gusty sky and fields. Open your door, go in. There, on the bed, an angel sleeps. He is waiting for you. In his dream, and yours and his, he lifts his head to greet you.

Soon, soon, soon, he says.

The night after talking with Rita for the first time I go for a walk by myself in the hospital halls. I'm not supposed to, but I can't sleep and need to get out of my room.

I have miles of halls to roam. It is a world of a place. There are three wings and a dozen floors, some dimly lit and deserted, some brash and busy with nurses and patients. I walk in oblivion, hearing and not hearing my name being repeated on the P.A. I cross a sky bridge, over a street, into a new building. Eventually, I come to a lobby with a wall of tinted glass looking out onto a courtyard. Across the way, inside an opposing wing, I can see another lobby, where people wait in chairs. As I watch, a man steps up to the window directly across the courtyard from me.

He stands with his feet apart and seems to stare at me.

Remembering is like something coming loose, an arm or a leg. I gape into the hole of my husband's face. Gleaming in the porch lamp, he is defined against the night. He floats there. I remember it. I have always known just this. He is before me, more than himself, more handsome and heroic, his eyes shining. I hear him say, *How dare you,* though he has not spoken. And I seem to respond, *Why don't you come inside?* though I have not spoken. And I am rebuked: a sudden blurring of his hand going up, an explosion from the right. There is no sensation of being struck, only I know I have been or will be hit.

The lawyers and skeptics, Nate's many defenders will accuse me. They'll say I'm inventing this, the revelation is no more substantive than a dream. They don't understand how it seizes me. There's finesse to the memory, precision. It's like a painting in a museum, too vivid to be real, yet more real than the thing itself. I am amazed at how true it seems, how unalterable and complete: Nate at the door standing in the light, waiting to knock me down.

I have no choice but to be convinced. I close my eyes and remember at once how I came down the stairs for a glass of juice. How I heard the car door slam in the distance and the slow footsteps on the gravel. I go to meet him at the door, which seems to open on its own. And Nate is there: jewels for eyes, a skin of light. His brutality is perfect.

After breaking the guestroom window, I sleep only a few hours before the phone wakes me. I listen to Bill at work ask my machine if I can come in early today to do the obits because the other girl's out sick. I pull myself out of bed to answer the call and say yes, I'll be there, don't worry about a thing. I wonder if I sound drunk. Bill doesn't seem to notice, though, and tells me to hurry if I can.

I leave the house, and it's a hot, hazy day that clings to my face. I'm feeling feverish and full of twitching as I haven't taken any pills for my seizures. It's as if my mind is stuffed with cotton. The air is like syrup, slowing my thoughts and movements. Still, I believe I can work. I believe I have no choice but to settle into the car and turn the key and let the car take me to town. As I drive, my soft, drugless mind turns these fields into an ocean. The world is ancient and vast. I drift through it, half-awake.

"*Good* to see you," Bill tells me brightly as I come into the office. His face clean of the mustache, he looks boyish to me. He was divorced not long ago. "Are you sure you're up to the obits?"

"I wouldn't have come in if I wasn't. It's a nice day, isn't it?"

As I walk away slowly to my cubicle, I try to stand straight, step carefully so as not to fall or start the seizure I feel inside me. I know Bill is watching, wondering if I should be at work at all. I should, I'm up to it. I'm going to do this quickly just like before.

You have to type, is the thing. You have to take the first one off the pile and begin. I know how to work the keys, the names start to come out of my fingers. There is a Sandra Henderson. Careful now, Sandra Hender*sen*. Don't make mistakes, families get upset. The last hurrah is not a typo. Be sure of yourself. Sandra Hendersen. She was seventy-nine and had a child and a grandchild and a dead husband in the ground. She will be cremated instead. There will be a ceremony at Greenlawn. Who will come to see her go? The family live far away in South Dakota. Another. David Reeker. An unfortunate name. The dead so often have them. Mr. Reeker died yesterday and has no surviving family. I read these notices like they are poems. I look for significant detail. As if dying could give the story of a human life a satisfying conclusion. For David Reeker, there is no clue. The obit stands as it is, absurd, meaningless, full of information. I type it. I've done four now. Over an hour has passed. It will be a long, long time before I reach the end.

Eventually, Bill, chomping on an apple, comes by and watches the screen over my shoulder.

"How you doing?" he says.

"Fine." My head suddenly jerks to the left.

"Fine?"

"Yes, didn't you hear me?"

"I heard you," he says, "but—are you sure you're okay? Do you need a rest?"

"No."

He looks at me. "I think you should go outside and get some air. Take a lunch break. I'll tell you what. I'm going to do some of these entries while you have your lunch. And when you come back you won't have so many left."

I stand there, dazed, considering Bill's face. It is not young to me now. I see lines around the eyes. He will be startled by old age. He has missed out on something, he has watched his love die.

"We've known each other so long, Bill." Though I feel I hardly know him.

"It's been a lot of years."

"I just appreciate your letting me stay around," I say. "I like being able to come to work. It's always been important."

"I know, Maggie." He touches my arm now, just below the shoulder. It's an awkward act, as if the puppeteer holding the strings of his life has made his arm make this touch. I look down at it, and I am still looking at it when he moves away and sits down in my chair. I am still feeling his touch when he takes an entry off the stack and says, "You go to lunch."

In the parking lot, the day swelters off asphalt and chrome. I'll walk to lunch along a busy street. I hug the shoulder of the road, noticing debris, socks, Coke cans, old gloves. The cars pass hotly, gustily, the eyes inside them turn my way. I feel the heat on the backs of my thighs.

It takes ten minutes to reach downtown. There is a block with many restaurants, but I don't want to eat. Walking along, I see an antiques shop and decide to go inside. As I enter, bells ring, a cat coolly slides off an old chair. The scent of musty furniture and wood rises in my mind as I shuffle into a shadowy room. Here beside me are glass cases filled with old lockets and pocketwatches, boxes full of antique postcards once sent to lovers. The room stretches far back, where Victorian couches and chairs commune with a display of old rifles and revolvers rescued from dead hunters. Behind the counter is a plump woman I wish would disappear so I might have this place to myself. It is luscious to be alone in an antiques shop. I move further in now, past old teacarts and silver trays, and notice a couple looking at furniture. He is small, passive, the woman large and cruel. They are starting a home, I think. She wants to buy the tackiest couch in the store and will make him sit on that couch for the rest of his life. They will never leave the couch until they die and the couch leaves them, returning to a store like this to wait for another couple.

I know I will make a purchase. What that will be is a mystery until I move behind a large oak wardrobe and see the one-armed mannequin in the tired red party dress. She is bald, with a cracked face, and tilted a little to the side, as if in danger of falling down. Even so, she's eye-catching in her smart mauve hat with not too broad a brim, pointy sunglasses with silver frames, and a white silk scarf around her neck.

"I am sorry to strip you of your costume, dear," I say, taking the glasses, hat, and scarf. "But I am in need of it more than you."

I take it all to the woman at the counter. She has her fingers immersed in a tray of tangled chains.

"Found something you like?" she says, as if talking to a girl of sixteen. I hand over my loot and say nothing. She walks away to an antique register, leaving me with the tray of necklaces. Some are studded with false rubies or emeralds. Costume jewelry, pulled off old widows exiting their own costume party. Maybe I should buy a talisman, I think, a charm to protect a woman in trouble. I pick out a braided chain bearing blue glass gems.

"How much is this?"

"Well, I don't know. Twenty dollars?"

"Fine."

"Well, all right then!" She beams at me, her face flush with tense cheer at the sale. She rings up the necklace, too, while I put on my hat, which fits, and the glasses and scarf. She comes back and sees me, gives a little gasp of surprise. "It all looks wonderful," she lies.

"Thank you. Will you help me put on the necklace?"

"Sure I will." I turn around with my back to her, and she clasps the gold braid together at the back of my neck. The six studs hang in a pleasant half circle on my skin, just above the blouse. "Well, I'm glad to be of service. You come in any time you want to. We get new accessories all the time."

"Good," I say. "Good-bye."

I slowly walk to the door, rather wanting to spend the day murmuring among the old things in this store. Dozing into dreams upon ancient couches would be nice, but the afternoon demands my attention. It always does. I lean into the heat as the store bells ring behind me.

Back at work, Bill's done all the obits but three. When I'm in the middle of the second one, my phone rings, and it's Nate.

"Maggie."

"Yes."

"It's me."

I keep typing. It's important not to make mistakes.

"I want to talk to you."

Richard Frake. F R A K E. He was seventy-one.

"I want to talk to you about some business."

He was survived by a wife, Evelyn, and three sons, who reside in Indianapolis. Evelyn is spelled with L Y N at the end.

"Will you stop typing?"

I keep typing.

"Maggie. It's me."

"You sound like you've been drinking."

"I'm in a bar. I thought we could meet. We could meet here. We could meet wherever you want."

"Where are you?"

"Downtown," he says. "At O'Connor's. The place on the corner of—"

"I know where it is."

"Will you come?"

I hang up the phone.

I read over Richard Frake. There needs to be a comma after the name, before the age. The cause of death is not right. The fax in front of me says it was liver cancer. I had typed cancer. I put in the liver. They want that in there, they will have it. Evelyn must have thought it important. Details are important. The period is missing at the very end. Now it's done. I put the fax to the side and look at the next one. The next one is very short. Eric Corn had no surviving children. There is only a matter of getting his age and cause of death and the time of the service, which is tomorrow at Holy Cross Roman Catholic Church on Riverside Drive.

I look out the window of the newsroom. The rain is beginning to come down hard against the glass. The reporters stand up to look because the thunder just cracked and lightning flashed, and they are reporters, who care about weather. They stand up in their cubicles and check out the rain. One turns to look at me, notices my scarf and necklace. I put on my sunglasses. He smiles.

I get up to check with Elsa, the librarian who some days clips the articles for the archives. She jumps a little in her swivel chair when the thunder cracks. I say, Hello, do you need help? Why are you wearing those glasses, Maggie? I bought them just now and like them and wanted to wear them, what do you think? They are very stylish. I am going to help you, Elsa. She says, You don't have to. There's plenty of time, and I've got most of it done. But I sit down anyway, because it's raining and not a good time to go outside. Let me help, I say, taking up a pair of scissors and a sheet of the sports pages. This will be easier with two people.

The reporter who smiled at me comes into the room. He wears a tan shirt and brown pants, has yellow teeth and rabbity fur for hair. He covers city hall like a pro, and nobody likes him because he's arrogant. He looks at me like he knows me well and smiles. He thinks I am cute in my sunglasses, but I am not being cute. He doesn't know what I am being, but cute is what I will never be.

Elsa is nearly finished with the clipping for the day. I take up the sports page, what is left, and cut slowly around the article about our minor league baseball team losing.

Is there anything else for us to do? Elsa says of course not. The day's news is all filed away. She picks up her purse, saying, I'm going home, see you later, I do like those sunglasses! And off she goes. Alone, I sit in the library, take the scissors, and put them in the drawer of the table. And the ruler, too. I don't know what else to do with myself. I put the red pencils we use to mark the articles in the tin cup. I stand up to go.

Outside, I walk through the warm rain without an umbrella. I pause in front of my car, wonde   drive it. You are not supposed to when you are likely to have   ou are not supposed to drive at all, in fact, if you have as many   do, but I know how to lie to the DMV. I also know how to stee   to the driving, so I get inside the car, turn down the visor, and tilt   mirror. Though it's wet, my hat looks smart. So do my glasses.

The traffic is easy. Also, a seizure starts slow, quiet, a soft turning about of light in the corner of your vision. I'll know when it begins. I'll have time to stop the car. Time to grab hold of a table or a door. Maybe a phone. Will I have need of one? At least I'll have time to stop the car.

I am not required to face him. I am required to survive.

"I'll keep driving."

And drive, and be home in minutes, and walk down the ravine to the bottom of the creek and swim. But then I park across from the bar. The way to do this: as if you are finding a stranger. As in an airport, and you do not know the face of the man you've come to meet.

It's a tight black box, a burnt-out cinder of a bar. The kind of place for desolate drinking, with the sweet reek of beer and smoke in the air. I stop in the doorway, adjusting to the darkness. I don't want to take off my glasses. I can just make out the red lights advertising Budweiser and schnapps and the gleam of brass trim on the stools. A heavy bartender stands below a television set tuned to a baseball game. I don't see anyone else.

I walk toward the bar and sit down. I am almost blind with these shades, but find this comforting. I say louder than I normally would, "I'd like a martini, please."

The bartender walks over to me, a shaker already in his hand.

"Straight up?"

"Please."

I watch him make the drink, expecting Nate to tap my shoulder. I

will turn and see him, and who will know what to say? We will have to be
civil, make conversation, inquire about the other's life. This is going to be
absurd, I think, absurd and impossible. But no one taps my shoulder.

The drink is made, and no one is near but this bartender, who says,
"Heck of a storm out there."

Relief—or is it disappointment?—settles inside me. I take my first
sip of the martini.

"It's just a summer shower," I say. "You know, I received a call from a
man who asked me to meet him here. He has red hair. I don't suppose
you've seen him?"

"He left ten minutes ago."

"No message for a Maggie Wilson, I guess."

"No, but I think his father is here."

A door opens in the corner of my eye. I see the imperial heft of him
emerging from the men's room. My heart surges. Acid fills my stomach.
Somehow this is worse than Nate, and I want to get out of the bar.

"Get me a scotch and soda," commands Dick Duke, throwing one
enormous leg over a stool two down from mine. "And leave us alone, if
you don't mind."

I turn to face him and throw out my hand for him to shake, a performance of bravery that only heightens my anxiety. "Mr. Duke, it's a surprise to see you."

He takes my hand like he's not sure what to do with it and lets go
immediately. "How are you, Maggie?"

"I thought Nate would be here. He called me and asked me to come.
He said nothing about you."

"He had to go. He asked me to talk to you in his place. So here I am."

"He said he would be here. He said that a few minutes ago. Did he
have somewhere else to go? Is he coming back?"

"Relax," he says.

The bartender gives him his drink. He takes a sip of it, staring at me
over the rim of the glass. He has noticed my sunglasses and hat, and the
judgment is evident in his eyes. He never could hide his disdain for
women. It's on the surface of his skin.

"Nate asked me to talk to you. He didn't want to do it. I don't blame
him. It's not so easy for me, either."

I can hear his heavy breathing, his calculation. He wants something very specific. Perhaps the meeting was his idea to begin with and he put Nate up to the phone call. I pick up the martini glass. It trembles in my hand, and I spill some down my chin, onto my shirt. Tears spring to my eyes, and this infuriates me.

"Why did Nate call if he didn't want to see me?"

"We have business to discuss."

"What do you want?"

"The house."

He turns all the way around on his stool so he's facing me directly, studying my reaction.

"We want you to sell it to us, Maggie."

I say nothing.

"I don't have to tell you the history," he goes on. "That land belongs to my family. It has for over a century. My grandfather was born there. My father was. Or did you forget that, too?"

"It belongs to me."

"Legally. Morally speaking, you stole it."

I take out my wallet to pay.

"You're not leaving yet," says Dick.

Somehow, the change purse opens and coins fall and scatter across the floor. I ignore this. Dick thinks I'm crazy. Maybe I am. I've never felt so jittery. I put a five-dollar bill on the bar and put my wallet away.

"Why are you wearing those glasses?" says Dick, when he sees that I'm not leaving, that I'm obeying him. "I can't see your eyes."

"You don't need to. I didn't even come to talk to you. Why are we having this conversation?"

"We want to buy the property. It's that simple. You had no right to it before, and you *sure* as hell don't have it now. You've got a lot of nerve, if you want to know. You look like a goddamn fool living in that house."

"That's a pretty way to persuade a girl."

"Nothing about this is pretty. I'm not asking pretty. I'm making a demand."

"On what grounds?" I regret the words as soon as I say them.

"You destroyed my son's life."

"He destroyed mine."

He slams down his empty glass. "What in God's name are you? Blind?"

I don't answer. I want to get up and leave, but am somehow compelled to endure this.

"We'll sue if we have to," he says. "I've talked to lawyers. I can do it. I'll see you up in the stand crying again, and I won't give a damn how much it hurts, because you *hurt* my son. You have no soul to sit there and—"

He stops himself. I take off my glasses, wanting to see him better now. His puffy face is crimson. His hair has gone completely white and his eyes are now surrounded with wrinkles that somehow improve his appearance. He looks like an unusually energetic grandfather.

"I'm not interested in your morality," I say. "I came here to meet your son. If he's concerned about the house, he shouldn't be. It's mine, and I've taken good care of it. In any case, he lost his right to it."

"Look me in the eye and say that."

His eyes are shot through with hate and something more: confusion, curiosity. I am a wretch to him, an incomprehensible.

"I'm telling you," I say.

"You're a stone-blind bitch."

It's two steps out the door. I finish the martini and stand.

"I need an answer from you. What are you going to do?"

Dangling on the point of this question, I see it's a way out. I could escape the house and leave town. I could go anywhere, as Manny has always promised. The thought of departure races through my mind, making my heart pound. Before I know what I'm doing, I say, "I'm going to leave soon. Perhaps that is some comfort to you. I don't know. It's not my concern. I want to know where your son is."

"You're moving?"

I nod, stunned by my revelation.

"When?"

"Next month," I say, trying to convince myself. "Next month I'm going to move and put the house up for sale."

"How much do you want?" He's all business.

"I have no idea. I'll talk to a Realtor," I say. "I'll talk to a Realtor or put an ad in the paper."

"You don't have to. Call me. Have your Realtor call me. You don't have to see me or touch me or talk to me ever again. I'm nothing to you. Sell me the goddamn house. We'll make an offer that counts. You want to make some cash? You want to walk away with a chunk of Duke money? That's fine. Fuck you. We'll pay it."

He turns around to tend to his scotch and soda. His eyes glisten with tears. This astonishes me. It makes my stomach turn over. Just then, the darkness begins to break into shards around my eyes. My head twitches to the left.

"Do you agree?" he says.

"Yes. Is that all?"

"You agree," he says, observing my crisis coolly. "You agree."

"And now I think I'm—"

I don't want him to see me go thrashing into the dark. I grab my sunglasses and purse. "I'm going now—"

He stands as I do and places a hand on my arm to stop me. His grip is strong, strangely familiar. "Do you really want to see Nate?"

I have spent all summer not wanting to see Nate, but I know I must. I want to see Nate the way you sometimes want to vomit. I nod and turn away.

Epileptics are not to drive or skip their pills. They are not to drink martinis in the afternoon. I walk through the door like there's a load balanced on my head. The sun hits me like feathers, like concrete. Outside, the street pulses into a nauseating confusion of chrome and glass, pavement and bodies.

A bus cozies up to a curb. A cream-colored bus, curling exhaust. I walk that way. The driver opens the door, sees me from atop her throne. She is enormous, full of authority. "Can I have a ride?" She says nothing. I step up uneasily with the light flickering, now chasing.

"It's seventy-five cents."

Okay.

I stumble on back. "It's seventy-five cents." And I stumble on. It's seventy-five cents to go gently back to where the light is vaulted and strange, and the sitting people, all golden statues, wait for me to join them. How do you do? The light in here is golden. The bus is moving. I'm glad for that, and glad it's soft enough a ride that to ease down and sit on the floor is no trouble. To lie on your side is not so troublesome. It's easy to withstand even this. Just find a soft place full of creamy light and easy swaying, groaning motion, and let the light—

Where is this bus going, the hospital? I ask a pair of shoes.

No, the mall, say the shoes. Do you need some help?

High up in the clouds and near the sun, I rest in a hospital cot. Outside my window, far below, parked cars glint like a mosaic design. Gazing down, I feel a rush of vertigo, a dazed peace. No one knows I'm here but Manny.

"Why aren't you talking?" I say.

"I'm worried," he says.

"Pretend you're not."

"The time for pretending is over."

"It isn't," I say.

"There's a bump the size of an apple on your crown. The time for pretending is over."

Manny's worried. I fell hard in the bus, and the seizure was long. I awoke to the grave faces of doctors.

"Talk to me about California," I say.

But he wants to be more useful than that. He is opening the cabinets next to my cot. Maybe this is my guardian angel, white-haired and teary-eyed, hankering for his gin and tonic. In the bathroom he finds a rag and wets it.

"Are you nursing me?"

"Someone's got to do something," he says, sitting beside me. He places the rag on my forehead. It's cold, cottony, smells faintly of soap. He moves it gently down my temples and jaw and under my chin and around my neck. After he's done, my face feels new and bare.

"What do you want to know about California?"

"I want to know how beautiful it is, in the hills and mountains. I want to know about the ocean, and how it is to swim in the ocean."

"It's salty."

"That's what I want you to tell me," I say.

"Salty and blue. And the sun is golden. And the sky is bluer than here."

"How blue?"

"A perfect, blazing blue."

He takes my hand from the bedcover, cleans my fingers and palm and wrist with the rag. Then he does the other hand. When he sees that I am crying, he touches the rag to my eyes, holds the rag there to blind and cool me, then washes my cheeks and feverish mouth. The cool is too good for me. I give up talking, shut my eyes, fall back into the pillows. Thinking, if my pillows and bed were the ocean, salty and enormous, full of caress and blue-salt, and if all the swimming in the world were up to me, I would be gone like a fish in the waves.

My body is an open book. While I was out cold, the doctors sneaked away with a tube of blood and discovered my Tegretol level had hit rock bottom. Dr. Stanzcik, baffled by this, comes to scold me in my room. He demands to know why I stopped taking my pills.

"To get to the other side of something. To get out of my body for once."

He considers this. "There isn't another side, Maggie, if I understand you. There's only this side. Thankfully. And now you've *got* to get better." He insists I stay overnight while the Tegretol level in my blood is brought back to normal, and in the morning I'll have an MRI exam.

Manny has come to share a small pizza with me and departed, leaving me with my sketchpad and charcoal, a smattering of magazines, and the road atlas. We argued briefly when he threatened to contact my mother, the last person I want to see, and I convinced him not to call. The nurses have also come and gone, and now I face a night alone in a white cell.

I get out of bed and walk to the table by the window and take the sketchpad and charcoal. I turn out the lamp on the nightstand so the room is pitch-dark and get into bed. The charcoal is exciting to hold. The rough page beneath my fingertips seems so broad in the dark.

There is only me now. There is only me in this room, with these hands and this mind. I can tell you that the doorway was such. I can draw it, and I can create the night with a dash of my hand, and the shining lamp reveals my husband so. I'm not drawing Nate. I'm drawing my memory of Nate in the doorway, facing me with an object in his hand. They would ask me, *Maggie, what was in his hand?* I would tell them, *I don't know. Why didn't you see it? I didn't look at his hands. I looked at his eyes.*

I looked at his mouth, which was almost smiling. There was no hint of violence to begin with. It happened too quickly, leaving no time to think. There was never any question of choice or regret corrupting the memory. There was only the impossible moment of being crushed. Perhaps this is what I meant by "the other side." I draw it, or try to. I draw the head and the face and the hand rising. It happens in an instant, like an age-old myth; one word is enough to conjure the night. Truth is like that. It travels with the speed of light and need not be narrated with a wealth of detail, evidence, testimony. That's where Hodge and Mary Starr are mistaken. They don't know what it means to be destroyed.

When I'm done with the first page, I turn to the next and begin again, staring into the dark. I can create a world here. To believe in yourself is the greatest peace, and I have so rarely felt it. I will draw for hours, repeating the same image, always not finishing, always on the verge of discovery. If I run out of paper, I can begin to draw on the cardboard. When I have filled that, too, I will be left with nothing but my own flesh and the bedding.

The door opens. Light floods into the room.

"Sorry, dear," sings a nurse, turning on the overhead lamp to my surprise. I blink crossly. "It's time for your bedtime pill." She carries it in the palm of one hand, a white plastic cup in the other.

I look down at the drawing in progress. Shown up in the light, it appears childish, clumsy, the work of a fallible hand.

In the morning, they slide my body into the tube for an MRI. The atmosphere in here is cosmic, the hiss of rain, stones knocking, and all the space in the world to think. But the machine is blind to thought. It sees only nerves, lobes, blood, and bone. It produces images of florid reds and yellows that blink like weather maps. The doctors are in love with these maps. They can see everything. But the result is always a non-answer. You're normal, they tell me. Your test results were fine. I might as well be a beam of iron ore, they learn so little.

Shortly after, I'm free to go and walk outside the hospital unassisted into the muggy bath, where Manny waits for me. He drives me to the bar where I met Dick Duke so I can drive my own car home, parking tickets and all.

On the way home, I let Manny speed ahead so I can make two stops without being troubled by his company. The first is an art supply store in a suburban strip mall. The selection of media is tempting and distracting. My needs are limited to paper and charcoal, but here are glittery paints and gels and bright-colored craft papers. I pass these by and find a large sketchpad, another pack of charcoal, though on a whim I grab several tubs of varied colored paint, a brush, a fistful of pens.

My second stop is the liquor store on the edge of Evansville. I find two bottles of wine and one of whiskey.

At home, there's a message on my machine from Mary Starr, who cheerfully announces she would be glad to see me next week. The shrill sound of her voice makes my heart beat faster. Now that she's called, I've no excuse not to go.

Hours later, I walk outside, looking forward to the relief of Manny's daily dose of gin. When I arrive, he is on his porch, as usual, but instead of the usual cocktail, there's lemonade.

"Home-squeezed. Can you believe that? You know how many lemons went into this?"

I sit down in my chair, silently outraged.

"Well over two dozen. Most ridiculous thing I've ever done, and my hands are killing me, so you better drink your lemonade and like it."

He reaches over to turn on the radio news, then thinks better of it.

"I just figured you'd been having enough to drink, Maggie," he says. "I understand you weren't exactly sober when you had that spell of yours, and after talking to the doctor—"

"It isn't your business, my doctor, my head, my medical state, is it?"

"If not mine, whose is it?"

"Mine."

"We don't always treat ourselves right. I know that from experience. How's your head?"

"Fine."

"Good," he says.

The fading sun shines for one last moment on Manny's face, lighting up all the papery wrinkles, the mole on his temple, his veined eyes. He was the one who found me. He was the one who first heard what he thought was a woman's scream, who inferred something bad had happened. Given my request for road maps, my nervous behavior, his long-standing dislike for the redheaded husband, he made an inference and reached for the phone, at which point he heard the car streaking away, back toward New Harmony. The car, he had always said. Nothing about a truck, Ben Hodge's vehicle. But he could never confirm that. He hadn't seen it.

"I'm going to leave," I say.

"What, right now?"

"I mean I'll move. Get rid of this house and land, go somewhere else to live."

Somewhere else. This sounds unreal to me. I have no idea what "somewhere else" means right now.

"Where are you going to go?"

"Let's not talk about it. Actually, it's not a plan at all. Maybe I'll go to Indianapolis for a while. Maybe I'll go back to school. I've no idea what's going to happen."

"I do. You're going to go on a road trip with a seventy-six-year-old man across the U.S. of A. I *did* buy road flares today."

"You're crazy," I tell him. "Road flares. We'll need a whole lot more than that to save us. Why aren't we drinking gin, by the way?"

"Hang in there and stay sober for twenty-four hours, think you can handle that?" Manny gives me a stony look.

"No."

"Then you're in serious trouble."

"I already knew that."

I stand up and put down the lemonade.

"What is this? Boycott? The sun's not halfway down." I walk off his porch and he follows me down the steps. "I squeezed five thousand lemons for you."

I turn around and blow him a kiss, and his shoulders slump in disappointment. I feel him watching me all the way through the trees until I become, I hope, invisible.

I open the bottle and pour the whiskey until the glass is half full. I add ice, a little water. Then I carry the glass to the windowsill and put it there against the pane and walk away.

I take my paper and charcoal into the living room. It is not really for living. I don't know what it is for, but there is a lot of space, almost no furniture. I sit on this childhood couch from my parents' basement and open the pad of paper. People say to those on ledges, don't look down. Same situation here, don't look down at your hands or their work. Just make the memory real. Move the charcoal fast and decisively, as if you know all there is to know, which you do.

I am convinced I am the only one who does know the story I'm telling. No one else can be allowed in. The house is locked. A strong, resourceful person could get in. Windows are easily shattered, as I well know, and a door is only a door, it can open all on its own. But here, in the confines of the page, there is only what I know. I want to shrink the entire story down so it will fit on one sheet.

I think of the whiskey in the kitchen window, waiting for me, as I draw the frame of the door and fill it up with night. I draw his face with eyes like chips of coal, a dark, deep gash for a mouth. His arm, rising up, ends in a black block. I tear off the page and begin again, and as I do, I remember his legs, the gleaming shoes, what I saw when he hit me. I remember a proposal in the rain, and his body pressed against mine in the back of a car as the highway burned with speed, and our lives are taking off toward one inalterable end in a jet to Maine. I draw this. I don't draw anything but wild, lurching lines, but I feel certain. I begin again, staving off the whiskey. I draw Nate's face, and as I do, it gradually becomes my own. I take one of the pens and unscrew the cap. I slide out the plastic receptacle of ink and bend it back and forth, until it breaks. Ink spills in drops, then all at once, a gush. I spread it across the page with my hands.

I go to the kitchen and see the glass of whiskey waiting. I open a drawer of tools, rummage about for a hammer and nails. I take these to the living room, which has since become dark. I grab a sheet of paper off the floor and stand on the couch and hammer the nails through the drawing, high up on the blank wall. I use two nails, one in each upper corner, then go back for another sheet. I create a pod of drawings in the center of the empty wall, a malformed diamond, each one holding a rash estimation of my husband, or more precisely, the violence in his arms. This makes my heart race. There is possibility here. Shown this way, one after another, the images build power. Together, they are more potent, more complete than the isolated scrawls. They hang precariously, with corners drooping, and all off-center, a kind of random collision of memories, all of which hold a common image. Not of a man, but merely a gesture toward a man. You cannot make out anything, really. It is childish, but has the force of omen.

I go inside the kitchen now, and in the light am shocked by the sight of my hands. They are black, gloved in charcoal and ink. I look at the whiskey on the windowsill. I walk across the room and empty the glass down the sink.

Mary Starr's assistant isn't at her desk, so I approach the office unannounced. I stand in the doorway, and Mary doesn't notice me. She's too busy putting some bound documents into her shiny leather briefcase. She's dressed in a prim black suit, and her hair's in a bun that sits on top of her crown like a tumor. It must be another day in court for the deputy prosecutor.

"Hello, Mary."

She jumps with a shout. "What are you doing here?"

She's outraged. Her face is ashen and sharp as a needle. I try to show no feeling at all.

"I called you," I say. "You said you could meet me."

"I remember. But I don't have time now. I'm going to court. You should have called before."

Of course, I am unwanted. Her cheerfulness on my answering machine last week was an act, as so much of what she does is. But something in the way I step into the room and look at her persuades her to put down her briefcase.

"I didn't mean to sneak up. Your assistant's not here, so I just came in."

"I understand. You want to talk. That's fine, really, I'm glad you do, but right now—"

I sit down. "I read it."

She tilts her head to the side, a show of disgust that reminds me of girls I knew in high school who were rich and entitled to everything. "I don't know what you're talking about, and, as I pointed *out*, I have to go. There isn't time to chat."

"It wasn't easy for me to come here. Will you please sit down and listen."

She puts her briefcase on her desk and folds her arms.

"Ben Hodge isn't telling the truth," I begin.

I prepared this speech in the car. I muttered it at stoplights so I wouldn't leave anything out. And I was ready. Only now, the words have escaped me.

"There are explanations," I blurt out, feeling foolish, desperate. "There are reasons to explain why he seems familiar with the house, with me, what I was wearing. He could have seen all these things through the window. He could have walked up to the window of the guestroom and seen everything that night . . ."

Mary clears her throat. "The curtains were completely closed when they found you. That's in the photos, Maggie." She sighs and glances at her watch. "This isn't the time for this. I can't help you now. I don't know if I ever can. I see you're confused. I was, too. We all were. This was a difficult case, a peculiar situation. But I believe, I am certain, I am one hundred percent sure that this man is telling the truth. Why? He knew the floor plan of the house, the decor of the living room. He knew what kind of juice you were drinking, what happened inside the entryway. He knew the guestroom, the color of the walls, the bed, the painting. He described it very precisely. He could not have known that by looking inside the windows."

"He could have. There are many windows, and he came often—"

"No, Maggie." She is almost shouting. Her face is taut, and it seems she wants to win this argument. "He saw things he couldn't have known of that way. Like where you were hit, where you were cut. And, no, there's no record of his requesting to see documents about the case, and many of these details weren't ever reported in the press. The fact is, he was there. A man on the verge of freedom confessed this crime. I'm sorry, Maggie. You want me to defend this. You want me to justify it, and so I will. And I'm right."

Her voice is resonant inside her small office. It is the same voice that proved undeniable during Nate's trial. "Don't talk to me that way, Mary."

She sits down, finally.

"Maggie."

"What?"

"Why are you here? What are you doing? Are you okay?"

"They were in the same prison in Carlisle, Indiana. Of course, you know that. Nate could have talked to Ben, convinced him to say something. Nate's very good at that kind of thing—"

Mary looks offended that I would say such a thing.

"I have thirty seconds more, and then I have to go. Maggie, we considered that. If you don't know, there are three facilities in the Wabash Valley prison. Minimum security, medium, and maximum. The prisoners in one don't communicate with those in another. Nate was in medium security. Before Ben's confession, he was in minimum. They didn't know each other. They'd never met. We talked to inmates who knew both men and asked if Hodge and Duke had communicated, and all six of the witnesses insisted they hadn't. So did the guards who watched them."

She picks up her briefcase.

"I'm sorry, Maggie. I don't know what else to say. We don't reverse convictions casually. This is the first time in my career I've ever done this, and I was *thorough*. I believe we made a mistake with Nate. *I* made a mistake, and I've killed myself over it, but now it's over."

I want to make her stop talking. I can't think of anything to say. She is too powerful, too full of evidence and logic and conviction.

"I don't mean to yell," she says now, in her soft voice. "You frightened me when you came in, and I'm late, and I suppose I feel a bit emotional about all this."

"But you have to believe me," I say. "What *I* remembered."

She looks as if she's sorry for me. "Privately speaking, Maggie, I don't think you were lying. I never thought that once."

I need to say something more, some last defense. I know there is one. But I can't think of the right words to say.

I get up and walk quickly out of the office, ahead of her. Without looking at her or saying good-bye, I hurry down the cement stairs and into the blistering lot. I run to my car, and just behind me, I hear Mary's heels, clicking on the pavement. She stands by her car door and watches me from a distance. I have to get out of her sight.

At home, I find a large man with the look of a farmer standing on my porch, peering inside the front windows. I don't know who he is, or recognize his black pickup. He waits for me on the porch, as if I'm the one who's visiting.

"Who are you?" I say, walking up the steps.

"Fred Cummings." His handshake is damp, long, and powerful. He presses into my space, this man of fifty-something, with a face like red steak. He wears frayed jeans and boots covered with mud. He is massive, a man used to pushing cows around.

"Who are you? Why are you here?"

"I'm not going to hurt you. I live ten miles that way."

Now I remember him. Fred Cummings, who owns an enormous farm nearby, who grew up with Dick Duke and used to be his best friend. He'd go deer hunting with Dick in the fall. I'd seen him only once, when he came to take shots at a target in the yard with Nate and his father.

"I came to ask you a few things," he tells me.

"So ask."

"You planning on moving?"

"Maybe."

"You don't know?"

"I don't really want to talk to you about it, Fred."

He folds his arms, standing with his back to the door, so I can't go to it. "Well, I'm here to find out when you're moving. Dick wants to know."

"Why doesn't he come himself?"

"I guess he tried that. Talking to you. Said you ran out on him."

His severe eyes won't look away from mine. I can't tolerate this intimidation. "This doesn't concern you," I say. "I don't even know you, and I can't talk about my plans. I want you to leave."

He stands there, a resolute block.

"Now!"

"All you got to do is give me an answer. When you gonna let Dick have his granddaddy's house back?"

"Not ever. Leave me alone."

"You sure about that?"

"Yes."

"All right. That's an answer. Not a very smart one, but it's an answer."

He walks off the porch, making the whole thing creak. I go inside and slam the door shut. I lock all three locks and fall to the floor, listening for the sound of the truck's wheels on the gravel. When I can't hear the motor anymore, I grab my hair in my hands and scream.

Don't die yet, I whisper into his ear. *There's so much life to live.*

But Nate is intent. Expressionless, he takes a blade and cuts deep into his wrist. I feel the seep and gush of it, as if it were my own wound.

I'm sorry, I keep telling him. *I'm sorry.* This isn't enough to stop the hemorrhage, which now really is my own. Death comes like dawn, by fluid, irreversible increments.

I wake from the dream and rise out of bed. I go downstairs to the living room. I see my drawings, spreading across the wall. Someday, I'm going to stop. I'll call the Realtor and pack the bags, throw out the furniture, move on, only now, still, every night finds me on the living-room couch with charcoal in hand, reminding myself over and over of what I saw. What I think I saw.

They asked me so many questions about my memory. I always had answers.

How did the door open?

On its own.

You mean he opened it?

It seemed to open like a ghost had pushed it.

And what did you see behind it?

I saw my husband. He was on the porch, under the porch light, and I saw his face. It was very white, and he was looking at me.

I remembered in the hospital. I walked through the halls one night, and it came to me, with such vividness and power I didn't question it.

And now I am faced with a blank wall. I've filled up half of it. I'm compelled to draw as if satisfying a hunger. I've never done anything like this. I've taken to paint as well as charcoal. I've covered Nate's face with layer after layer, creating dark purple and brown masks. I've cracked open all the pens in the house and spilled ink onto paper like blood. One very drunken moment, in the dead silence of four a.m., I found a razor and nicked the back of my arm. I watched the drip, drip, drip, as the room spun around me and the paper absorbed it. Ecstatic with possibility, I took the blade to photos of Nate and myself. I sliced indiscriminately and affixed our young heads to the paper with glue. I've ripped apart journal entries and court documents. I've placed the words in strips over the mouth of the man in the door, or in a blizzard of language all around his head. I've done all these things in a drunken daze, acutely aware of the things around me.

I am seated on the floor now, the sketchpad on my lap—when I hear that familiar motor come up the grade. This is not the truck I recognize now as Fred Cummings's. It's not Manny's old Chevy. It is a new car that has passed before and slowed down, but never stopped. Tonight it does, and I'm not surprised.

I open the front door before Nate arrives. I see him walking from a distance. He is shorter than I remember, stouter. He has a beard that ages him. He walks across the yard as if he still owned this land and expects to enter the house. But when he looks up, his eyes are afraid.

Seeing me in the doorway, he stops on the first step. All summer, I've been fearing this moment, dreading it, imagining something devastating and violent that would demand fight or flight. But now that he's here, I know he's been dreading this, too, and I am going to survive it.

Barefoot and in a nightgown, I walk out of the house and close the door. I do not want him to come inside.

"Hello, Maggie." He has not moved from the first step.

"I'd like to talk out here," I say, and my voice suggests there is nothing at all unusual about our meeting, at two or three in the morning.

He walks up the steps to the porch. I am even uncomfortable with this. It would be better to be in the yard, in the dark, where not so much is exposed. I had not realized how private the space is to me.

"What's wrong with the house?"

"I want to be outside."

He distrusts me, but doesn't know how to protest. "My father said you wanted to see me."

"Is that the only reason you came?"

He shakes his head and stares at me with an expression of quelled alarm.

"How do I look to you?" I ask him.

"Tired. Scared. How do I look to you?"

He is so different now. The beard, but more than that. He walks with an inward slouch. A quiet acceptance of shame lurks behind his eyes. He has a small belly, and his face is pillowed with a new layer of fat. "I think you look older, Nate."

"Prison does that to you." He cracks a thin smile, a self-deprecatory tic that he never had before. "That and other things."

I don't want to hear about how it was. Without explaining myself, I walk down the steps, away from the light cast by the porch lamp, and wait in the near pitch darkness of the yard. Just across the road stands a silent army of fragrant cornstalks. Nate is right behind me, staring into my back.

"I can't see you very well."

"Does it matter?" I turn to him.

"It's important that I see your eyes."

He can see them, as I can see his. They gleam in the dark.

"You're still living here, I guess. Is the old house holding up? Is it still full of ghosts?"

"Of sorts."

"Why the hell did you move here, Maggie?"

"That's my business."

"You can talk to me. I'm not a demon. You think I am, don't you? Do you still think that?"

I think of the drawings on the wall, his face multiplied by tens, stained with paint and charcoal, and, yes, I have considered him a kind of demon for a long time. Now that he's here, he seems shrunken and soft.

"I don't know what to think of you, Nate."

"Didn't you love me once?" An offhanded jab, sarcastic and wry.

"I did. I was twenty."

"A lifetime ago! I can barely remember it. It's like another man's romance. Do you remember?"

"Why do you care?"

"Actually, I remember it like yesterday. What else was I going to do for six years? I was just thinking of you. Did you get my postcards?" He smiles the way he used to, talking up friends and girls, showing off his voice. I can smell the booze on his breath.

"I got your letters."

"I wrote often, didn't I? I wrote lots of love letters for my wife. I'm sure you read every one."

"Stop it," I say.

He's silent.

"You've been driving by my house every night for the past week. Are you trying to scare me? You and Fred Cummings? I live alone in the country. I hear everything. I've got your old rifle in the closet ready to shoot at the first sound of glass breaking. If you've wanted to scare me, you have."

"I'm sorry you're scared. That wasn't my intention." He stares at me, his eyes wide open as though he can't believe he's really having this conversation. "What do you say we go for a stroll?"

I stay where I am.

"You're right. I kept driving by and chickening out, like I did that day in the bar. But tonight, I'm up to it."

He smiles from a long way off in the dark. Then his face goes stone-cold.

"What do you want from me, Nate?"

The question opens some trap door inside him. I've never seen him look so afraid. "Tell me why you never answered my letters."

I turn away from him and walk farther into the dark. I hear his voice behind me.

"No dice. How about that stroll, then? Come on." He takes my hand in his and begins to lead me toward the road. "I'm not a demon."

The still-warm asphalt feels good on my bare soles.

I pull my hand away, but follow him. I can't be hurt anymore.

Here you could not see anything at all were it not for the half-moon floating overhead. To the side, the cool corn field breathes the odor of late summer, moist earth. The experience of walking beside him, the hint of his cologne (why is he wearing it?), makes our marriage so immediate, so tangible. It's as if no time has passed at all, as if I've just now risen from the guestroom floor, bloodied and still shattered, to walk along this country lane with the man in the door.

"Can you tell me why you did it?" he says.

"Did what?"

"Put me in jail."

He is not accusing me. He is inquiring. I had not anticipated his calm in the face of this question.

"I told them what I remembered. I didn't lie, and I think you know that."

"I don't know anything about you."

We walk in silence for a time, and when he finds words, his voice is raw and scarred.

"There were days I was sure you did lie. And there were days when I thought you didn't know what the fuck you were doing. And then there were many days when I thought you'd told the truth. That I hadn't slept by the river. I'd come to the door and I'd knocked the shit out of you. I even imagined it. The feeling of—that act. And those were the worst days. The worst of my life."

I could run down the road. He wouldn't have it in him to follow. I can see how I would look to him, my white gown vanishing into the darkness. But I walk beside him, listening to every word. He speaks close to my ear, murmuring, a voice like a cold finger on my spine.

"All of that is over now. I am not guilty of anything. I live in Louisville and have a good job and an apartment, but it's not so easy stopping the nightmares. They're all about you. Loving you, chasing you, being chased by you, finding you dead in forests, you and all your lovers, you inside our house."

"What are you doing to me, Nate?"

"What have you done to *me*?"

"I told them the truth."

He stops and grabs my wrists in his hands. "You can't accuse me."

"Then don't come here."

"You have no right to do this. Not now, not after all this *time*." The word is his greatest wound, a private disaster. As he says it, his hands tighten around my wrists. His whiskey-scented breath is hot on my face. "Can't you admit you were wrong?"

I refuse to answer. He pushes my own hands into my gut and thrusts me backwards so I fall to the pavement. Stunned, the wind knocked out of me, I stare at the moon floating harmlessly above. I feel a breeze on my face, cool and sweet with the corn. I sit in the middle of the road, wrap my arms around my knees and make myself small, a child waking up from her nightmare.

"You never saw me. I wasn't there. You couldn't have seen me, and if you did, you didn't know what you were seeing, and you shouldn't have ever imagined I would do that. you shouldn't have lied, Maggie, about *me*. Do you understand that? Don't you?"

He needs an affirmation I can't give. "All I know is what I saw."

He lets loose a guttural scream. I bury my head in my arms.

"Look at me!"

He grabs my head in his hands, jerks it upward so I will look. Our eyes meet. His are desperate. "Tell me I didn't do this, Maggie."

I feel the electric pulse of a seizure flicker through me. My head jerks to the left. Nate lets go as if he's been shocked. I roll to my side and begin to shudder.

He watches it. I've never been this naked. Nate stands and watches as the seizure peaks, and I gasp with pain, and the darkness churns through me. I am limp on the pavement, and still he watches. I squeeze my eyes shut, willing him to disappear.

"You're a liar," he says, and there are tears in his voice. "You don't know what you're saying."

I hear him kick a rock down the road. I hear him walk away toward the house. I will not move a muscle until his car door slams and the motor starts and the car rolls over the road back toward the highway. But these sounds don't come. Only the call of an owl far away in the woods, the rustle of wind in the corn. I hear the squeak of the screen door opening.

Panic seizes me. I get up and begin to run. I pound the asphalt with my bare feet and leap into the yard and run through the grass. I take the porch stairs in a jump and crash through the door.

The closet is open. Nate Duke is in the living room, and he's holding his rifle.

"Get out!" The words lurch from me.

"What the *fuck* is going on in here?" he says.

He stares at the drawings, bewildered. I run to the lamp and yank the plug, plunging the room into darkness. I throw my body against his, arms flailing, striking his chest. Taken by surprise, he stumbles backwards, and I push him farther toward the entryway, wanting only that he will leave this room, this house, to get him outside again. In the corner of my eye, I see the glint of steel and wood, the arc of the rifle swinging through the air. The butt catches my forehead, makes a dull thud.

I am again on my knees. I collapse to the floor, head ringing. The sound of his running vibrates through my skull. It seems a long time before the distant motor ignites, before I hear the wheels carry him away at last.

Summer 2002

Windows and doors locked shut, the house sweats the odor of old wood. The window units pump the rooms full of stale air. A heat wave, a week of one-hundred-degree days, and the grass and weeds are tinged brown. A match would set things right, get the blaze going. I lurk inside. I have not left, but for two trips to the liquor store. I called in my resignation at work. I was drunk at the time. I said to Bill, the editor:

"I'm quitting. I'm sorry. It's over between us."

He laughed, and so did I.

"You're not serious, are you?"

"Of course I am. I can't come in anymore. You don't need me. You never did. You just felt sorry for me, didn't you?"

He said that wasn't at all true, that everyone had always thought very highly of me. "I'd hoped you'd become a copy editor some day, Maggie. I really did."

"Well. That's sweet. But."

"But what?"

"I'm getting out of here. I'm moving, Bill."

He asked me where to, and I told him California. He was impressed. He asked me what I would be doing there, and I said I'd let that take care of itself.

"Are you okay, Maggie? You sound—tired?"

"That's funny. All I do is sleep."

Which was and is true. I sleep through much of the day, and have abandoned Manny. He watches the sun go down all by himself. A few days ago he came over to knock on my door, while I was stirring in bed. I didn't go downstairs to see who was there, but saw through the upstairs window his little white head by the kitchen door. He called on the phone several times, but I didn't answer that summons, either.

218

What I have done is read. It is a relief to turn my imagination over to the lives and troubles of others. Mostly, I am drawn to the dusty tomes of local history long ago lent to me by Manny. I have learned a great deal about this home of mine. For example, the founder of New Harmony's second Utopian commune was an atheist named Robert Owen, a Scottish industrialist who left his wife, Anne Caroline Dale, in New Lanark while he built his short-lived "Owenite" kingdom in the Wabash Valley. I am curious about this absent wife. She was a pious woman who believed in the truth of the Gospels, truth you can't see but through faith alone. She preached to her children, but the sons sided with their father, a lover of empirical fact and adventure. He attracted his boys to the Indiana wilderness to start a bold new life while faithful Anne became sick and died in Scotland. There are pictures of the ill-fated pair in one of the books. He is, of course, rendered as handsome and bold, with an angular face that is proud and forthright. Bonneted Anne is rendered in murky pinks and whites. Her face is pasty and ethereal, her eyes smoked over with sadness. My book is mute on the subject of her death. She's a footnote. In this history, as in so many, a woman resides inside a house, waiting and suffering in obscurity.

If I'm not reading, I'm probably drinking or drawing. These activities go hand in hand. I've a routine. In the afternoon when I first wake, I pour a glass of whiskey. I put the glass on the windowsill in the kitchen and leave it there until I've earned it. To earn it, I go into the living room. I make sure the curtains are drawn, the windows locked. I open my sketchpad on the floor and sit, Indian-style, before it. I draw with the charcoal, or the paint. Each effort turns out differently, but always in the center of the page is the almost unrecognizable image of a doorway and a man. Sometimes a gun appears, floating in the corners. Sometimes I do. I am usually just a face. My eyes are always closed. My head is broken. It is like a melon cracked into pieces. I laugh as I do this. I don't feel pain or cry, because by this point I've earned one if not two or three drinks, and I am lost, my hands frantic and happy, as they fill in his eyes, two chips of coal.

Nine days have passed since Nate's visit. My head has stopped aching. I was in bed for a time and immobile. I am okay now, though I've noticed that I flinch when the house creaks.

The swims are a salvation. At dawn, just as the trees emerge blue and stony in the forest, I come out of the stale air. I walk with a towel into the ravine, and it is a relief to know the world continues to move, that wild-flowers have hid their faces at night and will rise up again. On the way, I find bloodroot plants that Manny has pointed out to me and dig up the tender roots full of dye for my drawings. I walk in the creek and let the cold water move over my sandaled toes and try not to think of anything at all.

I don't swim so much as linger, floating on my back, so I can see the subtle sway of high-up branches. I think of the future, though am not convinced it will come. If it does, maybe I will find myself at a university studying journalism. I will be in another state. I will have acquaintances with whom I won't ever talk about my past. They will be worldly people, strivers who have done much and traveled afar. Among them, I'll be a quiet unnoticeable woman whom people privately wonder about.

I often think of the words Mary Starr said to me in her office. I think of her conviction and how, for an electric moment, I believed, in my bones, everything she was saying. I think of Nate's arms around my back, his breath on my neck. *Can't you admit you were wrong?*

And I think of Hodge standing over the obit desk, spelling H-E-A-T.

I sink into the water now and hold my knees and know that if I did do it, this would be the place, and Manny would know where to look.

When I return, I walk inside the kitchen and make one last drink. I take it with me into the living room and look up at the wall. The drawings spread out from the center toward the side. They cover it completely now.

The more I draw it, the more unreal the memory seems. The more unreal it seems, the more I believe in it. This is irrational, I know, and the impossibility of these two responses coinciding makes me want to get to the end of the project, but there is no end. I sit down on the floor with the sketchpad and sip as I create something new. This man I'm drawing isn't Nate, but Hodge. His legs are like dogwoods, spindly and delicate, his body impossibly thin. He stands in a barren field, his angular head turned skyward and faceless. I place a sword in one claw, a Bible in another. I give him vulture wings, a sharp beak. He is the anti-angel, Utopia's evil son, and a preacher. I drink the rest of my whiskey, and take the bloodroot from the forest, break it open, and watch the dark red dye seep into the paper. It makes a strange cloud over the man, but does not hide him. He is like a dream now. He is a lie, as Nate is a lie, and all these memories are. I begin to laugh, and just behind the laughter, the familiar panic runs like a mouse in the walls. With hammer and nails, I put Hodge high up near the ceiling. He stands out, red and terrible, among the others.

Fatigue overwhelms me. I curl upon the couch and fall asleep for a long time, as the sun begins its climb.

When I awake, someone is in the house. The kitchen radio is on, playing a familiar pop song. I hear footsteps on the floorboards. My head reeling, I rush into the kitchen and find Manny emptying a bottle of whiskey into the sink.

"Sleeping Beauty. Welcome to the living."

I watch the last of the whiskey gurgle out of the neck. I feel so sad and terrified and angry, all at the same time. The other bottles of wine, also emptied, are on the counter.

"How did you get in here?"

He holds up a pair of keys and smiles.

"Get out."

"Rule number one of Manny's New Regime: Maggie obeys his orders."

"I said get out."

"Rule number two: Manny does not listen to what Maggie says if he doesn't like it."

"I don't want you here now."

"That would fall under rule number two. What's for dinner?"

He goes to the refrigerator and looks inside, raising an eyebrow. "Not much to go on." He opens a cupboard, pulls down a box of pasta and a can of tomatoes. "I see linguini," he says. "I see marinara sauce. All we're missing is—well, everything."

"Manny. I asked you to leave."

He finds a pot under the counter. He fills it with water as if this were his house and I wasn't standing behind him, fuming. He places the pot on the stove and ignites the gas with a kitchen match. Then he opens the windows.

"It's hot," I complain.

"Better than this stuffy air. It's time to clean the lungs, clean the body. Maybe we'll go on an all-citrus diet. And by the way, our trip to the Golden Coast was supposed to start last week, while you were in here drawing God knows and drinking rotgut. I won't have it. I'm fed up. We're making some changes. We're opening windows and throwing shit out the door."

He pushes the door open and strides into the dining room. I grab his arm and pull him back before he goes all the way in. "Stop it, please. I can't have you in there. It's my space. Please, Manny, just leave me alone *for once.*"

He takes my hands away gently. He looks at the boxes of documents, now scattered about on the table. Glancing only briefly at the living-room wall to his right, he turns to me and says quietly:

"What do you say we just burn all this tonight? After dinner, of course."

His eyes sparkle with intelligence and daring. I turn around and walk into the kitchen and stand by the empty bottles. I hold one up to confirm its emptiness and put it down. Manny, behind me, says, "What do you say? Are you ready to do that?"

"Do what you want."

"It's all about you. Are *you* ready to do that, Maggie?"

"All right."

"Good. A night of festivities. I don't suppose you have any garlic?"

We hardly talk as we make the meal. I feel like a child who's been scolded. I wish he weren't here, though it is also a relief to have him nearby, stirring stewed tomatoes in a pan, adding some onions I managed to find, sprinkling in spices. The tinny radio and the simmering water fill up the silence. I keep remembering there's nothing to drink in the house.

We have dinner outdoors. It rained during the afternoon, finally breaking the heat. The table is damp so we sit on towels and eat on a tablecloth.

"About our trip," says Manny. "I've been making a few preparations."

He's brought out a shopping bag. Placing it on the table, he starts to remove his loot: a sack of gumballs, cheese puffs, Gummi Bears. Two ponchos, Swiss Army knives, a St. Christopher medallion for our car.

"What's that for?" I say, picking up the medallion.

"He's the patron saint of traveling, I think. In case we need some divine help. I also picked up reading material." He holds up a few romance novels and some history books about the Wild West. "No chance we'll be bored, if that's what you're worried about."

"I'm worried about survival."

"It's not so bloody hard surviving. You're healthy. Sort of. And I'm indestructible. You are coming, aren't you?"

"I don't think so."

He sits down to his pasta and tomatoes, dejected. "That's ridiculous."

He finishes the meal in a hurry and announces he's going to get the lighter fluid from his garage. I go inside to find the one bottle Manny didn't see. In the dining room, on the table, beside the folders bearing Hodge's name, stands one drink more. The end of some sherry. I pour it into a glass and sip it quickly. I open a transcript from the trial, and there is the testimony from Manny, the one who found me. The man who has always been closest to all of this.

I went to my kitchen to get a bite to eat. Then I heard a woman's scream coming from the Duke house. Followed immediately by glass breaking. I went to my bedroom to look through the window. I could see one window was lit, that someone was there, and I began to worry. I picked up the phone and called. It rang many times, and no one answered. I'm deciding what to do next, when I hear a car door slam shut and then the sound of a car screeching away. That's when I decided to go have a look.

I close the transcript. I look at all the documents before me. There are so many. I could read them and read them, but there is no reason. All the facts in the world don't change what happened to me that night in the hospital, when I saw the truth in a flash that has only grown brighter.

Manny has sneaked up behind me, holding the can of lighter fluid. I drain the glass, and he scowls at me. "Maggie, lift that box."

Together, we take the boxes outdoors and across the grass into his backyard. In three trips, we've brought everything. The dining room is suddenly empty, but for the walnut table and chairs.

In his backyard, he pulls a rusted metal drum away from the side of his house. It's half-full of old, compressed leaves. The inner sides are charred black. He takes all the documents out of the top box and dumps them into the barrel.

"Want to do the honors?"

He hands me the lighter fluid and a box of kitchen matches. I take the can and hold it upside down over the stack of papers. I feel empty inside, full of dead space. I strike a match and drop it in, and there's a soft *whoosh.* Flames leap into the air. The motions and police reports and affidavits begin to burn.

We watch the fire grow as it feeds on the paper. I pick up the next stack of documents. One by one, I toss them into the flames until my arms are empty, and then I pick up another stack. I feel some new excitement, an adrenaline rush as I throw in the heavy white volumes. They send up a spray of red-hot ash.

"You never have told me about that night."

He stares at me through the flames. "What do you want, Maggie?"

"To know what you know."

"You ask me these questions. You ask me over and over. But you're the one who's supposed to know what happened. Aren't you?"

I don't say anything.

"Don't you understand everything, Maggie?"

"Don't make fun of me."

"If you did, you wouldn't be living here. You wouldn't have read all this garbage or keep asking me questions. You *don't* know what happened, do you?"

"I was there."

"Stop it. You were there, but what does that mean? Maggie, do you want to know how I found you?" he says. "Do you want to know what I really *do* know about that night?"

"Yes."

"Your face was smashed against the floor. Blood was pouring out of you, soaking the rug. Your body was covered in it. Your hair full of it. You were *clobbered,* broken to pieces, limp. The medics weren't sure if you'd live. I paced that hospital eight hours, praying my guts out. If ever I saw that man who did it, God help me, what I would do to him. He's lucky he's behind bars."

"Manny!"

"You were this close to death, and you made a *mistake* about Nate, and so did everyone, and I don't give a damn. You're alive. That's all that matters to me."

I turn away and stare at the forest.

"Look at me, Maggie."

"You don't know. Nobody knows that."

"*Look* at me."

I turn around to face him. "Where was the car parked? In the road or the drive?"

"Jesus! The road, Maggie. I heard the screech of the tires when he drove off, and it wasn't the sound of a car on gravel. So what does that mean? That Nate wouldn't park on the road? Maybe. But the point is, you don't believe yourself anymore."

Manny comes behind me, puts his arms around me, but I move away.

"You have to believe in me. Someone has to," I say.

"I've always believed in you."

"You don't!"

"Whatever you saw or remembered—it seemed true, felt true, and it was true. But it was also wrong, and that makes all the sense in the world. Come here, Maggie."

"I need to be alone."

"You need that like you need a hole in your head."

I walk away from him. I begin to run through the trees. He calls my name, but I keep running toward the house.

I throw open the kitchen door and run inside, find my keys on the table, and go at once back into the night. I see the flames leaping from the barrel, Manny's small shadow beside it, as I hurry to my car.

I tear into the road, and the land grips me. I can't escape from it. I want to be somewhere impossible, a hidden acre where there are no men with stones or Bibles to throw at you. I concentrate on the blur of yellow dashes in the headlights. I'm thinking of what's open at this hour, where I could go. Manny doesn't believe me. No one does. Mary Starr's one hundred percent sure, and a car accelerating on a gravel drive does not screech.

Seventy-five isn't fast enough. The skeletal barns and homes blast past me. A tin sign flashes in the distance. Mary's Hideaway, Nate's favorite spot, a bar you don't leave sober. I brake hard and turn down the dirt lane. I take it through a field, around a stand of trees, and find the low, brick building with a flat roof and no windows. A place I don't belong, but where else can I find what I need right now? The sky has crashed into darkness. Anything could happen here, and I don't care.

It's a bar the size of a garage. There are the backs of two men, the only patrons. They turn as the door squeals, and one face belongs to Fred Cummings, the other to a stranger. A woman ministers to their needs behind the bar.

I go to her and say, "Can I have a martini?"

Fred squints at me like I've said something rude.

"What do you want?" I say.

"For you to leave."

I keep my eyes on the bartender, a plump woman about my age, squeezed into a halter top and skintight jeans. The man whom I don't recognize calls her Jane and asks for another.

My drink comes. I take a long sip of it, feeling the chill of the gin between my teeth.

"I've never seen a woman with more nerve than you," says Fred, his voice sluggish.

"Leave her alone." That's Jane.

"You know what this woman did?"

"You don't know anything about it," says Jane. "Just drink your booze and keep to yourself."

He turns to me. "So, have you changed your answer about the house?"

"No."

"Dick Duke's liable to come out there and throw you out with his bare hands. That's what I'd do."

"Well, no one asked you," snaps Jane. "Did they?"

Taped to the mirror behind the bar are Polaroids of hunting conquests, this being the place to go after a fresh kill. The fuzzy deer heads loll on the ground, their hides slit open. I look at my reflection, then at Fred's. I know I should leave, but I don't have anywhere to go. I drink the martini in big gulps. It takes fast effect. I close my eyes and feel myself spiral a long way down, never touching bottom.

Fred gets up and walks over to me. He leans against the bar, forcing me to look at his face, and when I do, he starts to speak quietly. "I knew Nate when he was this tall, see. And I never believed any of your horse-shit."

I shut my eyes again and feel emboldened by the gin. "You weren't there," I say.

"I know Nate's an honest man. That's all I need to know."

"I saw him in the doorway. I can draw you a thousand pictures. I can show you and show you. Why doesn't anyone care about that?" I look up at Fred and Jane and the man. They are all watching me with puzzled faces.

Fred shakes his head. "Would anyone mind if I threw this whore out?"

"Fred!" says Jane.

"Would anyone other than her mind if I just—"

"The Lord don't ask you to judge the guilty," says the man I don't know. "He'll do that all on His own."

Somehow, that logic has authority over Fred. He sits down on his stool, and I'm alone again with my drink. I finish it and order another. I sit there and concentrate on getting it down fast without thinking about what Manny said. But that's impossible to do.

I stand and pay with a ten-dollar bill. I walk out of the bar very carefully, one step after another, knowing full well that once I get outside, back on the road, there won't be any more hiding places.

I brace myself for the driving. It seems I have to get somewhere. I float over deserted fields, eyes wide open, hands gripping the wheel. This travel is a kind of nausea to pass through. In time, I appear in New Harmony. I come to the square with the museum, home of the two-headed calf, to the Utopian dormitories. I pass Carnation Street, where Ben Hodge let his mother die. I drive outside the town and arrive at the labyrinth of hedges.

Here is a place not on the map. The labyrinth is a lake of darkness. I get out of my car and walk haltingly inside. There are no dead ends here, no such thing as a wrong turn. It is designed not to frustrate but to embrace you, draw you in where you can create your own world.

I try to remember it again, my husband in the doorway. When I close my eyes, I see the drawings, the wild charcoal scrawls. Rita once said to me, "You want to finish the story, Maggie. You feel it in your gut," and she was right. It was a physical need then and still is. That is what it means to be destroyed: you're always trying to end your story, but you no longer have that power.

I make a turn and walk inward toward the brick hut in the center. I snake around in the bushes a long time until I stumble over a root into a clearing. The hut is closed for the night, the gate locked, as if there were anything inside to steal. I sit down in the dirt, lean back against the brick wall, and look up at the sky. It is so quiet here. I feel as if something in me is collapsing, a wall of defenses against the man in jail. He is here with me. Everyone says he is. When I leave, he'll be there, in every city I travel through, a random pair of eyes in the corner of the room, watching my movements.

Beside me is an empty beer bottle. I could break it against the wall and cut myself. Because I was wrong, and everyone knows it now but me. My head falls against the bricks. The hedges spiral upward into the stars, and exhaustion overtakes me. My eyes close, and in half-sleep I see myself breaking the bottle and making the cut. A long ways off, a car comes to a fast stop, braking hard so the tires scream. I open my eyes with a start, as if someone has just said my name. Oh God, I think over and over. There's nothing at hand to fight back with now. If I've done what it seems, then—

I'm on hands and knees, gagging, eyes wide open, my skin cold with fear. I can't stop until something smelling of alcohol rises up.

Tell me I didn't do this, he'd said.

No one will tell me anything here, and I don't know what to do.

In the living room, I rip the drawings down, one after the other. I don't look at them. I throw myself into the violence of tearing the paper off the nails. In a matter of minutes all the sheets litter the floor. I gather them up into a pile and carry them outside.

In Manny's backyard, I find the drum and the matches in the grass. I drop all the drawings inside but one, which I hold up in the near pitch dark. I can just make out his face even now. It's only paper, only charcoal, something to burn and forget. It catches flame from the match, and the flame eats the drawing. I drop it and stand by the barrel, watching the blaze. I watch until the papers curl into a fine black skin.

When I turn to go home, I see Manny standing outside the house.

"Do you want to spend the night on my couch?" he calls.

I walk toward him and say yes.

Sunlight shines into my eyes. My name is being called. I sit up, not knowing where I am. I see Manny's guitar leaning against the wall, his duck lures on the shelves, and a sepia-toned map of Indiana.

"Maggie! You awake!" It's Manny, shouting from the backyard. I look out the window and see him holding the bucket of chicken feed, scattering it on the ground. "There's someone here to see you."

The memory of the night before is like a kick in the gut. I fall back into the couch.

"Maggie!"

I stand up in my underwear as Manny comes toward his house with his pail of chicken feed. I find my shorts and T-shirt, and clothe myself in a hurry before he sticks his head in.

"Are you awake yet?"

I go outside. The heat wave has really broken now. It's nearly autumnal, breezy and dry. I come around to the front of my house and see my mother on the porch, ringing the bell over and over. She's in her robe. She wears tennis shoes with no socks. It's a four-hour drive from Indianapolis, and it's not yet seven a.m.

"Mom?"

She whirls around. "Maggie! Thank God!" She runs down the porch steps, grabs hold of me, and squeezes. "Where have you *been?* Why didn't you call me last night?"

"I didn't even get your message—"

"I called so many times I lost track, and you're never out late, and I had no *idea.* I thought something terrible had happened, and maybe it has." Her face is swollen with fatigue, her eyes red.

"Everything's fine, don't worry," I offer lamely, and I see she's not convinced.

I lead her into the house and go into the kitchen to find her a tissue.

She follows me, and her eyes at once home in on the empty whiskey and wine bottles on the counter, the very thing she didn't want to see.

"What is that?" she snaps.

"Nothing."

When I give her a tissue, she's trying to regain composure, knocking tears away with the back of her hands in a way that makes her look girl-ish. I love her. I haven't felt that in months.

"Let me fix you some breakfast," I say. I open the refrigerator and find a bit of bread, a tiny lump of butter. "I could make toast. I also have cof-fee."

"I don't want toast *or* coffee."

"What do you want?"

"I want to know that you're okay. Is that too much to ask? Do you think I don't have a good enough imagination to picture you dead in a hundred ways when you don't answer the phone for twenty-four hours?"

"Mother, I'm sorry. I'm fine. I'm not sick or dead or hurt. I'm fine."

She glares at the garbage heaped up in the can as she says, "You're not. When you are, you call me, you answer the phone."

"I was at Manny's last night."

She asks me why, and I don't know how to begin. I close my eyes. "I'm tired is all, and it's been a hard time, and I think things are going to change very quickly. I don't know if that's good or bad, but this place isn't for me anymore."

She looks at me wistfully. "I would have driven across the entire country to hear those words."

A swell of nausea reminds me of the fast, wretched drinking I did last night in the Hideaway.

"You look as bad as I must," says my mother.

"I'm okay. Really."

I begin to cry. I try to stop and say something sensible, and the cry-ing only gets very big and physical inside me. My mother holds me. There's the humid atmosphere of home in her robe and hair. It is the odor of worry. I know how she suffers. She burrows her warm body into mine, and I feel her voice vibrating into me when she says, "Let me help you. It's all I want to do now."

"I want to leave," I say.

"Of course."

"I want to leave soon."

After a nap, we spend the day shopping in Evansville, where she buys me a hundred dollars' worth of groceries, a fancy lunch at a café, and even a new dress. I play along, wanting to please her. At the mall, I try on everything she throws at me in the dressing room, and choose a plain yellow sundress I have no need for. I observe my skinny self in the mirror as she chatters about a vacation she and my father want to take with me in Michigan. A friend of his has a cabin by a lake, which is really a wonderful lake, good for swimming and fishing and whatever I'd like to do. As if the future were a holiday, as if there was nothing at all in the world to worry about now. I come outside the changing room, and she loves how I look. She says she'll buy it, and how about some shoes? The more she talks, the more afraid I am, the more it seems I'm not yet ready for life.

As we drive back to the house, I want to curl up into a ball and withdraw from her company. But she's here, beside me, chattering on about Realtors and packing and ordering a U-Haul truck.

That night, she titters around my oven, checking on the meat loaf like it's a baby. Manny has brought his guitar and is strumming chords in an awkward succession that starts to resemble "All the Women I've Loved Before," then falls to pieces. I stand in the corner with my glass of juice and tell myself I can get through this.

"Where've you been all these months?" Manny calls out to my mother.

"Just waiting for an invitation, that's all!" She opens the oven and lets loose a blast of meaty steam.

I don't know why it's a challenge, having bounteous food and company, love and loud voices inside this kitchen. I feel somehow they are working against me.

"Maggie looks nice, doesn't she?" sings my mother.

"Like a movie star, though I wish we could get her to smile."

I am self-consciously wearing the new yellow dress, feeling costumed. I grin a little for Manny, and he frowns at me. "Don't complain. I'm about to eat two slices of my mother's meat loaf. What more do you want from me?"

I actually eat three. For the first time in ages I revel in food, eating steadily, feasting on the smells and tastes and saying little.

"That's a good girl," my mother says, placing more potatoes on my plate.

I eat everything she gives me and hope they won't ask the questions they do.

Where will I go?

When?

What will I do?

Do you want to go to school or work or travel?

I feel it's impossible to answer these questions. I have no idea what to do with myself. I try to smile the questions away, dismiss them with lame jokes: Oh, I'll just go to Hollywood to work as an actress. They laugh, only Manny's eye is on me. He sees everything I'm trying to hide.

"I'll go home," I offer. "For the first few months, perhaps. I'll figure it out from there . . ."

"Well, I'd still like to take you to Hollywood, if that matters."

"Who knows?"

Manny talks about the road trip he still wants to happen. He says he made the cross-country drive once before in his life, when he was young, a tender nineteen years old, riding back from San Francisco with his Indiana girl in the car. He talks of the mountains, the Great Plains, the little things you see when you're off the interstates, how lost you can become. He is trying to reach me.

The dinner goes on and on. The meat loaf, the salad, boiled potatoes, and finally, perversely, brownies. I can't touch mine. She insists. She wants to see me eat a brownie, because they were my favorite dessert as a child. I give in to this, getting a few bites down, and there is heat lightning outside warning me of something just on the other side of this well-lit room. We raise our glasses of juice and have a toast to my imminent homecoming. My mother is assured. I see that in her smile.

She leaves in the morning. It's a long drive, and she has work Monday. I give her hugs and promises to call the Realtor, to rent the truck and pack my things. As she drives away, I watch her car drift over the hill, out of sight.

Alone again, I hear the tight screech of crickets. The humidity presses against my eyes and ears. I walk onto the porch and stare at the white door. I open it and see my face in the mirror. If Manny's right—? The question keeps ringing inside my mind. If Manny *is* right? If Nate is right? If Mary Starr is? I've got to move, to keep the panic at bay.

I want no remnant to remain. I take several garbage bags upstairs to the bedroom. I take down the photographs of my parents and the Wabash and throw them into a bag. I will act like Ben Hodge's brother and be furious, throwing away even the useful and valuable if it has been tainted by this time and place. My clothes and books and rugs and lamps must go. My hair and body, too, have to be cleansed. I anticipate a transformation. In the near future, somewhere, I am going to take on a new persona. Or so I tell myself. You can begin with the physical things. Shoes, something as useful and pedestrian as that, go in the trash. Jade earrings and gold bracelets given to me by my grandmother go in a separate category for items to return to their rightful owners. I open the nightstand drawer and dump out its contents. There's a set of prayer cards given to me by the receptionist at work, in hopes I would one day come to her church. I wonder why I didn't ever go. In my new life, I will do such things, take advantage of everyone's pity and turn it into understanding. There is a small book of inspirational poems from my mother's best friend, stationery for letters I long ago stopped using, an address book full of out-of-date numbers. I flip through it, noticing names of friends I haven't thought of in years. So many connections abandoned. I save the address book and throw everything else into the trash.

In the front parlor, I pitch books into a Goodwill box. I strip the room of the cornhusk dolls and magazines and pewter mug decorations, the painting of the ocean. When I'm done, the shelves and sills are bare. I sit down on the couch and feel a ball of terror in my stomach, pressing against my ribs. I've not many rooms left.

I take Rita by surprise at the end of the day. Her office is already dark. She's tidying up her desk when I walk in. "Can we talk?"

"Oh, Maggie! There you are."

It's as if she'd momentarily misplaced me and I'd done nothing wrong. I apologize for running out on her, and she waves it off. "I ask way too many questions." She winks. She hugs me at once, her bare arms slender and warm. She holds me tightly a long time.

"You know, I've been inside all day. What do you say we do this out by the river?"

I'm grateful for the suggestion. To sit down in her familiar chair would invite more tears, I suspect. In silence, we walk a block to the riverfront, a cement quay overlooking the slow, brown current. We pass the gaudy white casino boat and watch a barge loaded with coal ease down the center of the Ohio. It's refreshing to see the windy expanse of water, the people milling about on the walkway.

"I don't usually meet with patients out here, but it's such a nice day. It's almost like fall."

"You're not angry with me, Rita?"

"Don't be ridiculous. Are you angry with me?"

I shake my head, wishing she didn't have to ask.

"So how are you?"

"Not so well."

She sees through my confused smile, sensing my circumstance in an instant. She puts her hand on my back and rubs. "What's happened?"

I wish I could say everything without uttering a word.

"I started to draw a while ago," I offer. "Like you suggested. I bought paper and charcoal. I sat down and drew my memory of that night. I drew Nate standing in the door. There were dozens, maybe hundreds of drawings."

"How did they affect you?"

We pass a couple and a child, a threesome holding hands, the little girl swinging between the adults. She flashes me a brilliant smile, a potent dose of love it seems I'll never have a right to.

"They scared me into belief again, but the world was telling me otherwise."

In a thin voice, I relate my encounter with Dick Duke. I tell her about the seizure that left me in the hospital, my meetings with Mary and Nate. I tell her about what Manny said to me the night we burned the documents.

"He heard the car on the road," I mutter, as if this means anything to Rita. "He believes it was Ben. He told me that."

We lean against a railing, and beneath us water and silt slide away. It's a vertiginous drop. As I stare into the murk, a part of me trembles. Rita takes hold of my hand. "Take a deep breath. Relax. Tell me what you want right now."

I am reminded of what it feels like to pray, a sensation of gravity and weightlessness at once. "I want to know I didn't do this."

Her eyes ask me to go on.

"I want to know I did the right thing, but I didn't. No one believes me. Everyone says I was wrong. Even you probably think so."

"I don't judge you. You have to know that," she says, her eyes blazing with conviction.

"It doesn't matter if you do or not. I'm starting to—fear myself. If I did this to Nate? And it seems so, it seems to be very possible, Rita, and that's *horrible.* I still tell myself it *was* Nate, and I can remember it, but the more I do the more it feels like a story someone invented."

"You're not to blame."

"Don't say that."

"Did you do what you thought was right?"

"What's right? Everyone believes Hodge's word, not mine. My word is broken."

"I believe the spirit of your word," says Rita. "I don't know the facts, but I listen to you speak and I hear you trying to make sense of extraordinary circumstances. You can't be persecuted for that. You can't persecute yourself."

"I do."

She promises me this will change over time. It's important to live in the present, to look forward. She asks me about the future, and I tell her about my plan, shifting as it is by the day. I'm finally going to leave with Manny on his road trip, and when I return, I'll move into a new apartment in Indianapolis. I'll find a job to keep me afloat while I apply for graduate school in journalism. Rita approves of all this. She says I'll make a very good and sensitive journalist, and she's always thought I was up to such a challenge.

We walk slowly back toward downtown, and she asks me to continue to see someone when I move to Indianapolis. She writes on the back of her business card the name of a woman she knows and respects. She tells me she has a lot of faith in me, that I've been through the worst of it. I hardly hear her words. I am focused on the idea that I will never see this woman again, will never look into her eyes as I struggle with the facts or what I wish were facts. To leave her feels like an admission of failure.

When she opens her arms to me, I want to say, Stop, wait, there's more to say!

But soon I'll have to get back in my car and drive home. One thing will lead to another, the packing of bags, an interlude of travel, a new apartment, an hourly job, a new set of faces and problems.

"I'm not ready," I say, hugging Rita good-bye.

"Yes, you are."

Her embrace is soft, vigorous, unreasonably affirming. She kisses both my cheeks, and I say thank you, though it is hard to say much.

I have one more task in Evansville. It brings me to the tallest building in town, the tenth floor. When I get out of the elevator, I'm met by a middle-aged receptionist who greets me with a cheerful hello. I give her my name and tell her I'm here to see Dick Duke.

"There's a Maggie Wilson here to see Mr. Duke," she says into her phone. "Does he have time?" She's put on hold and hazards a bald stare at my face. She recognizes me, I'm sure, for I recognize her as the same woman who sat in that chair years ago.

She puts the phone in its cradle and glares at me. "Go on back, Maggie."

I don't know where "back" is, but begin to wander into the halls of cubicles and offices, feeling like an intruder. These are different quarters now, but it's not hard to find the head honcho. He still takes up the corner office with the best views. He stands in the doorway, shirtsleeves rolled up, his face caught in an expression of exasperation.

"Maggie!"

I stand before him, my heart pounding.

"What do you want?"

"I need to talk to you in private," I say.

"I'm in the middle of everything, and you just show up." He checks his watch. "Can't you make an appointment—"

"It has to happen now."

He turns abruptly around and walks into his office and stands at the door, ushering me in. He closes the door behind me. It's suddenly silent. I'm inside the sunlit cube of his power now, and he wants me to know it. He stands behind a monstrosity of a desk adorned with tiny white models of office parks, and waves a hand at a chair. I sit.

"What is it?"

It's like I'm approaching a ledge, steps away from leaping into a freefall. "You can have the house," I say.

"What?"

"I've got a truck rented. I'm packing up. Soon I'll be gone. There won't be any trace at all."

He sits down, a somber look on his face. "What's your asking price?"

"I don't want your money."

He squints at me.

"That's what I came to say."

The most foolish financial decision I've ever made, but I can't have it otherwise. I couldn't tolerate living off this man's wealth, and I don't want to sell the house to someone else. It's easier—even necessary—to walk away with no indebtedness.

"What's this all about?"

"This is about you getting what you wanted, even more than that. Are you going to take it?"

He doesn't like being talked to that way. "I said I would pay."

"I told you I don't want your money. It's that simple."

His voice is suddenly quiet, mercenary. "All right. You'll need to sign some papers. I can have my lawyer draw them up and send them to your house. Are you ready to give me your address?"

I give it to him. He writes it down and looks up at me, over spectacles. Despite what I've just announced, there is hate in his eyes, as potent as it ever was. He seems to stare at me for minutes. For the first time, I see what I've done. This is the father of a man I put in jail.

"What else?" he commands, expecting something more.

I see Nate in a cell, enraged and powerless. I see the letters he wrote me, piled up and unopened. I hear the words of the one note I did read: *Your silence is incredible. It's this prison I'm in, the brick piled up to the lights.*

"I don't know what to say."

"You could apologize."

The word's a blast of cold sun on the weakest part of me. His demand leaves me speechless until the useless words fall out.

"Yes. I'm sorry—if I did this to him." My voice breaks off, my eyes fill with tears. I tell this to a man who wants me dead, whose hatred does not ever end.

"There is no if anymore."

"You can have the house, I said. I'm leaving and never coming back. You won't see me again—"

The twitching around my eye begins, a quiet convulsion. He sees me flinch and peers at me, as if trying to sort out a riddle. There's no solving it. His eyes go dark and hard.

"My lawyer will write you in Indianapolis."

I almost want him to say or do something more, to fill the silence this horror creates inside me. As the seizure grows, I stand and stumble away from his desk, aghast at what I've done. Somehow I get outside the door.

In the hallway, I lean against the wall and endure another spell. As it slowly grinds through me, I start to walk, one foot after another, clumsily accelerating with each step, as if someone were chasing me. The world is splintered into shards of light, the apology hot in my throat. Not until I'm in the elevator, descending, does the fit die away, my vision become whole.

I drive into a country clinging to summer. Tired leaves hang on the trees. The corn droops. I want to disappear without trace, to vanish like mist, but there's work to do. I'll go home and finish the packing. I'll drive a truck to Goodwill with furniture I don't want and spend more time out by Manny's barrel, feeding photos and journals and records into flames. I'll destroy these treasures without thought and move on to the next pile. There will be diminishing heaps and then, finally, no heaps at all, a bit of lint in a corner, some lost pennies and a photo or two, and that occasional piece of clutter that pierces through all the years like an arrow—one of his cufflinks? A cartridge from his gun?

I only have to spend a few more nights dismantling the scaffolding holding up my life. Then, on Friday, my parents will come with a pickup to carry away what I'll need in Indianapolis, and I'll head off with my neighbor for our jaunt out west. A valiant effort on his part to distract me, and I love him for it. He's already packed. Being a collector of maps, he has dozens of them for the road. They are pure possibility, the best kind of information. I suspect I won't want to follow them much. I'll try to get us lost, as I meander now away from the usual route. I turn from the highway leading toward New Harmony and take a one-lane road called Butternut Ridge.

Carson lived on this road. The last man I ever made love to. I wonder about him. I wonder if he would want to speak with me someday, or if he damns me, too. I think of Nathan's letters and all their venom I never tasted, the revulsion in his father's eyes. I was wrong about everything. Most of all, I was wrong about love. It should not be so hard to tell the truth about the face of a man.

An explosion goes off in my mind. I gun the gas. I could take this car a long way. The tank is almost full, and packing can wait.

I take another turn, hoping this road leads nowhere I can remember. I notice up on a hill a small church, the size of a pillbox, white and plain. It seems I've never seen it before. There are few corners of this area I don't know, and to come across this old church struck by sun excites me. My stomach drops as the car takes a hill at full speed. The road carries me across a crop-laden field. I turn down another lane. Just when I think I'm losing my way, my eyes fall on a familiar trailer, and my heart sinks. I know where I am now. It's hard to get truly lost in the country. There simply aren't enough roads to take. A few minutes later, as it always does, the gray house appears in the distance, waiting for my return.

I park in the drive and stare at that door, my door, forever in its place. An impossible conviction takes root in me. I'm going to go inside and scour the rooms, purge them of every speck of me. I'm going to be like a fire that levels this house. On Friday morning, I'll get in the car and, without looking back, burn up the road with three desperate and saving words: I can leave.

ABOUT THE AUTHOR

Raised in Indiana, Paul Jaskunas attended Oberlin College and Cornell University. The recipient of a Fulbright grant to Lithuania, he has worked as a journalist and teacher. He lives in Washington, D.C., with his wife, Solveiga.

A CONVERSATION WITH
PAUL JASKUNAS

Q: You've received a lot of praise for the convincing way in which you wrote *Hidden* from a female perspective. How did you develop your heroine's voice?

A: I don't know if I did anything to develop Maggie's voice I wouldn't have done with a male narrator. I simply wanted to write my way into her world, inside her crisis, and imagine its details. More than anything, the challenge of the book was imagining the emotions of brief moments in time: her picturing the scene of the crime, waking up in that cavernous home, firing her ex-husband's gun. These realities carried the story along. As an abstract idea, narrating from a woman's point of view is scary, but writing isn't abstract work. It's quite vivid and tangible—both the people and places taking shape on the page, and the physical act of putting words on paper.

Q: *Hidden* is set in the utopian community of New Harmony, Indiana, and Maggie finds solace in the labyrinth that the town's founders built. How does the religion-based setting come to bear on the action of the novel?

A: Maggie is not a religious woman—she doesn't belong to a church or pray—but she sometimes conceives of what's happened to her in apocalyptic terms. The attack was a kind of death that ushered her into a new life, one that gives her a unique vantage from which to view the local history. The first utopian community in New Harmony was steeped in rapture faith and the desire to create an earthly Eden. This is a dark and male-dominated fantasy, the dangers of which Maggie can recognize at once. In a sense, she has experienced her own rapture, one she's still struggling to escape throughout most of the book. In the labyrinth, she seeks but does not find solace; what comes to her there is a deeper recognition of the trap she's in.

Q: You go into great detail about Maggie's medical troubles since her attack—particularly, you describe her seizures vividly. How did you research this?

A: I didn't research this aspect of the book. Most of the passages describing her seizures spring from my experience.

Q: How would you describe Nate's relationship with his father? How does Nate's family history influence his behavior?

A: The worst thing that ever happened to Nate's father was his wife's leaving him. The novel doesn't probe this wound, but as I felt my way into the story, I recognized Dick as a kind of misogynist. Over the years, he's taken out his bitterness against his children, especially Nate, who he used to discipline with occasional violence. All this leaves Nate with a lot to deal with as a man. But he doesn't deal. I don't think he recognizes his childhood pain as a handicap at all. He writhes in his father's shadow, hating it, yet incapable of escaping, and the familial misogyny surfaces in destructive ways.

Q: You've used photos, newspapers, journals, and court transcripts as tools for Maggie to uncover her past. To what extent do these documents act as stand-ins for Maggie's memory? Can she ever really know the truth?

A: If I sit down and write about, say, having coffee with a friend, I'll more likely recall that moment and its particulars in the very way I write about it—my friend's words, the sound of his voice, the way his hands look to me. The same goes for photographs. These images, casually taken, later despised or cherished or laughed at, shape what and how we remember our lives. In this sense, the journals and photographs Maggie goes back to are the stuff of her memory. Not a 'stand in' at all, but the essence of how she recalls the time. The transcripts and police reports form a more threatening account, a public narrative that is foreign to her private recollection.

Q: The atmosphere of *Hidden* often feels akin to Southern Gothic. Do you find the landscape of Indiana to be as threatening to Maggie as the people?

A: The land in southern Indiana is lush in summer, desolate in winter. It promises quiet charms, plenty of handsome farmhouses and pastoral views. Yet there are also the corners of decay, so many out-of-the-way bridges and barns and junkyards where you will feel perhaps too alone. I have spent time in this part of the state, as a child and young adult, and always have been moved by the loveliness and the ominous isolation of its towns and homes. Maggie is at times grateful for these qualities. A part of her wants to hide, to be alone. Yet sadly the setting becomes a danger to her.

Q: At the end of the book, Maggie has come to realize that she can leave New Harmony behind. Can she really? What exactly is she leaving?

A: She is leaving the men. She is leaving Nate, who's anger and jealously and culpability haunted and haunt her. She is leaving Ben, his sinister claim on her, his devious stalking. She is fleeing, too, Dick Duke, the man who last throws guilt in her face, the one who most potently blames the victim of the crime. She leaves all these destructive claims. By going into the heart of the mystery and coming out intact, she can get away from them. But I feel she will be burdened, in her relationships especially, by fear, distrust, and regret.

Q: It is unclear in the final pages of *Hidden* whether Maggie knows for certain who attacked her. Has she made peace with not knowing, or has she figured it out?

A: By the end, Maggie has faced all records of this one terrible night. She has exhausted the Hodge account, and she can accept the soundness of the case relied upon by the court in exonerating Nate. She can recognize these facts as facts. What she can't do is dismiss the force and vividness of her memory. She will always hold in her mind the vision of Nate standing in the door. The emotional truth of this moment can't be erased. Is she at peace with not knowing? She knows. She knows too well the truth of her memory and knows the facts that have set her husband free. The mystery of her predicament is uncovered but not solved.

ACKNOWLEDGMENTS

Dan McCall and Lamar Herrin were forthcoming with encouragement and candor throughout the writing of this book; I admire and thank both writers. Warm thanks, also, to Amy Scheibe, whose editing inspired me, and to my agent Erin Hosier. The Constance Saltonstall Foundation for the Arts and the U.S. State Department's Fulbright program provided key financial assistance while I was writing and revising *Hidden*. Rebecca Morrow read the book several times, never failing to offer generous critiques. I am indebted to Marguerite Young's compelling nonfiction work about New Harmony, Indiana, *Angel in the Forest: A Fairy Tale of Two Utopias*. Finally, thank you to all my family, especially Richard and Sharron Jaskunas, who led me to a love of books.